One
Night
With a
Cowboy

Don't miss these hot cowboy romances from
eKensington:

TUCKER'S CROSSING *by Marina Adair*

TEXAS WIDE OPEN *by KC Klein*

ONE HOT COWBOY *by Anne Marsh*

One Night With a Cowboy

An Oklahoma Nights Romance

CAT JOHNSON

BRAVA

KENSINGTON PUBLISHING CORP.

www.kensingtonbooks.com

ACKNOWLEDGMENTS

This book would not have been possible without the many and varied contributions of the following:

Justine Willis and Alicia Condon of Kensington for taking an interest in my cowboys. Author Eliza Gayle, who was there from day one when this book wasn't even a spark of an idea yet. My Oklahoma contacts, John Dollar and Valerie Jones for the OSU details; and Jamey and Lizzy Martin of Joseph's Fine Foods for allowing me to borrow their location and their famous fried bologna sandwich for my story. Sebastian Junger's book *War* and the accompanying documentary *Restrepo* he filmed with the late Tim Hetherington, both of which were invaluable in my Afghanistan research. My military consultants for all their answers and input: Sean Abbot, Gary Crowley, George Peavler, and Travis Taylor. Dee Young and her hubby for the ROTC information. Carley Tucker for her in-depth college professor tutorial. And finally, every single one of my cheerleaders who provide ongoing emotional support, chief among them Helen Seely, Angel Shaw, Kimberly Radicy Rocha and Shannon Taylor.

Any mistakes made or liberties taken with the facts are my own.

Chapter
One

"Dr. Hart. Please, sit down." The dean clasped Becca's hand with her own cold and slightly bony one and then indicated the seat in front of her oversized, mahogany desk.

"Thank you, Dean Morris." Becca sat in the leather wingchair, feeling a bit like a child as its size dwarfed her.

She glanced around the stately, well-appointed office and let her mind wander as the dean of the faculty at Vassar College settled herself on the other side of the desk.

One day perhaps this office could be hers. *Rebecca Hart, Dean.* Becca's doctorate in English literature more than qualified her for the position, though she'd need a lot more years under her belt—years her boss obviously had, plus some. The woman had to be seventy if she was a day.

Maybe that was what this impromptu meeting was about. Was Dean Morris retiring and she wanted to inform the faculty personally? Becca tried to wrap her head around the idea and think of who might be replacing her. Probably Harold Wexler, the stodgy old Brit who'd been teaching at Vassar forever—at least it seemed that long to the bored students in his classes.

"Dr. Hart, you've done an exemplary job here. Both your internal and external performance reviews have been exceptional . . ."

She glowed with pride as her heart rate sped. Were they going to promote her to associate professor? Or maybe she was going to be awarded tenure. It had been four years since she'd completed her doctorate. That would be faster than usual for an assistant professor to be promoted to an associate, but as the dean had said, Becca's performance had been exceptional. At this rate, she'd rise through the ranks and be a full professor before she turned forty, which rarely happened.

Her chest tightened with excitement. Finally, all her hard work was paying off.

"However—" Dean Morris continued.

However? A lump lodged in Becca's throat. *However* was not a good word to hear after a long string of compliments. It negated, in a surprisingly painful and sickening way, each and every thing the dean had said before it. She swallowed hard.

"—donor dollars are down. Expenses are up. I won't bore you with the budgetary details, but suffice it to say the college has had to make some very difficult decisions recently. I'm afraid our department is being reduced, and consequently your position has been eliminated." Dean Morris did look moderately saddened. It didn't soften the words or the impact on Becca as she wondered if she could make it to the ladies' room before she threw up.

"Eliminated?" She was being downsized?

"Being the most recently hired faculty member, and without tenure . . ." Dean Morris spread her hands and let the sentence trail off.

Becca could read between the lines. The department couldn't fire any of the other professors without due cause no matter how good or bad they were at their jobs, because they, unlike her, were tenured.

"Of course. I understand." Her nausea was replaced by anger. She was a better teacher than half of the department, even if she had been there the least amount of time. Students literally fell asleep in Wexler's class. It was so unfair.

The dean leaned her elbows on the desk. "The semester ends in just a few weeks. Of course we'd like you to finish out the term. I'm sure you'd agree this far into the semester, continuity for the students is the main concern, but if you wish to take the rest of today for yourself, I'd understand."

She didn't have any more classes this afternoon, but she would normally do a few hours of work in her office before heading home. Nice of the dean to wait until after she was done teaching for the day to drop this stink bomb in her lap.

It was amazing what a person could endure and still remain polite. She wanted to rant. She wanted to scream. Instead, she smiled, stood, and grasped the dean's hand. "Yes, I think I will. Thank you, Dean Morris."

The trip back to her own office seemed eternal, but once there she grabbed her bag and car keys. Without checking if she had voice mail on the desk phone, or even looking twice at the stack of paperwork she could easily do at home, she turned. Leaving the office and the work behind her, she escaped down the hallway toward the exit. Thankfully she didn't see anyone, because she was running low on social niceties right about now.

She unlocked her car and tried not to notice how her hand shook.

Unemployed. The word echoed through her head like a death knell as she attempted to quell the rising panic. She pushed the feeling down and tried to think logically about the new state of her life. Yes, she had lost her job. But she had her condo, a small sum in her savings account, and she still had her boyfriend—almost fiancé really—Jerry.

Jerry had a good job with a steady salary and health benefits.

Her benefits—new panic rose as she realized she'd be losing her medical benefits through the college's group insurance. Maybe this was a sign. The universe telling them the time had come for her and Jerry to finally talk about marriage. They already lived together, which was almost like being married, just without the paperwork.

Sure, things hadn't been all sunshine and roses since he'd moved in. They had their issues, but that was to be expected in any long-term relationship. It was time for the two of them to commit to a lifetime together. Marriage was the logical next step and the perfect solution to her impending uninsured status.

While she navigated onto the road leading off campus, she pulled out her cell phone and pushed the button for Jerry's number. As she listened to the ringing through the speakerphone, Becca decided they'd have a small wedding. She'd never wanted anything large anyway, but especially not now with her recent unemployment. Just a hundred, or maybe a hundred and fifty of their closest friends and relatives. It would be lovely to have the ceremony outdoors along the Hudson River. Then maybe the reception at the old inn in Rhinebeck. Yes, something simple and tasteful. Perfect.

Jerry's voice mail came on, so she flipped the phone shut. She was almost home anyway. She could call his office when she got there.

Everything would be fine. She would marry Jerry, find a new teaching position; maybe they'd even buy a small house. She gave herself a mental pat on the back that she could find the silver lining in even the darkest of situations. With newfound optimism, Becca pulled into the driveway of the condo complex. She drove to the back of the building to where her assigned parking space was located, but as she rounded the corner, what she saw had her slamming on the brake pedal.

The car rocked to a stop and she sat, unable to comprehend what was happening in front of her. She didn't park, mainly because a truck already filled her spot. Not just any truck, but a rental moving truck. One Jerry was currently loading with his prized jumbo-size, flat-screen television.

Becca inched her car forward until it was just feet from the nose of the truck backed up to the curb, then she threw it in park and cut the engine. Her vehicle, sideways the way she'd left it, was blocking a whole bunch of parked cars. She didn't care.

She knew the moment Jerry noticed her there. The panic was clear on his suddenly pale face. Then again, he was always pretty pale, even in summer. Too much time spent indoors on the sofa watching that damned television he loved so much, she supposed. His wide-eyed, deer-caught-in-headlights expression was new, though.

Swinging the driver's side door wide, she stepped out. Leaving the door open, she walked around her car and stopped by the side of the truck. She was glad she was wearing her favorite suit. She felt powerful in this suit, and the length and cut of the pencil skirt made her legs look amazing. *Take that, Jerry.*

"Jerry, what's going on?" She had a feeling she already knew the answer. So much for that wedding.

"Becca. Uh, wow, you're here. I was hoping to be all cleared out by the time you got home from work." A deep frown creased the brow beneath his prematurely receding hairline. She predicted he'd be bald by forty. She'd noticed she could already see hints of his scalp through his thinning blond hair. "Why are you home so early anyway?"

That was his response to her question? Why was she home earlier than usual?

Oh, no, he wasn't going to get away with answering her question with a question. Especially since her question was why, after living together for almost a year, he was secretly moving out while he thought she was at work. After the day she'd had, she was in no mood to answer questions for this cowardly man.

"Where are you going, *honey*?" Her overly sweet tone brought an even more fearful expression to his face.

He let out a breath and leaned his khaki-clad butt against the edge of the truck. Who loaded a moving truck in light-colored khakis? He was going to get filthy. Good. She took great, though admittedly immature, satisfaction in knowing he'd probably have to throw those pants out when he got to wherever it was he was slithering off to, the damn sneaky snake.

Jerry finally raised his pale blue gaze to hers, before he yanked it away again to study the driveway at his feet and then the tire of the truck. "Well, you know things haven't been going that great with us lately."

Her brows rose sharply. "You could have fooled me."

Her mind latched on to his coming home smelling of beer just the other night, after which he'd proceeded to have sex with her for what seemed like a solid hour before he finally gave up and admitted he was too drunk to finish. Then he'd rolled over and started snoring, leaving her lying there unsatisfied and too awake to fall back to sleep.

Men who were unhappy with a woman didn't still want to have sex—especially bad sex—with her. Or did they? Maybe they did. She couldn't be sure of anything anymore. The world seemed turned upside down. It was like she'd awoken in an alternate universe and she was now living Bad Luck Becca's life instead of her own.

Jerry stood again, but stayed close to the truck. He continued to keep his distance, leaving a good bit of space between them. Maybe he wasn't quite so dumb after all. "I've been thinking about moving out for a while—"

"Then perhaps you should have mentioned that." She crossed her arms over her chest.

"—so when one of the guys at work had a roommate move out, he said I could have the room." He ignored her interruption and finished with his rambling explanation, as shitty an excuse as it was.

"How convenient for you." She glared at him.

"Becca, I think we need a little break from each other." Jerry took one step forward.

"A break?" Her voice rose in both pitch and volume. A break. Ha! She'd like to see something break, all right. Like perhaps Jerry's big-ass television after it fell out of the truck and broke his foot.

"Yes." He took a step back and retreated to his original position.

"Fine." She couldn't be here any longer or she might take a tire iron to Jerry's TV as well as his skull. She spun and walked around the hood of her car, back to the dri-ver's side.

"You're leaving?" He took a single step after her. Now that the bulk of the vehicle was between them, chicken Jerry must have been feeling brave.

She paused, her hand on the open door. "Surely you didn't expect me to help you move?"

"No, no, of course not." He frowned, but she wasn't convinced the thought hadn't crossed his mind. "It's just, I thought you'd want to talk or something."

She glanced at what she could see of the inside of the open truck, already packed pretty full with a jumble of boxes, bulging trash bags, furniture, and loose items. It was total chaos, but not even her obsessive-compulsive need for organization could make her help him now.

"The time for talking is long past, Jerry." Becca got in and slammed the car door shut. She turned the key in the ignition, but then hit the button to roll down the window as a thought hit her. "I paid this month's cable bill out of my account. I expect you to leave me a check inside for it."

Jerry wasn't going to get away with moving out with no notice and then stick her with all of the bills, especially now in light of her recent change in employment status. Not to mention he'd upped their cable television package to the biggest, most expensive one the company offered the moment he'd moved in last year. She'd cancel that as soon as possible.

He nodded meekly as she slid the window shut.

Feeling moderate satisfaction at the thought of taking Jerry's money, she pulled to the end of the drive and stopped. In front of her was a four-lane road. Now what? Shaking so badly she probably shouldn't be driving, she flipped on her blinker and aimlessly chose to turn right, mainly because she didn't trust herself to cross traffic at the moment. She drove a short distance and then pulled into the parking lot of the first shopping center she came to.

It took her two tries to dial her sister's office number correctly. When she finally heard Emma's voice answer, Becca's last bit of composure broke.

She drew in a shaky breath, tinged with a sob. "Em? I need you. Can you meet me at your place?"

Chapter
Two

"It's only been a month since the end of the semester, Bec. These things take time."

Nowadays, time was the one thing Becca had plenty of, since she was sans employment and all. Money, on the other hand, not so much.

"You don't understand, Em. There are practically no positions available in my field." Becca buried her face in her crossed arms on the table.

"Then you'll do something else. Oh, I know. You love books. You should become a librarian. Ooh, or work in the bookstore on Route Nine. That would be fun. They have that coffee shop inside." Emma sounded so excited about this new idea, Becca was inspired to throw something at her.

They might both have the same color hair and blue eyes, but Emma really embraced the role of the stereotypical bubbly blonde sometimes. Becca couldn't even dignify her sister's eternal optimism with a response. All she could manage was a shake of her head, which seemed too heavy at the moment to lift from the table.

She heard the sound of liquid being poured into a glass. Finally, her sister was doing something helpful and refilling her wineglass rather than dispensing less-than-useful career advice. This kind of compassionate behavior Becca could totally get behind. Rallying, she sat up and reached for the glass filled with deep, claret-colored liquid.

She drew in a long, slow mouthful and let the flavor dance on her tongue. Perfect. "Thank you. I feel better now." She let out a sigh.

Emma laughed. "You're welcome. If only I could solve your job situation as easily."

If only. Wouldn't it be nice if life were like a store? Aisle one—career opportunities. Aisle two—love and lust. Customer satisfaction guaranteed or your money back. Don't see what you want? Visit the customer service department and place a special order.

"So you haven't found any openings for an English professor at all?" Armed with her own replenished glass, Emma slid her chair around the kitchen table so she could see the screen of the laptop Becca had shoved out of the way during her latest bout of self-pity and frustration.

"Not anywhere I want to teach."

"Becca. In this economy, can you really afford to be so picky?" Emma looked every inch the older sister as she reprimanded her.

"What? Do you *want* me to have to move out of New York State and never see you?" She cocked a brow.

Emma squinted at the page up on the screen. "The University of Chicago? Correct me if I'm wrong since I don't have a doctorate or anything like you do, but last I checked Chicago was not in New York."

Becca scowled. "There was nothing around here. I had to geographically expand my search."

Emma narrowed her eyes and continued to look doubtful. "Fine, and what have you found in your newly expanded search? Anything?"

"There's one position available in Oklahoma, but that's

obviously not going to work." She dismissed even the idea of it with a flick of her wrist.

"Why not?" Emma frowned.

"Oklahoma? Emma, be serious." Becca had to laugh. Her, a New Yorker born and raised, in Oklahoma? The notion was absurd. She'd always lived just a train ride away from Manhattan. She needed culture, theater, museums, and world-class restaurants. Chicago. Philadelphia. Maybe she'd be all right in those places, but not in Oklahoma.

The persistently judgmental expression on Emma's face had Becca sighing. She moved her wineglass to the side and dragged the computer forward.

"All right. See for yourself." A few clicks of the mouse and the website for Oklahoma State University's Stillwater campus popped up, including images of the school's pride and joy, the OSU Cowboys football team. She angled the laptop toward her sister. "See?"

"OSU. That's a good school. Their football team did really well last year."

"I wouldn't know." She screwed up her face at the idea that last year's college football team standings were even on Emma's radar. Vassar didn't have a football team. There the school sports were things like fencing and crew team, pretty much the polar opposite of OSU. To prove her point, she pointed to a link on the screen. "Click on the rodeo team link."

"Rodeo? Wow." Emma leaned forward and looked far too excited.

"Emma, seriously, what do you know about rodeo?" Hell, what did Becca know about rodeo? Nothing, that's what, and she'd be fine if it stayed that way. "I've worked at Vassar. I can't apply to a school with a rodeo team."

"Oh, who cares if there's a rodeo team? It's not as if they're going to expect you to teach it, silly. The position is in the English department, right?" Emma cocked a brow.

"Yes, and that brings me to the next issue. Take a look at the course list."

So far her sister hadn't reacted at all as expected. Who would have guessed Emma cared about college football or rodeo? But she was confident the uninspired English curriculum would be the nail in the OSU coffin and get her sister off her back for not wanting to relocate to work there.

Emma scrolled down the web page of English course listings and nodded. "Shakespeare. That's one of your specialties, so that's good."

"Fine, they have one Shakespeare course. Where's the Chaucer? Where's the literary interpretation of the great philosophers? Where are the Old English and the study of Beowulf in the original language? I based my thesis on the impact of fifteenth- and sixteenth-century writings on modern literature, and the only thing they offer is Shakespeare?"

"Well, maybe they have a different focus there. There's History of the American Film." Emma glanced up. "That looks like fun. Maybe you could spin it to be how Chaucer has influenced modern films or something like that. I think that could be really interesting."

Becca, who'd made words her life and her career, had no more for her sister at the moment. All she could do was shake her head.

"I'll be back." She stood and, rather than say something she might regret, headed for the bathroom.

"I really think you should apply. Look. There's even a link on the English department page to send in your résumé." Emma's voice followed her all the way down the hallway and to the other side of the condo.

"No." Becca shut the bathroom door with enough force

it should leave no doubt in Emma's mind she didn't want to be disturbed.

She'd find another position, eventually, and it wouldn't be at a university that specialized in cowboys.

The ringing of the phone interrupted Becca's new favorite daytime talk show. She frowned at the number but didn't recognize the area code. With a sigh and one eye on the recipe the show's guest chef was in the middle of preparing, she hit the button to answer. "Hello?"

"Dr. Hart?" An unfamiliar male voice came through the earpiece.

"Speaking." She employed her most scholarly phone voice.

Just because she was unshowered and still in her pajamas at noon, enjoying what she'd always in the past thought of as crappy daytime television, didn't mean she shouldn't act professionally. No need to behave like an animal even if she didn't know who the hell was calling her and interrupting what looked like a really good recipe she might need if she ever did decide to get dressed, go food shopping, and cook a decent meal for herself again.

"This is Mark Ross. I'm associate dean for academic programs and head of the English department at OSU. I reviewed your résumé, and we're very interested in meeting with you about the position."

"Uh, what?" Perhaps that response was a bit less professional than she would have liked as her brain spun trying to figure out how OSU had gotten hold of her résumé. Granted, she had polished off a bottle of wine with her sister the other night, but she hadn't been nearly drunk enough to send her résumé and forget—

Her sister.

She stifled an angry growl. That had to be the explanation. Like pieces of a puzzle, things fell into place in her mind. She'd left Emma alone with her computer browser open to the OSU site when she'd gone to hide in the bathroom and pout. Her newly updated résumé document, clearly named as such, was saved right there on the desktop, and Emma had crazy good computer skills from her job in graphic design.

That sneaky, little—

"For the associate professor vacancy in our English department . . ." The man was trying to refresh her memory about the position he thought she'd applied for just days ago. The one, according to her reaction to his call, she'd already forgotten about. He must think she was an absolute dolt.

"Oh, yes, of course. I'm so sorry. There was something distracting me here. Um, did you say *associate* professor?"

"I did."

She hadn't reached the associate level yet at Vassar before she'd . . . left. She refused to think the word *fired,* and *let go* wasn't much better. But OSU wanted to hire someone at the associate level and they were interested in her? She hated to admit it, but that grabbed her interest. "And you want to talk to me about the position?"

"Yes. We'd love to meet with you in person, if it's possible."

"In Oklahoma?" That had come out sounding a bit disparaging. She hoped he hadn't noticed.

"Yes. I do realize you're in New York, but I can assure you, we'd only request a live interview with a candidate we're extremely interested in. I certainly wouldn't make you travel all the way here otherwise. Your education and work experience are very impressive."

Hmm, the flattery didn't hurt. Neither did the fact her savings account and the extension on her health benefits were both going to run out if she didn't find a new position soon. What the hell. How much could it cost to fly to Oklahoma in the middle of the summer anyway? It definitely wasn't the vacation capital of the world.

"Okay. I'd be happy to meet with you, Dean Ross."

"Would a week from Monday be too soon? Say, eleven o'clock?"

"No, I think that should be fine." It wasn't like she had anything else to do.

"Wonderful. I'll e-mail you the details."

"Thank you, sir. See you a week from Monday." Her thoughts a whirlwind, Becca disconnected the call and immediately dialed her sister's number.

When Emma answered, Becca pocketed her excitement and dragged her annoyance back to the surface. "Emma Madison Hart, what did you do?"

"Um. I'm not sure. What do you think I did?"

She could imagine the guilty look on Emma's face. She flashed back to when they were children and Emma was in trouble for something or another, only this time Becca was in the disciplinarian mother role rather than being the giggling sibling enjoying her older sister's troubles.

She let out a huff of frustration and realized why their mother had so often done the same. "Did you submit my résumé to OSU?"

"Um, yeah, I kinda did. Can I blame it on the wine? Wait, how did you know I sent them your résumé? Oh, my God, did they call you?"

"Yes, they called me. Imagine my confusion since I never applied there." The volume of her voice rose.

"Okay, I get it. You're mad, but what did they say? Did they offer you the job?" Emma's excitement was beginning to infect Becca, just as she was trying to stay mad at her sister for interfering.

"No, but he said they're very interested and they want

a live interview." She'd tried to keep the stern tone in her voice, but it was difficult. The news still sounded good.

"I knew it!"

"Stop acting like you did something wonderful." She scowled. "You did a very bad thing, Emma."

"You'll get over it. So when's the interview?"

She wanted Emma to see what she'd done was wrong, but it was just too hard trying right now, so she gave up. Becca couldn't undo Emma's years of practice in sisterly meddling with a single lecture anyway. "A week from Monday."

"Yay! I'm so happy for you."

"Oh, don't get too excited, and get out your credit card, because if I have to fly to Oklahoma to interview for a job I didn't apply for, then you're coming with me."

"Fine. Gladly. I've always wanted to see Oklahoma. What day do we fly out?"

She sighed, not believing for one minute her sister's secret lifelong dream had been to see Oklahoma. "I don't know. How long does it take to fly there? The interview is at eleven o'clock."

Through the phone, she heard the distinct sound of fingers tapping the keys on a computer. Emma was probably already looking up flights. She shook her head. She'd never meant for Emma to enjoy her punishment for meddling.

"It's good it's at least ten days in advance, so the cost of the flights is still reasonable." Emma proved she was doing exactly as Becca predicted she would. "We can fly in on Sunday and get a hotel room. That way you can get settled and see the town before your interview."

"A hotel room?" She groaned. This was sounding more expensive by the minute.

"Of course, silly. We can't fly in and out in the same day.

I'll pay for the room as an early congratulations gift for the new job. I'm sure you're going to get it."

"Fine. We'll stay overnight." She rolled her eyes. Inviting Emma had been a bad idea, but at least she was paying for the room.

"Oh. My. God." Since that exclamation had been delivered in Emma's excited voice, rather than her more ominous *uh-oh* tone, Becca wasn't too concerned, but she still had to wonder what else could possibly be sprung on her today.

"Now what?" She drew in a deep breath and braced herself for whatever her sister might reveal.

"There's a rodeo the night we arrive." Emma practically squealed the news.

"A rodeo?" Becca laughed. "How do you know?"

"It's on the website for the hotel. There's a listing of local events. It says there'll be over one hundred vendors there selling food and all sorts of Western stuff. Belts. Purses. Boots. Purses made out of boots. And the tickets are only ten dollars. That's crazy. We are so going to this."

"Emma, you're the one that's crazy. We're not going to a rodeo." She realized she was frowning even harder than before. If she continued talking to Emma much longer, she'd need Botox to fight the wrinkles her sister was giving her.

"Too late. I just ordered the tickets. We're going, and you're going to have a great time. Besides, you can't interview for a job without experiencing some of the local culture first."

"Culture. Mmm, hmm. Sure." She let out a derogatory snort.

"Yes, culture. Cowboy culture. Cowboys have a long and illustrious history, you know. Mmm, mmm. I can't wait to get there and see some up close and in person.

Make sure you pack your jeans. Ooh, do you still have those cowboy boots you bought a few years ago?"

"Maybe. I'm not sure. I only wore them once." Becca shook her head at the ridiculousness of this all. She should be planning what to wear to her job interview, not worrying about what to wear to this rodeo she didn't want to go to in the first place.

"Well, go look. Then right after I'm done with work, I'll come over and we'll plan your rodeo outfit."

Some forces of nature were impossible to fight. Emma on a quest was clearly one of them. Defeated, Becca sank back into the cushions of the sofa with a sigh. "Fine. See you later."

Chapter
Three

"Hey, Tuck. Check out those two blondes walking in."

Tucker Jenkins grunted as Jace's elbow hit the exact spot on his rib cage where Son of a Gun had stomped on him last night. The bull's hoof had only glanced off his safety vest or Tuck probably would be warming a hospital bed with a collapsed lung tonight rather than riding, but that didn't mean the bruised ribs didn't hurt like a son of a bitch. He sure as hell didn't need his friend poking him, and over two buckle bunnies no less.

Without bothering to check out the most likely overly endowed women Jace was so excited about, Tuck turned toward him. "What's with you and the bimbos lately? Ever since you and Jacqueline broke up, you're like a dog in heat. I swear."

"That was mean and uncalled for, but I'll forgive you since going without female companionship for as long as you have tends to make a man ornery. I can only imagine you must be getting pretty tired of only having sex with the four sisters on Thumb Street." Jace's sandy-colored brows drew low beneath the brim of his black cowboy hat. "And the girls I was looking at are not bimbos, thank you very much. These two happen to be classy."

Ignoring Jace's jab about his only pleasure coming from his own hand for far too long, Tuck decided to focus on

Jace's taste in women instead. "Classy? Ha! I doubt that. You don't generally go for the high-class type."

"I could. For these two chicks anyway." The sound of Jace's voice rose and took on a defensive tone.

With a huff of defeat Tuck gave in and finally turned toward the entrance. Who the hell could these girls be that his friend thought they were such a big deal it warranted such an overly long conversation?

He didn't need Jace to point out the newest objects of his attention. There were only two blondes in the immediate area worthy of all this discussion, and they happened to be walking in his direction. The two looked so much alike, they had to be sisters. That fact, back in his younger years, might have held really intriguing possibilities of the sexual nature for Tuck. He'd had an unfulfilled sister fantasy since high school, when the Gibson sisters had shunned him and most of the other guys in their class in favor of the star players on the football team. He'd filled quite a few nights of his misspent youth dreaming about both of the Gibson girls, and thanks to the obsession they'd fueled, he'd also enjoyed a threesome a time or two while on the road competing.

However, those types of exploits and those single days—before the U.S. Army and a divorce had aged him beyond his years—were long past. Still, he was only thirty, not dead. He could appreciate the sight of a tempting female or two. He had to admit the one blonde, the woman looking like she'd be more at home on Rodeo Drive than at a rodeo, sure captured his attention.

Tuck knocked his cowboy hat back a bit and took a better look at the rear view as she turned and began to climb the stairs leading to the upper level seating of the arena. Dressed in black from the leather of her boots, to the enticingly tight denim of her jeans, to the low-cut but tasteful blouse, she definitely stuck out from the rest of the colorful crowd.

He saw the minute she noticed him watching her. She'd just turned to walk along the upper level. Her gaze met his, and she literally stumbled in her shiny, high-heeled, city-girl cowboy boots. She had to reach out and grab on to the arm of the blond woman walking next to her. Interesting. Apparently, he'd caught her eye just as she'd captured his. It was nice when things worked out. She continued to glance at him and then drag her gaze away, only to peek again a second later.

Feelings Tuck hadn't let himself own up to in a long time started to heat him. They began somewhere deep inside his core and radiated outward, filling him with warmth and anticipation. Jace was right. Tuck had been too long without a steady woman warming his bed. He hadn't let anyone inside his world, either for a night or for the long run, since that string of rebound flings he'd indulged in right after the breakup to try to forget his cheating ex-wife.

In his head Tuck knew one bad apple didn't spoil the whole barrel, and a woman who would run around on her husband while he was deployed in service to his country was surely the lowest of the low, but it was taking a while for the rest of him to believe it enough to take a risk on getting close to anyone again.

A twisting low in his gut accompanied by a familiar stirring in the region just below his championship belt buckle made Tuck decide he might be willing to explore things further with this girl. Not that it mattered much if he might be ready for something more involved than a quick tumble, because from the looks of this woman, she wasn't local. This area wasn't exactly a tourist destination, and she had *just passing through* written all over her. He doubted she'd be around long enough for him to get attached or hurt.

That was fine. Better actually. He should ease back in to having a social life slowly. They could enjoy each other for a night or two and then part as friends. No chance of a long-term commitment or the hurt that would come with the end of it. Just two attractive adults having a good time. His scarred heart could certainly handle that. And his dick was apparently on board with the idea as well.

"I get the one in black." When Jace didn't respond to his claim on the woman, Tuck glanced at his friend. He found Jace standing openmouthed and staring at him.

Finally, once the look of shock had passed, Jace laughed. "All right. You got it, Tuck. Oh, and there's a fresh box of condoms in my gear bag. You know, just in case."

Glancing at her again, he didn't bother denying his interest. Jace had known him too long for Tuck to try lying to him now. They'd been riding in local rodeos together since they were horny teens on the prowl for any willing female. As concerned about their post-competition activities as they were about the ride. It was no use pretending he wasn't picturing this woman and him rolling around naked. If she was willing, he sure was.

Tuck nodded. "Good to know. Thanks."

"Anytime. And about damn time you got back on the horse."

"Yeah, it is." Tuck nodded, not even mad at his friend's comment since it was true.

He leaned back against the rail, glad the women's seats were at this end of the arena, above the bucking chutes where he and Jace usually hung out before their event. This way he could keep an eye on them. Make sure his blonde didn't go anywhere before he had a chance to lay the old Jenkins charm on her, if he could remember how after all this time.

"I'm just glad there's two of them." Jace let out a snort of a laugh as they stood side-by-side watching the women work their way along the upper tier.

"Why's that?" Tuck frowned at the odd comment.

Jace shot him a sideways look. "Because when Tucker Jenkins is at the top of his game, no other guy stands a chance against him."

"The game being women, you mean?" Tuck laughed and shook his head. "I've been out of that game for a very long while." Between the years he'd been married and this past year, when he'd been too hateful to trust himself near any nice women, he was sorely out of practice.

"It's like a bicycle, I suppose. Just hop back on and *ride*." Jace waggled his eyebrows and smirked.

Shaking his head at that immature euphemism, Tuck glanced up and saw the two women had finally found their designated seats. Now their heads were bent close to each other as they talked, glancing in his direction. Oh, yeah. That was a good sign. He might be out of practice, but he knew when he had a woman's attention, and he sure had hers.

He knew he was staring—his mother would be appalled at his rudeness. And he knew the object of his newly awakened desire knew he was staring at her, but now he'd made his decision, he wasn't about to pussyfoot around. He'd never been subtle to begin with.

His heart rate picked up speed as adrenaline surged through him. He had a feeling making a play for this woman would be less like riding the bike Jace had compared it to and more like riding a bull—potentially dangerous but exhilarating and, if it worked out, totally worth the risk.

"Their seats suck. They're way the hell upstairs in the top tier." Jace was obviously keeping an eye on them as closely as Tuck was.

"You're right. We should bring them down to the floor." He hadn't brought a woman back behind the chutes to watch him compete in a very long time. Hell, lately there hadn't been any he'd wanted to bring down there with him. This woman, however, made him want to.

Again it seemed Tuck had managed to surprise his friend. Jace's brows rose high, but he nodded. "Uh, all right. If you want to. Sure. I'm game."

"Good. Let's go." He pushed aside any lingering doubts and strode up the steps, his legs easily spanning two at a time. A few inches shorter, Jace had to scramble to keep up.

Tuck smiled when the blonde's eyes popped open wide at the sight of him coming toward their section like a bull charging out of the gate. She looked as if she was ready to bolt, but her friend—or sister or whoever she was—was all smiles. That was all the encouragement he needed to not second-guess his course of action. He had her companion's approval. From past experience, he knew that could be the biggest part of the battle.

He heard the sound of Jace's boots on the stairs behind him. His backup. His wingman. Hopefully, they both wouldn't get shot down.

Up close, she was damn attractive. He'd learned the hard way that wasn't always the case, but this timeless distance only improved the view. She somehow managed to look sophisticated and naïve at the same time. Her wide eyes, full of surprise and a little bit of terror, were as blue as the cold brook running through the woods behind the house where he'd grown up. Her hair was as golden as a hay field . . . and just the fact he was thinking corny romantic stuff like this made Tuck want to turn around, run back down those stairs, and do something safe—like hop back on Son of a Gun.

He gave himself a pep talk as the distance between them shortened to mere yards now. This was just some innocent flirting. Okay, maybe not so innocent if the night turned out the way he hoped, but it certainly wasn't serious. He wasn't going to bring this girl home for dinner with his mamma. Hell, he probably wasn't going to get to do anything with her at all, because judging by the expression on her face, she'd rather crawl under the seats and hide than talk to him.

Too late now. He'd reached the point of no return as he stopped next to her.

"Hi. I'm Tucker Jenkins and this here is my buddy Jace Mills." Tuck hooked a thumb at his friend on the step below him and forged boldly ahead. "We couldn't help noticing you're pretty far away from the action in these seats. We were wondering if you'd like to come down below where we hang out and watch from there."

"We'd love to." The other blonde smiled and stood so fast, it earned her a shocked look from the woman who had Tuck's pulse racing. She continued, "I'm Emma, by the way, and this is my sister Becca."

Sisters. Yup. He'd thought so. Strange though, as much as they resembled each other, it was only one sister—Becca—who kept his attention stuck like glue.

"Wait. Are we allowed down there?" Becca looked even more uncertain as her glance shot between her sister and him, but despite her doubtful tone, Tuck had to admit her voice sounded as sweet to him as an angel's.

"Sure." He nodded. "As long as you're with us, you are."

"See. It's fine. Don't worry." Emma pulled Becca out of her seat, so now they were all standing on the stairs as a stream of people trying to get to their own seats pushed past.

Tuck couldn't care less if he was in the way. All of his attention was on the woman in front of him. He could see the dynamic between the sisters already. Emma was the adventurous one trying to push Becca out of her comfort zone, while Becca, the rule follower, was obviously the more conservative of the two, the worrier. Strange she was the one who made his heart race. In the past he would have gone for the other type. Maybe time and events had mellowed him. Or maybe there was something to all this chemistry stuff.

"Very nice to meet both of you ladies." Jace extended his arm and pumped each woman's hand in turn.

Thank God at least Jace was keeping up the niceties while Tuck was deep in his own head trying to figure out how to warm Becca toward him. Maybe some good old-fashioned small talk would help. Hell, it was worth a try.

"So, first time at a rodeo?" He directed the question directly to Becca, hoping she wouldn't be able to avoid answering.

"Yes." Her flushed face broke into a small, tentative smile aimed in his direction. "How could you tell?"

Tuck returned the smile. It wasn't at all hard to do. "Your boots look too good for you to have stomped around places like this very often."

"That's very observant of you." Her gaze dropped to his own well-worn boots and traveled back up as Becca did some observing of her own.

His knees nearly buckled from the intensity of her stare. He raised a brow at her perusal. She caught the move and yanked her gaze away as her cheeks turned a deeper shade of crimson.

"Well, I try." Tuck also had to try to mentally talk down the arousal her little head-to-toe inspection of him had caused.

Damn did she look attractive when she got all embarrassed. That didn't help the situation in his jeans, either. He didn't come across many women who blushed. He was finding he liked it. A lot.

He pulled himself out of the pool of her eyes enough to

notice both his friend and her sister had become very quiet. He glanced at them and yup, just as expected, the two were watching them like proud parents at their kid's first school dance. As if this weren't hard enough already, the dead last thing he needed was Jace playing matchmaker.

Though if Becca's sister were half as nosy about her love life as Jace was about his, at least he and Becca would have something in common. An alliance to build upon. That was good. He'd gladly take that common ground while he regained his footing in the treacherous dating waters. Then hopefully later tonight he'd need the supply of what was in Jace's gear bag.

Tuck turned his attention back to Becca. "How about we get you downstairs and settled? The opening will be starting soon."

Becca hesitated. She glanced at her sister and then looked back at Tuck. Finally, she nodded. "Okay."

"Good." He grinned and grabbed her hand. At that, both her eyes and her sister's opened a little wider.

City girls sure were easy to rattle if a little hand-holding shocked them. He decided he liked that, but he couldn't even begin to imagine how she was going to react later if and when he dropped his jeans and introduced her to Tuck Junior.

He laced his fingers with hers and held tight, having no intention of letting go as he led her and the others down the stairs. One quick glance over his shoulder told him Becca's sister was following with a smile on her face. And behind her, with his attention glued to Emma's butt while he walked and wore a smile of his own, was Jace.

Quite the mix of characters they had here. If nothing else, it was sure going to be one hell of an interesting evening.

Chapter
Four

As they descended the stairs, Becca struggled to match the long stride of the cowboy at whom her sister had practically thrown her. Tucker—even his name sounded cowboy, which fit in perfectly with the rest of him. From the hat to the boots and all the many parts in between.

Glancing around, she found herself amid a sea of cowboy hats. She was definitely in Oklahoma. A stranger in a strange land. Speaking of strange, she was feeling more than strange to have her hand captured in his much larger, work-roughened one.

He led them to the lower level where he nodded to a man wearing a T-shirt marked SECURITY. That single nod was all it took to gain all four of them access to what looked like a restricted area. It relieved the suspicious New Yorker in her. He must at least be familiar to the security personnel and not some kidnapper who came in off the street. That was something anyway. Of course Emma wasn't one bit concerned. The free spirit who was her sister would likely get them both killed one day.

Becca scowled at the thought as they wound their way down another flight of stairs toward an area that bustled with rodeo competitors and staff, and she felt even more out of place.

The definite scent of manure assaulted her nose. A

glance to the right had her tripping over her own feet as the source of that particular odor was revealed—a dozen or so bulls. Really big bulls with long horns, and nothing keeping them contained except for some pretty flimsy-looking metal railings. At least they looked flimsy to her as one bull rammed the boundaries of the pen and the whole thing shifted a good six inches.

Torn between which she should be more worried about, the animals ready to stampede or the cowboy still clasping her hand in his iron grip, she glanced behind her. Emma was still there, looking triumphant. Perhaps Emma should spend less time gloating over Becca's current situation with Tucker and pay more attention to the other cowboy. The one bringing up the rear . . . and concentrating solely on Emma's butt.

Becca glanced down again at their intertwined fingers. Her bastard ex-boyfriend Jerry hadn't been a hand-holder. Not in the beginning of their relationship, and definitely not near the end. She wasn't sure how she felt about this man who'd plucked her out of her seat to bring her to his domain. Kind of like a Neanderthal dragging his chosen mate by her hair back to his cave.

Part of her railed against the whole concept. While other parts of her, parts lower, were all aflutter. She'd never dated a really manly man. She'd been with other English students while she was in college, but if their hands got dirty it was because they were erasing the chalkboard or dusting the lesser used books on the shelves in the campus library. Then came Jerry who pushed papers for a living at his job in sales. Not one of the men in her past had ever made her feel quite so . . . dominated.

Just the word had her womanly muscles clenching as Tucker stopped walking and turned to her, his eyes focused solely on hers. "This good? You'll be able to see the bucking chutes from here."

She eyed the immediate area, feeling every inch of her New York roots and like she didn't belong anywhere near this wild place filled with men and beasts. "Wow. This is really close."

To her right was one cowboy bent over strapping on a pair of leather chaps. Next to him, another one wrapped surgical tape around his own wrist. Meanwhile another guy pulled on a vest covered in sponsor logos, making her feel even more out of place and like she was intruding on their private space. Kind of like a female sports reporter who'd stepped into a testosterone-laden locker room full of jocks in nothing but towels.

At least these cowboys weren't naked, just making some final preparations, and they didn't seem to care she was there. They were right out in view of the rest of the public, who were kept on the next level by the guard their little foursome had swooped right past thanks to Tucker's lead.

She yanked her gaze away from the various vignettes and spotted the other demographic of people. Scattered around the male competitors were girls. She definitely wouldn't call them women. Nope. They were girls. Young, bouncy, eager-looking girls who seemed much closer to her students' ages than her own.

"That's the whole idea, sweetheart. To enjoy rodeo properly, you gotta be close enough to see the snot fly." Tucker grinned, his blue eyes crinkling in the corners as he did. He dropped his hold on her hand and moved to stand slightly behind her and to the side.

The snot comment had her laughing, until she felt the weight of his right arm drape casually around her shoulder. "You're right. This is much closer than our seats. We'll definitely be able to see the snot from here." She swallowed hard.

Again, he took her by surprise. Had Jerry ever put his

arm around her shoulders? Probably not. Jerry was only a few inches taller than she was. It would have been a stretch for him. But Tucker was so tall, he could easily see the arena over her head. Even so, he stayed turned toward her, his gaze remaining only on her.

How was he so focused on her and only her when the girls surrounding them could easily make up a cheerleading squad? All right, the *sweetheart* comment had made her feel a bit better about being old enough to chaperone the group of girls hanging out among the cowboys, but the whole thing was still perplexing. Particularly how that intense stare of his remained trained on her rather than moving on to the perky young thing whose top didn't cover her belly button or hide the outline of her nipples.

It was a mystery to Becca.

As a bull rammed the railed enclosure one more time, she jumped and wondered if maybe they were standing a little too close. Bull snot was one thing. Horns and hooves were quite another. She'd seen videos of the running of the bulls in Pamplona. It wasn't something she wanted to participate in, there in Spain or here in Oklahoma. Yet somehow she trusted Tucker. Even without really knowing him, she had a feeling he'd save her if a crazed bull should barrel through that fence and charge her. But they should really invest in some stronger fencing, in her opinion. She eyed the enclosure one more time.

"Uh, he's not going to break out of there, is he?" Her voice sounded a bit squeakier than she would have liked. Squeaky was not sexy. Though being trampled and covered in snot wouldn't be so good, either.

"Nah. He's just flexing his muscles a bit. He's fine." As he swiveled his head to look toward the bull still making the disturbance, she allowed herself to look closer at the cowboy who was so calm about the commotion.

He was probably close to thirty. Older than the barely

twenty-something females hanging out nearby, but not too old he couldn't take advantage of them if he really wanted to. Certainly not too old to be hanging out with them rather than her.

Maybe he had a daughter of his own. That could be one explanation for what was keeping him from partaking of the bimbo buffet within reach. She did the math in her head. Tuck could have a twelve-year-old if he'd started young.

Kids usually came with a wife. That thought raised a whole new and very troubling concern. As he gripped the metal rail, she glanced at his left hand—no wedding ring. Not even a white stripe of skin where one had been recently. Phew. She breathed a sigh of relief and tried to calm her racing heart.

Maybe for tonight she should stop over-thinking things, or at least stop analyzing everything quite so much. Though old habits were hard to break.

How nice would it be to not think for a little while and just be? Emma seemed to be able to live in the moment with no problem, but Becca wasn't sure she'd ever done that before. Maybe tonight was the time to give it a try.

"Thank you." She glanced up at Tucker.

"For what?" He glanced down and his eyes met hers. Again the intensity of his gaze unnerved her, and she broke eye contact first, looking around them.

"For bringing us down here. Making sure we can see." Making sure they didn't get trampled to death . . . She shrugged. "For everything."

"My pleasure." The dimple in his chin was so tempting, she found herself staring at it. She imagined nibbling on that and more of him. She yanked her gaze away and tried to get hold of herself.

"Hey, you girls want a couple of beers?" Jace's question

broke into her naughty imaginings about what parts of Tucker she'd like to bite.

"Thanks. That would be great." Emma answered for both of them, just as Becca had opened her mouth to say no. Stone-cold sober, she was already picturing her mouth all over Tucker. She hated to even think what would happen if she had some alcohol in her.

"You be okay while we're gone?" Tucker squeezed her shoulder as he asked the question.

He touched her so easily, so casually, yet it still had her swallowing hard. "Uh. Sure."

"Okay. Be right back." He winked and turned on one boot heel, treating her to the tempting view of the back of him.

Tucker Jenkins sure did wear his jeans well. He should probably be the spokesmodel for the brand. Come to think of it, the name of a jeans company was embroidered down the arm of his shirt. He probably was a spokesmodel.

This was all so different from what she had expected when Emma first declared they were going to a rodeo in Oklahoma. She let out a breath and tried to absorb it all.

"Oh, my God. He is so hot." Emma's eyes were opened so wide, Becca was afraid her sister's eyeballs might pop out and roll after the two cowboys walking away.

"Which one?" Not wanting to give her sister the satisfaction of knowing she was melting inside from five minutes in Tucker's presence, she played innocent.

"You know very well which one." Emma screwed her mouth up into her usual annoyed expression. "The one who's been holding your hand and looking at you like he wants to eat you for dinner."

"In case you haven't noticed, there are two of them, and the other one seems to like you just fine." She cocked a brow at her sister. If she was going to be devoured for dinner, then Emma was going to be right there on the table next to her.

"Can't blame him, really." Emma grinned. "I'm a very likeable person, you know."

She ignored Emma's joking. "You're really okay with hanging out and drinking with two strange men we only met a few minutes ago?" She might be very interested in getting to know Tucker a little better, but she'd be damned if it was because her sister had decided it for her.

"Of course, I am. And they're not strange, they're just strangers. There's a difference."

"Emma Hart, sometimes you scare me. Strangers are just as bad, or are you forgetting all those stranger-danger assemblies we had to sit through back in middle school? You really need to be a little more selective about who you're willing to go out with. What do we know about these guys?"

"We know we're not up in the nosebleed seats anymore, thanks to them. They're polite. We know they're paying for our beer. What's not to be okay with? I even hope you'll have breakfast with one of them in the morning."

"Emma!" Okay, the idea had already crossed her mind, but still, Emma was her older sister. Her job was to talk Becca out of having casual sex with strange men, not talk her into it.

"Come on, Becca. You were living like an old, boring, married lady while you were with Jerry, and since breaking up you've been living like a nun. It won't kill you to have a little fun."

"It might. What if they're serial killers who stay one step ahead of the law by traveling with the rodeo?" She tried to imagine a string of bodies and missing persons strewn across the country, coincidentally matching up with the rodeo circuit, but she couldn't. That image didn't fit with the man who'd asked with genuine concern whether she'd be okay if he left her for a few minutes. The same guy who'd just stopped on the way to the concession stand to take a picture with a little boy all dressed up in miniature cowboy gear to match Tucker's big-boy outfit.

She watched Tucker take a marker from the boy's mother and sign the boy's cowboy hat, before tipping his own and turning toward the beer vendor to join Jace there. Okay, maybe she was being ridiculous and these cowboys weren't serial killers on the lam, but that didn't mean she was going to give Emma the satisfaction of knowing.

"You like him."

Becca turned to see her sister's smug expression. Crap. Emma knew her so well, she could read her face like an open book. It was true. Stranger she'd just met or not, she did like Tucker.

She struggled with herself before finally giving in and rolling her eyes. "All right. I'll admit he seems nice. On the surface."

"Ha! I told you so."

With a groan, she shook her head. This was why she didn't want to admit anything to Emma. "What did you tell me?"

"That you should apply for the job because Oklahoma could be a nice place to live and work. That you'd have fun here at the rodeo. And that cowboys were hot." Emma let out a sigh of appreciation. "Mmm, mmm. Look at all these strapping, handsome men, and they're all gathered for you under one roof right here in Perkins, Oklahoma. Which I might add is conveniently located a short drive from Stillwater, where you have a job interview tomorrow and will be living if—when—you get the position."

She ignored Emma's self-satisfied tone. "Anything else you'd like to add to your I-told-you-so?"

"Nope." Emma shook her head and shot Becca a grin.

"Good. Now it's my turn. First of all, I didn't get the job yet, and who knows if I even will? Furthermore, I have yet to be convinced Oklahoma is such a great place to live or work. It's only been a few hours since we landed. We've seen nothing but the airport, our hotel room, and this arena. And lastly, the rodeo hasn't even started yet, so how do you know it'll be fun?" Becca crossed her arms and narrowed her gaze at her sister, but all Emma did in response was smirk.

"That all?" Emma asked.

"Yes. Why?" She frowned, already exhausted from both the travel and all this banter. How long would it be before the guys got back with their beers? Maybe then Emma would leave her alone.

"I notice you didn't deny my third point. That cowboys are hot." Emma's brows rose with a challenge.

Becca's gaze hit on Tucker and Jace, walking toward them now, each with two big plastic cups in their hands. Tucker's long legs ate up the distance between them, the cowboy boots making him swagger just a bit. His hat was drawn down low enough over his eyes that it emphasized the strong line of his jaw. She let out a breath. "Fine. I'll concede these two particular cowboys happen to be hot, but nothing more."

Emma sighed, loud and long. "You won't give even an inch, will you?"

"Nope." She finally broke her gaze away from Tucker's tempting form to glance at Emma.

A small smile bowed her lips as she saw Emma watching the two men's approach as well. Her sister finally glanced her way. "That's okay. Time will prove me right."

Becca had a bad suspicion it might, but she couldn't worry about things like Emma gloating right now. She was too busy wondering, and worrying, what her nosy sister might do or say next to embarrass her.

"And when they get back here with those beers, you drink up. You need to relax. You obviously forgot how to flirt during all the time you were with that ass Jerry."

"I can flirt just fine."

"You're doing a pretty shitty job of it tonight."

"That's because . . ." Becca couldn't say. Maybe she had been out of the dating world too long. Maybe Tucker was just so far removed from any man she'd ever been attracted to before she was out of her comfort zone. It wasn't like she could talk Chaucer's *Canterbury Tales,* or Broadway shows with him. The fact was, she was so attracted to him in a raw animal kind of way, she'd be happy to not talk at all. She let out a sigh but refused to tell Emma any of that, so she gave up. "Oh, be quiet. I flirt fine."

"Whatever you say. Just drink some beer. You need it." Emma kept her voice low as the men descended the stairs toward them.

Becca couldn't reply to Emma's suggestion she get drunk so she'd flirt better, because there was the hotter-than-hell cowboy handing her a cupful of beer. She took it, needing two hands to do so it was so big.

"Thanks." She glanced up into those eyes hidden in the shadow of his hat, making them look even more sultry.

"You're welcome." His lips curved, looking soft in comparison to the dark stubble covering his cheeks and chin.

Jerry had gone an entire week without shaving once when he'd taken vacation time from work, and he still didn't have stubble nearly as thick as what she suspected was Tucker's five o'clock shadow. She'd never known she'd been into the rugged-type of man, but this look was sure doing it for her tonight. Becca took a sip of beer, hoping the icy-cold foam sliding down her throat would cool the parts lower that were really starting to heat up.

Her gaze hit upon Tuck's big hand wrapped around his

own cup, and the tingle deep inside her increased twofold as she imagined what those long, thick fingers would feel like running over her body. God, she'd gone so long without good sex. She'd probably never even had the kind of sex Tucker could offer. The getting-thrown-down-and-sweaty kind. Becca's attention moved to his biceps, straining the fabric of his button-down shirt. Yes, sir. He could definitely pick her up and throw her onto the bed. No problem.

She watched the cup press against his lips as he took a sip and then frowned at the dark liquid and ice cubes she could see through the plastic. She glanced at Jace's cup, and it, too, contained the same colored drink.

"That's not beer," Becca accused.

He swallowed and then smiled. "No, ma'am. It's pop." She couldn't help smiling, too, at how Tucker called soda *pop,* as he continued, "I admit I'll ride hung over, I won't lie to you and say I haven't, but I'm not crazy enough to drink before I sit my butt on a bull."

"A bull?" Her eyes opened wide at his revelation. "That's what you ride?"

Next to Tucker, Jace laughed. "Yup. What did you think we did?"

"I don't know. I mean I saw the bulls over there, but I guess I thought you rode horses or something. Or maybe you, like, herded the bulls and roped them." Becca shot Emma a glance and saw her laughing and shaking her head.

"I told you bull riding was one of the events. I read the entire schedule to you right off the rodeo web page the day we booked our flights. Remember?"

Becca remembered the day. She just tended not to listen too closely when Emma started talking incessantly about things that didn't really interest her. Though she sure found Tucker interesting—and now he was smiling at her.

"Roping bulls." Tuck grinned wide as he captured her in his gaze. "You're absolutely adorable."

"Um, thanks." Her cheeks heated at the compliment.

Um, thanks? She stifled a groan at her reply. Dammit, Emma was right. She couldn't flirt for anything. She took another sip of beer.

"And to be fair to your sister, Miss Emma"—Jace tipped his head in Emma's direction—"Tuck and I do occasionally ride horses and do some roping, too. We rope calves, or steers. Not bulls."

"You do?" Becca asked.

Emma's attention turned to Jace now. Becca was happy to see her sister wasn't exactly immune to cowboy charm, either. "Calves and steers? That's really interesting."

"Yes, ma'am." Tucker dipped his head in agreement. "Jace and I competed in team roping for a few years once upon a time."

"Until someone backed out on me." Jace shot Tucker a look.

Tucker's brows rose in response. "Circumstances beyond my control and you know it. And you could have found another header if you wanted to."

"Yeah, yeah. Like just any other header would do." Jace scowled at Tucker and then glanced at Becca and Emma. "I'm a heeler, you see."

"Ah, of course." Becca nodded and tried to look as if the entire conversation about headers and heelers hadn't gone right over her head. She knew about headers and footers and other document formatting–type lingo, but this rodeo reference was totally new to her.

Tucker laughed, deep and low. A sound that went right through her core.

"I'll explain the different events to you while we watch." He shook his head, still grinning. "It's been a long time since I've had to explain rodeo to a city girl."

She got a twisting of irrational jealousy in her belly, not that she'd ever assumed she was the first woman this cowboy had charmed. "Oh, really? Have you had to explain this stuff to a lot of city girls?"

That elicited another hearty chuckle from Tucker. He leaned lower, closer to her ear. "Never one as cute as you."

He straightened again right after he spoke, but the warmth where his breath had wafted across her skin remained. It intensified and spread through her. Becca swallowed hard. She glanced at Emma, who luckily was getting a lecture from Jace about something rodeo related, judging by how he was pointing out things to her in the arena. Good. She didn't need Emma watching her. She knew there was no hiding from her sister the blush creeping across her cheeks. After the big serial killer stranger-danger rant a moment ago, she was in for a big I-told-you-so from Emma for letting Tucker get to her.

"Your sister said you flew here. From where?" Tucker was asking Becca a question, so she couldn't worry about Emma's imminent lecture anymore.

"New York."

Tuck nodded. "Yeah, I shoulda guessed that."

"Why?" Her brows knit in a frown. She'd worked very hard to make sure she didn't have any sort of regional accent. She was certain she'd done a good job of keeping any New York influence out of her speech.

"That wasn't an insult, sweetheart. Just an observation. All the New Yorkers I've known have a certain . . . way about them. I would have recognized it, if I wasn't too busy noticing other things, I suppose."

"Oh, really? You get a lot of New Yorkers in this part of Oklahoma?"

"No, not so much. But I do know a few folks who weren't born in this state. You know, one or two." Grinning, Tucker continued on, either oblivious to or just plain ignoring how she had reacted to his comment. "So, how long you here for?"

"We leave tomorrow." Emma, suddenly back in the conversation with Becca and Tucker, answered for them both.

"Really? Well now, that's a real shame. I guess we better make the most of tonight then. Don't you think, Tuck?" Jace asked his friend.

"I guess so." Tucker tipped his head in agreement and took another sip of his soda, but his attention never left Becca as his gaze held hers over the rim of his cup.

"I agree. We definitely should." Emma shot Becca a look heavily laden with suggestion, which she tried her best to ignore.

"There are some good bars around here. Some of them have live music on weekends. How would you ladies like to go out after we're done here? Maybe you'll get to experience a real live Oklahoma honky-tonk while you're here."

"We'd love to go out afterward." Once again, Emma answered for them both.

"You up for that?" Tucker looked specifically at Becca, making direct eye contact.

The problem wasn't Tucker. It was her. She'd been miserable and monogamous for so long, she was afraid she'd forgotten how to let loose and have fun. If she'd ever really known how to begin with. Looking at Tucker, she realized he was the perfect guy to relearn with.

She swallowed hard and gave in to temptation. "Okay."

"Good." He smiled wide. His eyes twinkling beneath the brim of his hat captured hers and made her heart beat faster. She could picture those eyes holding her in their trance as he leaned in for a kiss . . . or more.

Damn. She was in big trouble. She and Tucker could have one hell of a crazy night together. The kind of memories that would last her a lifetime. Then she could fly home and never see him again.

This plan wasn't like her at all. She didn't do one-night stands, but right now, after all she'd been through recently with Jerry and the job loss, the idea of throwing caution to the wind in favor of some mind-numbing fun seemed a little too tempting to pass up.

Becca took another long swallow of beer. She needed all the courage she could get.

"Another?" Tuck's gaze dropped to the increasingly low level of the beer in her cup.

"Um." Oh, what the hell. She nodded. "Sure. Thank you."

Chapter
Five

"You like her."

"What? Who?" Tuck stoically did not respond to Jace's question. Instead he kept his gaze on the concession stand attendant as the kid poured two more beers.

"You know damn well who. So how we gonna work this?"

"Work what?" This time Tuck wasn't playing dumb, but knowing his friend, he was almost afraid to find out what Jace was talking about.

"Getting them alone. They must have a hotel room nearby since they're not local, but I'm thinking they're most likely sharing one room. So one of us is going to need to get another room."

"I think you need to slow down and not put the cart before the horse." Tuck shot Jace a warning glance.

"What?" Jace's eyes opened wide. "What the hell are you talking about?"

"You can't assume we'll be giving those two anything more than a couple of beers."

"The Tuck Jenkins I know would never say something like that."

"No, probably not." Tuck let out a snort.

The man he used to be a year ago, right after the divorce, would have been fine with screwing a girl behind the building or bending her over the sink in the men's room. In fact, that had happened in the restroom of this very arena. He'd been pretty shitfaced and it was all a little hazy, but he was sure it had been here. Which meant it had also been exactly one year ago during the Independence Weekend Rodeo.

He shook the memory away. He was a different person now. Jeez, at least he sure as hell hoped he was. Besides, he could tell Becca wasn't that kind of a woman and he didn't want her to be. Her careful consideration of each and every question, from moving from their seats down to the floor, to deciding whether she wanted another beer, was one of the things he liked about her.

Sure, he'd like to get naked, even get a little kinky with her, but he'd also like to wake up next to her in the morning. He hadn't thought that about a woman since the divorce. He pushed thoughts of his ex-wife away and turned to Jace. "Let's see how things go. Okay?"

"Okay." His friend eyed him closer than Tuck was comfortable with. "You do know, your divorce? It was nothing you did. Brenda was always a bitch. I knew that from the first time I met her. I always thought you deserved better."

This conversation had taken a turn for the serious. The last thing Tuck needed or wanted right now was serious, or a concession stand analysis of his failed marriage. He laughed and tried to lighten things up. "It would have been nice if you'd told me before I put the ring on her finger."

Jace shrugged. "If you'd made me your best man instead of *her* brother, maybe I would have."

"This again? It's not like I had a choice." Tuck rolled his eyes, not believing they were on this subject again after all these years. His own brother would have been the logical choice for best man, but as he'd said, Brenda had forced the issue.

"Correct. You didn't, because she was a bitch." Jace spread his hands wide. "See the logic here?"

"Yes, I do. Now help me carry these drinks." Tuck handed two of the cups off to Jace. "And next time, open your damned mouth before I walk down the aisle. I don't care if you're the best man or not."

"Next time, I'll let you know exactly what I'm thinking. In fact, I think I'll start right now by saying if you don't take that pretty little thing to bed tonight, you're going to regret it the rest of your life."

Didn't he know it, though he truly hated when Jace was right. Tuck picked up the last two cups and turned away from the concession stand. He scanned behind the chutes. It was easy enough to spot Becca in the crowd, even from a distance. Her gaze met his and his heart rate picked up speed.

Crap. One night wasn't going to be enough with this girl. He knew that already and they hadn't even gotten naked yet.

The announcer's amplified voice coming over the sound system interrupted Tucker's suspicions he should probably run in the opposite direction, far away from Becca, without looking back. Otherwise, there was a good chance he was going to be drowning eyeball deep in something he wasn't sure he was ready for.

Luckily, he couldn't think too much more about that now because it was showtime. He glanced at Jace. "Come on. We better get back."

"I was waiting on you." Jace frowned before he turned and led the way back to the chutes and the two women.

Tucker let out a slow breath, thinking one more time it would probably be less risky—and less painful—riding the rankest bull in the State of Oklahoma than opening himself up to a woman again.

Loud music reverberated off the walls, sending the

adrenaline coursing through Tuck's veins. He'd competed for so long, such cues as the roar of the crowd, the announcer's echoing voice, and the pounding base of the music pumped into the arena all caused a visceral reaction. It all combined to tell his body it was time. He was like a warrior preparing for battle, every cell in his being ready, except his battle was against a bull and it would last only eight seconds.

Worse, the bull riding was the final event. He had an entire evening to sit through, feeling hyped enough to crawl out of his skin, just so he could jump on that bull and expend some of this energy.

His gaze hit on Becca, and he decided there was a much better way to get rid of some of this restlessness. The image hit him of tangling his hand in her hair, pulling her head back, and claiming her mouth with a long hard kiss.

That would certainly be nice and there was nothing he would enjoy more, but instead Tuck smiled and handed her the beer. "Here you go."

"Thank you." Her focus went to his cup. She smiled. "Soda pop again?"

He tipped his head. "Yes, ma'am."

"You will drink later on, won't you?"

Hmm, she'd warmed up a bit while he'd been away. What had done that? Was the beer kicking in? Or perhaps it had been a heart-to-heart with her sister, who seemed to be all for their spending time together later. Either way, something had swayed Becca toward him. Gone was the slight hesitation before her every sentence. Instead was a bold flirty city girl he'd definitely be happy to get to know a lot better, not that he hadn't been into her already. Now that she'd gone and added another layer to her complexity, she was even more tempting.

Maybe that kiss wasn't out of the question after all . . . a bit later.

"I surely will. As soon as my feet hit the dirt after my ride, I will gladly join you in a drink."

"Your feet, or your face. Either one." Jace grinned wide.

Tuck shot his supposed friend a less than happy glance. "Thank you for your confidence."

Jace's eyes crinkled in the corners with his smile. "You're very welcome."

He turned back to see Becca smiling.

"I look forward to it."

Tucker raised his cup to her in a toast. "As do I. So, let me tell you what's going to happen tonight."

Her brows rose. "All right."

Her smirk told him she was thinking about something besides rodeo. He laughed and shook his head. "In the events, I mean." They could discuss the post-competition activity later. He'd look forward to that. "It moves pretty quick. You can't keep the animals cooling their heels in the pens or the chutes for too long."

"Of course." She nodded knowingly, but he suspected she'd probably never owned anything bigger than a goldfish. Or maybe one of those little dogs fancy women carried around in their purses. That was fine. He was a very good teacher. He'd certainly enjoy their lessons.

With that image in mind, Tuck continued. "The action pretty much alternates between the two ends of the arena. The bucking chutes are at this end and the ropers' boxes are at the other end. So you're gonna see bareback bronc riding here, then tie-down and team roping down there. Then saddle broncs at our end and steer wrestling at the other end. There's a break so they can set up the barrel racing for the women—I'll explain it to you when we get to it. Then there's an event for the kids. Mutton bustin'."

"Mutton? Like people eat?" Her eyes opened wide, making him smile.

"Yup. Sheep. The little kids—like five or six years old—

ride those and try to hang on. Then the maintenance crew drags the arena and the bull riding closes the event."

"They save the best for last, huh?" Becca's lips looked too damned tempting when she smirked all vixenlike. It would be very easy to bend down and take a taste.

Tuck swallowed hard. He certainly hoped there would be one more event at the end of the night. A private one between him and Becca. "They certainly do."

"I look forward to the end, then."

So did he. So did he.

"So, right now there will be some exhibition riding. The barrel racers will ride in with the colors. Once the flag is brought out there will be a prayer and the singing of the national anthem. Then there will be some riders in the ring, warming up the horses, both the rough stock and the trained stock . . ." He paused when he realized Becca likely didn't know the difference. "I'm sorry. Am I going too fast for you?"

"No. Don't worry. You're definitely not going too fast." Becca took another swallow of beer, but her eyes stayed on him.

Tuck drew in a deep breath, deciding to cut her off for a while after this drink. He wanted her. Hell, yeah. But he wanted her because she wanted him, not because he'd gotten her drunk.

That thought gave him pause. It was just another thing that had changed in him since a year ago. Back then he'd be pouring shots into a girl if it meant it would get her out of her pants quicker. Sure, he'd had to step quick to avoid getting puke on his boots once or twice after that, but what did he care? He was quick on his feet, and quick to get in and out.

That was back then.

Not anymore, and definitely not tonight. Tonight, with

Becca, he intended to take his time. And he wanted her to be acutely aware of every single second of it. He glanced at the clock on the scoreboard. It was dinnertime, and judging by the way one beer had loosened her tongue considerably, he was betting she hadn't eaten. "Hey, you girls want to try one of our Oklahoma delicacies?"

Again Becca's brows rose. "Sure. What did you have in mind?"

He smiled. They'd get to that later. "The arena specialty. Foot-long corn dogs. Ever have one before?"

"Foot-long, huh? Impressive." Emma laughed. "And no, I can't say I've ever had a corn dog."

"I've never had one before, either, foot-long or other."

The expression on Becca's face was so devilish and inviting, Tuck had to yank his gaze away before he did something he shouldn't, like take her in back and show her something else that was long. Not twelve inches, but long enough for his purposes.

Jace shook his head. "Oh, you girls don't know what you're missing."

He swallowed hard. "I'll go get us a few."

"Thank you." Emma smiled at both him and Jace, but it was Becca who kept drawing his attention.

"My pleasure." Tuck shot a glance at Jace that told him to follow and then headed up the stairs one more time.

"What's up?" Jace matched his stride. "I've seen you buy girls drinks, but you're not usually one to feed them."

"She's getting drunk." Or at least her sudden easy flirtatiousness led him to believe she was.

"Yeah." Jace nodded. "What's the problem? That's a good thing."

Tuck frowned. "You can be a pig sometimes. You know that? Anyway, I figured they could both use some food in their stomachs."

Jace shook his head.

"What now?" Tuck was getting pretty annoyed at Jace's judgmental head shaking tonight.

"You're different. That's all. It's not bad, just different. I'm trying to figure out what changed. Is it you just getting older? Or is it this woman?"

"It's me trying to be a decent guy and show two out-of-towners some hospitality. Stop reading into things." He certainly hoped it wasn't this woman who had him suddenly acting like a gentleman, because she was flying away tomorrow.

Chapter
Six

Becca watched Tucker bend at the waist. Mmm, mmm. He was sure built nice. From the top of his felt hat to the tips of his worn leather boots. Those leather chaps he'd just slung around his hips weren't too bad, either.

He reached back to buckle the chap straps first around one jean-clad thigh, and then the other. And she'd thought the rodeo would be boring. Ha! She could watch Tucker do this all day. Buckle and unbuckle. Bend and stand.

She let out a sigh filled with pure contentment. "All right, Em. I'll admit it. Cowboys are hot."

Next to her, Emma laughed. "Oh, yeah."

"Go ahead and say it." Becca shot a sideways glance at her sister.

"Say what?"

"Another I-told-you-so. I know you want to."

"Nope." Emma shook her head.

That was a surprise. "Really? Why not?"

"Because I'm happy to see you happy." Her sister smiled in her direction. "Becs, I'm really glad we did this together."

"Oh, sure. Me, too. All New Yorkers should attend at least one rodeo in their lives," she teased.

One of Emma's brows rose sharply. "Don't think I didn't hear that sarcasm. And I meant the whole trip, silly.

No matter what happens tomorrow with your interview and the job, I'm still glad we came."

Becca smiled. "Me, too. And thank you."

This hadn't exactly been on her bucket list of things to do before she died, but nevertheless she was very glad she'd done it. Her attention went back to Tucker again as he bent to get something out of his bag and the chaps acted as a frame for his very nice rear asset.

"For what?" Emma frowned.

"For making me come here to the rodeo even though I didn't want to. For being a little sneak and applying for the job even though that was still very wrong of you. For all of it."

Thanks to Emma's meddling, Becca wouldn't have to live with regrets. She wouldn't have to wonder what if? And if nothing else, at least they'd have good stories for the folks back home about their whirlwind Oklahoma adventure.

"Don't be silly. No thanks necessary. My favorite thing is making you do things you don't want to." Emma grinned.

"Yes, I know." As sincere as her thanks had been, she still couldn't help laughing at the truth of what Emma had said. That was the kind of relationship they had, and as annoying as her sister could be sometimes, Becca didn't think she'd want it any other way.

"Love you, Bec."

"Love you, too, Em."

"So, I'd like to make a proposal. More of a pact, actually." Emma glanced at her sister before turning back to watch the two cowboys again.

Becca's brows rose. "All right. What's your proposal?"

"Whatever happens tonight, there'll be no judgment on my part. No walk of shame in the morning. In fact, I hope I don't see you again until breakfast before your interview tomorrow. I want you to have a good time. I want you to get the thoughts of that bastard Jerry and what he did to you knocked so far out of your system you can't even remember what he looks like. And if riding that cowboy all night long is the best way to do it, then that's exactly what I want you to do. Okay?"

Her heart beat faster at the thought of what Emma was suggesting. Two city girls out at the rodeo with a couple of cowboys they'd just met was one thing. But Emma telling her to spend the whole night with one of them was quite another. She was still having trouble wrapping her head around what an entire night with Tucker might be like, but parts lower, female parts long ignored, were warming to the idea nicely.

Finally, she gave in to it all. Her sister. Her desire. Tucker. "Okay."

Emma smiled wide. "Good."

The fact she was giving Emma the satisfaction of being right about everything—from applying for the position at OSU, to coming to the rodeo, to a night with a cowboy— proved how woozy Tucker's mere presence made her. The two beers she'd had over the course of the last couple of hours probably helped with that a little, too, but she was far from drunk. Well, maybe she was a bit intoxicated, but on cowboy pheromones, not alcohol.

Her gaze fixed again on the men. They'd moved on to working with what she now knew after her private rodeo tutorial with Tucker were their bull ropes.

Next to her, Emma let out a sigh. "I don't know what it is about cowboys that makes them so irresistible. It must be all the leather."

"Could be." Becca couldn't exactly put her finger on the allure, either.

Maybe it was the leather. Or the easy way they said ma'am and darlin'. That hint of a drawl in Tucker's voice reminded her every time she heard it that she wasn't in

New York anymore. Since she had particularly bad memories for one particular New York man, as well as a certain New York college that had let her go, that was a good thing.

Of course, it could be the jeans and boots and the swagger, which seemed to come as a package deal on all the cowboys. But most likely it was the sheer amount of attention Tucker paid to her, as if she were the only woman in the room when that was far from the case. Except for the few times they'd gone to get food or drink, or take a bathroom break, the two cowboys hadn't left their sides for the whole night, until now when they had to prepare for their rides.

She'd gotten the promised explanation on all the night's competitions, but it was the details about the bull riding, Tucker's event, she'd listened to most intently. It wasn't hard listening to Tucker speak. She let the soothing warmth of his voice wash over her. She had memorized every detail as if there would be a quiz later. Except for that one part when she'd gotten distracted watching Tucker's mouth, but that wasn't her fault. When a man that attractive licks his lips, a girl's got to look. And imagine . . .

He straightened now and said something to Jace, who was getting ready next to him. When Tucker glanced in Becca's direction and saw her watching, he smiled and winked. That one move, just a wink, made her knees go weak. She swallowed hard and knew with complete certainty, she was going to do it—she was going to spend the night with him.

"Em, should we have some sort of signal?"

"What kind of signal?" Emma asked.

"If I want you to, you know, leave us alone." Becca couldn't believe that suggestion had just come out of her own mouth. Or that she was planning on doing this. Then the practical side of her took over. "But wait, that'll leave you alone for the night in a strange place—"

Emma held up one hand to stop her. "Oh, no. Don't you dare back out of doing this because of me. Don't worry about me. I'm the older sister and I can take care of myself. You worry about yourself, but you're right. We do need a plan and some signals."

"Agreed. So what should they be?" Becca could plan out an entire semester's lessons, but it seemed tonight she was incapable of coming up with a simple strategy to signal her sister when it was time for her to be alone with the cowboy. She was so far out of her comfort zone, it wasn't even funny.

"Relax. It doesn't have to be anything complicated." Emma shook her head. "Jeez, you have been off the market for too long."

She let out a snort. "Tell me about it."

"How about if you want to be alone with Tucker, you say you have to go to the ladies' room and of course, I'll go with you," Emma suggested.

"Mmm, hmm." Becca thought that plan seemed simple enough. She and her sister always went to the ladies' room together anyway. Didn't all women?

"Then when we come back, I'll say I'm tired and I'm going to turn in for the night, but you should feel free to stay out with Tucker and enjoy yourself."

"Okay." Becca nodded. "But wait. What about Jace?"

"I'll ask him if he'll walk me out to the car, and then once we're away from you two, I'll tell him you want to be alone with Tucker."

"Oh, my God. No. Emma, you can't say that." Appalled at the thought, Becca felt her face heat with shame. This was a bad idea.

"Will you stop, please?"

"I can't. This is too embarrassing. I don't even know Jace." Or Tucker, for that matter.

"Fine. I won't tell him that."

"Then what will you do?" She had a bad feeling Emma was humoring her and would end up saying exactly what she wanted anyway.

"I guess I'll just have to come up with another creative way to occupy him so he doesn't want to go back inside and hang out with Tucker." Emma shrugged, but there was a sly and very suggestive smile on her lips and a sparkle in her eyes.

Becca let out a loud breath filled with frustration. Now not only were her own morals plummeting, she'd dragged her sister right down along with her. She leaned closer to Emma, aware they weren't alone. "I can't ask you to sleep with him just so I can be alone with the other one."

"I don't have to sleep with him." Emma mimicked Becca's hissed whisper, but exaggerated it. "I haven't had a nice long make-out session in a while. I bet he can really kiss."

"You're right." She liked this idea. "I don't have to . . . you know . . . go all the way with Tucker, either. We could just kiss." That would be nice, and far less out of her comfort zone than having sex with a stranger.

Emma spun toward her, eyes wide. "Oh, no. You're going all the way."

"Why?" She took a step back from Emma's intensity.

"Because you need it. Desperately. And besides, don't tell me you don't want to."

Becca pursed her lips. She did want to, but she still hated when Emma was right. "We'll see how it goes."

"Yes, we will." Emma sealed the pack with one definitive nod. "Did you stay on the pill after you broke up with Jerry?"

Discussing birth control for her one-night stand in the middle of a rodeo—could this be any more embarrassing? Blood rushed to her cheeks. "I can't believe you asked me that. And keep your voice down."

"What? It's a valid question. Even as cute as he is, I'm not sure I'm ready to be an aunt to a tiny Tucker quite yet. Though I could buy lil' Tuck one of those adorable cowboy outfits they make for babies. Oh, he'd be so cute."

Becca couldn't believe the direction this conversation was headed. And she wished Emma would lower her voice and be a little more discreet. She eyed the people milling around near them and tried to judge whether they'd heard the whole appalling discussion.

"Yes, for your information I did stay on them. But I'd still prefer to use . . . other protection, too. I barely know him. We need to stop talking about this now." Becca glanced around them again.

This topic was embarrassing enough, but to be having it in public was making it even worse. No matter how low she tried to keep her voice, she was still convinced the people moving around behind the chutes could hear.

Emma smiled. "Okay fine, but I know you. You're still thinking about it."

Unfortunately, yet one more time, Emma was completely right. Even worse, the cowboy in question, the subject of all of their conversation for the past five minutes, was on his way over. "Shh. He's coming. Not another word."

"Yes, ma'am." Emma smirked but Becca couldn't deal with her smart attitude now.

Instead she planted a smile on her face and aimed it at the cowboy heading her way. "Hey. Almost your turn?"

Tucker grinned. "Yup, almost my turn. I just wanted to check and make sure you were good before I got too busy to come over. I'm gonna have to help Jace pull his rope. He's up before I am. Unless they change the lineup, I'm a few riders after he goes."

She pushed aside naughty thoughts of what she'd like to pull on Tucker. Jeez, apparently months without sex, mixed with a hot cowboy and a couple of beers, brought out the bad girl in her. She'd have to remember to avoid that combination in the future. "We're fine here. Thanks."

"Good." He hooked a thumb in the direction of the chutes, where Jace was already climbing up. "I'm gonna go help."

"Sure. Of course. Do what you have to." He turned to go and she called after him, "Tucker?"

"Yeah?" He glanced back at her.

"Good luck."

"Thanks. See you after." His smile lit his face and warmed her heart.

Becca nodded and watched him head for where Jace had just climbed inside a really small-looking metal enclosure. She frowned and looked closer. "Holy cow. Emma. He's in there *with* the bull."

Actually on top of the bull. She hadn't been paying much attention to what had been happening around her. She'd been too distracted by watching Tucker and then talking with Emma about her crazy ideas of what was going to happen later. But now Becca looked closer, she noticed every one of the teeny tiny metal cagelike areas contained a bull, and cowboys were straddling the railings right above them.

"Of course he is." Emma laughed. "Haven't you ever seen bull riding on television?"

"No." If bull riding was on television, it wasn't on the stations she watched. Though she supposed *Masterpiece Theater* and BBC had a different demographic from the audience interested in extreme sports.

There were so many cowboys surrounding Jace, Tucker included, Becca couldn't see much more than the top of his hat every once in a while. The sound of metal clashing had her eyes opening wide, just as the bull reared up and tried to climb out of the chute. Its front legs were actually on top of the metal railing, all while Jace clung to its back.

Tucker grabbed the back of Jace's vest and held him while another cowboy waved a hat in front of the bull's face and tried to get him to back down into the chute.

"Oh, my God. Emma, this is really dangerous." She couldn't take her eyes off the action.

"I know. What did you think it would be like?"

"I don't know." She didn't have the mental capacity to defend herself to Emma.

All she could think about was that Tucker was going to be the one inside what amounted to a metal prison with a deadly bull any minute. Meanwhile, Jace's bull's front legs were still hooked over the top rail. The animal was going to get hurt. Jace could possibly get crushed. And this was a sport?

The bull finally dropped all four feet back onto the ground again. Another cowboy tied a string above its head to keep it from trying to jump its way out of the chute again. But the single length of thin rope tied between the two top railings of the chute didn't look nearly strong enough to keep down a crazed beast. They couldn't expect Jace to ride this bull now. They should get him a different one. A better trained one.

"Why aren't they pulling Jace out of there?" she asked Emma, not that her sister would know the answer.

"When they act up in the chute like that, it's best to just nod and go. The less time they spend in there, the better for both of them." A woman stepped up next to Becca, leaning her baby's feet on the railing both she and Emma were pressed against in an attempt to see better.

Becca turned to the stranger. "But can't he request a different bull?"

"Doubtful. They have a few extra on site for re-rides, but an animal has to really act up pretty badly in the chute for the stock manager to replace him. Jace will be fine. I've seen him weather worse."

At that, Becca's brows rose with interest. "You know these guys?"

"Oh, sure. I'm married to one of them."

Married. That announcement had her throat closing to the choking point. Surely neither Jace nor Tucker would spend the night flirting with them if they were married. And with a new baby, too. But she hadn't noticed this woman here before. Maybe they hadn't expected her to come.

She glanced at Emma to find her sister looking as shocked as she did. Becca forced herself to be calm as she asked, "Which one is your husband?"

"Dillon McMann. He's the one in the pink shirt."

"Oh. Mmm, hmm. I can see him. Nice shirt." Becca finally let herself breathe.

"I'm Cassie, by the way, and this is our daughter Cheyenne." The girl, who looked young enough to still be in college, if not high school, just like the rest of the females back behind the chutes, jostled the baby. "Can you see Daddy? He's going to be up soon, baby girl."

After shooting Emma a glance filled with relief, Becca drew in a long breath and tried to slow her speeding heart, which only kicked up again as the clash of metal hitting metal made her jump. Then Jace and the bull were out from behind the confines of the chute and spinning into the middle of the dirt-covered arena.

The ride went so fast, Becca felt as if she'd blinked and missed it. One minute Jace was being flung around like a ragdoll, and the next he was on the ground and running for the fence with a bull hot on his heels.

"Way to go, Jace!" Next to her, Cassie yelled above the cheers of the crowd. It seemed no one but Becca was disturbed that Jace was clinging to a railing six feet high while a horned bull circled the ground below him, as if waiting for him to get down so he could charge.

"What just happened with Jace?" Becca asked, not sure if it was a good ride or a bad ride. "I'm Becca, by the way."

"He covered his ride." Cassie frowned. "You're here with Jace tonight?"

What to say to that?

"Um, no. Well not really." She glanced at Emma for help.

"Jace and Tucker saw how bad our seats were, so they invited us down here to watch with them. I'm Emma, Becca's sister."

"Hi, there." Cassie nodded. "So, you're out-of-towners and first time at a rodeo?"

"Yes." Apparently that was obvious to everyone. If she did get this job, she was probably going to have to work to look more like she fit in.

"Good score for Jace. Eighty-six." Cassie got a faraway look in her eyes as she listened to the announcer's babble, most of which went right over Becca's head.

"Oh, that's good." Not that Becca would know a good score from a bad one. "So, uh, Tucker should be up soon."

Another gate clanged open and she jumped once again at the sound. As one more cowboy and bull charged out of the chute and into the arena, her gaze swept the group of men. She was looking for one in particular and was having trouble finding him.

"Yeah, he's climbing into the chute now."

She had been so busy worrying and talking, she'd missed

that. The cowboys were once again all clustered around one chute, and it was impossible to make out what was happening inside it. "This is nerve-racking. I don't know how you can be married to one of them and watch him do this."

Cassie laughed. "You get used to it. It's in their blood. Most of these guys would rather go without food than not ride. And believe me, during the lean years when he was hurt a lot or having a bad streak, it's actually been a choice between paying an entrance fee or eating that night."

"Wow." Becca had had no idea. And here she'd been letting them buy her and Emma drinks and food all night. Not that she was much better off financially since her unfortunate termination, but still. She leaned toward Emma. "We're paying for drinks at the bar later."

Emma nodded. "Definitely." She must have been listening to the conversation, too.

Sexy but poor. Becca knew that no man—not cowboys in general, or Tucker in particular—could be totally perfect. There had to be something wrong and now she knew what. Cowboys, and most likely Tucker as well, had no money . . . but at least he wasn't married to Cassie. So that was good.

Her gaze stayed on the chute where all the action was taking place. She didn't realize she'd clamped on to the rail until Cassie's hand patted hers. She glanced down and saw her own white knuckles wrapped in a death grip around the metal.

"Don't worry. Tuck's a veteran rider. One of the best, and this bull is nothing compared to the one he drew last night." For a young girl, Cassie had a very wise look in her eyes. Or maybe it just seemed that way because Becca really wanted her to be right.

Becca nodded, trying not to overanalyze why she was so concerned over the well-being of a man she'd only met a few hours ago. The truth was, she could barely breathe as she watched and waited for this ride to be over.

She was about to thank Cassie and ask her more about the bull when the sound of the gate crashing open had her attention snapping back to the chute, just as Tucker's bull charged into the arena.

"Go, go, go! That's it, Tuck!" Cassie cheered the man on the bull while Becca watched silently and wide-eyed.

Unlike Jace's ride, which was over in the blink of an eye, this one seemed to go on forever. Like it was happening in slow motion. The bull spun and bucked. Tucker, with one arm held high in the air, absorbed the shock of every one of the bull's moves with a counteraction of his own.

The sound of a buzzer had her jumping, startled by the loud noise that broke through her attention when she'd been solely focused on Tucker. Then she breathed a sigh of relief. She knew enough about the sport after her tutorial to know the ride was over.

Yet Tucker was still on the bull's back. He held on for what seemed like forever, though it was probably only a few more seconds before he reached down and yanked the end of the rope tied around his gloved hand. He leaped off even as the bull continued to spin and buck away from him.

The other men in the arena scrambled. It took a while to get the bull out the gate, but Tucker was off and out of danger. That was all Becca could focus on. She let out a shaky breath.

The announcer's voice reverberated through the air, and Becca looked to Cassie for interpretation. "What did he say?"

"Eighty-seven-point-five. Decent score. It probably should have been higher, but his bull wasn't a great bucker. The bull score was probably low, and Tuck is such a good rider technically, sometimes he makes it seem too easy so the judges don't score him as high as they should."

"I'll never learn all this." Bull scores? Judges? She shook her head and sighed.

This sport was far more complicated than she'd assumed. She'd thought the rider just got on and tried not to fall off before the buzzer. Apparently there was more to it than that. Just like how there was much more to cowboys—and Tuck—than she'd ever imagined.

"That's a funny thing to say." Emma shot Becca a sideways glance. "Especially for a person who didn't want to come in the first place."

Becca scanned the cowboys again and found Tucker. He'd just bent to retrieve his bull rope from where it had fallen to the ground. After receiving a slap on the back from one of the bullfighters, he turned. She saw his gaze sweep the area. When it hit on her, he grinned and began striding directly toward where she stood. With a wide smile, she waited for him to arrive.

"Emma, save your I-told-you-so for later, please. I have a bull rider to congratulate."

When he reached them, he initially focused on Becca, but then turned the brilliance of his smile toward Cassie and Cheyenne. She missed the attention immediately. It was as if someone had turned off the sun. She watched as he leaned low and gave the baby a kiss on her blond curls.

"Look at you, getting so big. And how is Mamma doing?" He straightened up and gave Cassie a kiss on the cheek, and Becca found herself inexplicably jealous of the attention he was lavishing on both mother and child.

"We're doing good, Tuck. Great ride. Perfect, as usual." Cassie beamed up at Tucker, and Becca's frown got a bit deeper.

He laughed. "Not exactly, but thanks."

"The judges were blind. You should have scored higher."

"Nah, I could feel his spin was kind of flat and even. I dressed it up the best I could, but I knew it wasn't going to be a winning score on that bull. He wasn't getting any height in the rear with his bucks." Even though Tucker was still mostly talking to Cassie, he reached out and ran his hand up and down Becca's arm before turning his attention back to her.

They stood so close, she could absorb all the changes in him since the ride. There was a bright, almost manic look to his eyes and a tension that radiated from every muscle in his body. His hand trembled just a bit as he'd reached out to touch her. If she'd seen these symptoms in a student, she would have assumed it was from drugs. Seeing them in Tucker, she knew—he was on an adrenaline high. Suddenly she understood the appeal of this crazy sport. Why the riders got so addicted to it. Why a young guy like Dillon would risk life and limb and use the money he needed for food just to ride.

"Cassie, did you meet Becca and her sister Emma? They're from New York." Tucker smiled at Becca.

"I sure did." Cassie produced a knowing smile, and Becca couldn't help wondering how many of Tucker's women Cassie had stood next to during these kinds of events.

She tried to push that thought aside and be cordial. "Cassie was kind enough to explain things to me."

"Good. I'm glad. Sorry I couldn't be here—" His steel blue gaze was focused on her, chasing away any suspicions or doubts.

"Don't be silly. You had to ride. We were fine here."

"Good." Tucker glanced over his shoulder to where Jace perched on the railing next to where Dillon straddled the top of the chute, about to climb in. "I should go help."

"Of course. Go."

With a parting smile, Tucker ruffled Cheyenne's hair

and spun away. Becca watched him go and then realized Cassie was watching her watch Tucker. She couldn't help herself, she had to know. Becca glanced at Cassie. "So, uh, Tucker. He's uh . . ." Once she'd started, she didn't quite know how to finish.

"Yeah?" Cassie kept her eyes on her husband, all while jiggling the baby in her arms.

"He seems nice." Jeez. No one would ever know Becca had a doctorate in English the way this conversation was going.

"He is." Cassie turned to her and smiled. "A girl could do way worse than Tucker Jenkins."

Next to her, Emma cleared her throat. The sound had a distinct I-told-you-so tone to it. She didn't need her sister telling her what she already knew. If she was going to have a fling—one night with a cowboy—she doubted she could do better than Tucker.

All that adrenaline running through him with no outlet—God, what would sex be like with a man who literally vibrated with energy the way he was now?

Explosive. Unforgettable. The exact opposite of how sex with Jerry had been.

Becca realized that, against all common sense, she was dying to find out.

Chapter
Seven

"Can you see the end of the line yet?" Angling his head so the rodeo fan in front of him wouldn't hear, Tuck whispered the question to Jace.

"Anxious to get out of here, are ya?" Jace grinned.

"What do you think?" He turned away from Jace to smile at the young boy and scribble some semblance of his signature on the program the kid had thrust toward him.

It was nearly killing Tuck, having to stay the extra time after the competition ended to sign autographs for the fans with the rest of the guys. He glanced up from the next random item he'd been signing and found Becca watching him. It ramped up his need to be alone with her another notch. Now, he felt as if he were running at full throttle.

"I think this might be the last few," Jace mumbled low.

There was no use pretending Jace wasn't just as anxious to get done with this little duty as Tuck was. Not that they didn't love the fans, but there were two blondes waiting to be shown a good time, and Tuck, for one, sure as hell didn't intend on letting them down.

He forced his attention back to the last two fans in line, signing a T-shirt and another program before he stood and blew out a burst of air. "That's it. We're done."

"Yes, we are." Jace capped his marker and stood, too. They both made their way from behind the table in the fan zone and over to the women who'd patiently waited for them for nearly an hour. "So what would you girls like to do? There's that joint down the road, unless you have another idea."

Jace asked the question of the girls, but Tuck knew his own answer regarding what he wanted to do, and it didn't involve a bar or alcohol.

"Hmm. I'm wondering if the place nearby will be really crowded because everyone who was here tonight will go there." Emma pursed her lips. "I have an idea. Our hotel is only about ten minutes away and it has a really nice bar. Do you want to go there?"

Emma's suggestion of the hotel bar, so close to all those rooms with beds in them, was incredibly enticing. Tucker's attention remained on Becca as he waited for her reaction to the idea. She swallowed before saying to her sister, "I think that's a good idea."

It was all Tuck could do to stop from whooping with joy at her answer.

"Right? I thought so, too." Emma nodded. "That way if one of us wants to leave early—you know, because they're tired or whatever—they can since our room is right upstairs."

"Mmm, hmm. That's right." Becca wore an expression that seemed almost a mix of determination and anxiety.

The body language she broadcasted was so loud it seemed blaring. As if she battled within herself, and for once raw need had won out over logic. He would bet tonight's pay that didn't happen often to her. That was fine with Tuck. He'd waylay any of her leftover doubts the minute he got her alone. Which brought Tuck's immediate thoughts to exactly how fast could they get to the hotel and how best to get her alone once they were there?

"I think that's a very good idea. Jace? You in?" Tuck glanced at Jace and noticed his brows rise.

"Sure. Sounds good to me."

Tuck didn't care what Emma's motivations were for suggesting the hotel bar. It didn't matter whether she wanted the freedom to leave so she could be alone with Jace, or if she was playing matchmaker for Becca and himself. As long as the results were he and Becca, alone and sweaty, it was all good.

He turned to the girls. "How are we going to do this as far as vehicles? I've got my truck here and so does Jace."

Emma pulled a set of keys out of her purse. "How about I lead the way in our rental car. Then Jace can follow behind me in his truck and Becca can ride with you in your truck and bring up the rear. That way in case we get separated, she can give you directions to the hotel."

"Good idea." Tuck wasn't about to tell them he had GPS in his truck and could program in the address of the hotel to find it. Or that he lived in this area and probably knew every back road and business establishment there was, including whatever hotel they'd gotten a room in.

Nope. He kept his mouth shut, sparing barely a moment of sympathy for Jace, who'd be driving alone. Poor Jace wouldn't get the pleasure of Emma riding in his passenger seat, but Tuck would sure enjoy having Becca in his. Having her in his lap would be better, but getting her in his truck was a damn good start.

"Ready to go?" He turned his attention to Becca.

After a glance at Emma, Becca nodded. "Okay."

Tuck's gaze dropped to her mouth as she answered. Soon, he hoped, he'd have the pleasure of experiencing those tempting lips. He shifted the weight of his gear bag from one hand to the other, very aware of the strip of condoms Jace had so generously stashed in it for him.

Okay, so maybe Tuck wanted to do much more than just kiss Becca. At least he would be prepared. Fine motto—be prepared. It could make for a very good night.

He took Becca's hand in his, loving how she looked surprised once again at the action, but didn't pull away.

"Let's go." With a smile and her hand captive in his, he led the way toward the parking lot. Tucker pushed through the door and held it wide for Becca next to him. "So, was your first rodeo what you thought it would be like?"

"Actually, it was much more than I expected." The tone of her voice and the heat in her gaze as she looked at him had Tuck warming to the core.

"I'm glad." He blew out a slow breath to steady himself.

How far away was that damn truck of his? He was having trouble remembering where he'd parked. It seemed like a lifetime ago he'd pulled into the parking lot thinking tonight would be like any other event. That he'd hopefully win some cash and not end up on the wrong end of the bull. He certainly hadn't expected this.

Spotting the truck finally, Tucker squeezed Becca's hand tighter. He steered them in the right direction. Though any place they ended up together would be just fine with him, he knew her sister and his friend would be waiting at the exit of the parking lot for them. As tempting as making a break for it to be alone with her was, it wouldn't likely happen for a little bit yet.

Meanwhile, she was being awfully quiet again. He glanced at her as they reached the passenger side of his truck. One push of a button on his key fob, and the door locks released with a click. He opened the door for her. "This is it."

She glanced at the truck and then back at him. "It's big."

"The bigger the better, I always say." He grinned wide.

"Oh, really." Her brows rose, and he didn't miss the smile that tugged at the corners of her mouth.

Admittedly the truck was high, but he was never opposed to helping a lady up with a boost. Especially a lady he couldn't wait to get his hands on.

Damn. How long before they could be alone?

"Up you go." He stepped forward and wrapped his fingers around her waist and lifted.

She let out an adorable little squeak that had his heart, and parts lower, clenching, before she grabbed the handle inside and pulled herself into the seat. She looked good up there. He could get used to having a cute little thing like her in his big good ol' boy truck. Lucky for him she was flying away tomorrow, so he and his scarred heart wouldn't be tempted to keep her around and risk further damage.

After making sure she was tucked safely inside, Tuck slammed her door and strode around the truck to the driver's side. He dumped his gear bag behind his seat and was once again reminded of what it contained. He'd obviously been without a woman for too long; the condoms he'd gotten from Jace, and the possibility of being alone with Becca to use them, were all he could think about.

Jace had been right about Tuck's total lack of female companionship lately. Tuck was paying for that drought now. Just being close to this pretty blonde was making him feel like a high school kid hoping to get lucky after the prom.

Whatever. Too late to do anything about it now. He'd just have to try to enjoy the anticipation. But whatever was making his hands shake as he shoved the key into the ignition did not make him like his sudden bout of schoolboy nerves one bit. He glanced at Becca, hoping she hadn't noticed.

He backed the truck out of the space and maneuvered his way down the row and toward the exit. Tucker spotted Jace's truck waiting and pulled behind him. He flashed his lights to let his friend know he was there and then glanced at Becca. "So, what did you think of the bull riding?"

"I think it's dangerous and you, and all the other guys, are possibly a little bit crazy." She laughed.

"All right." He laughed, too, but didn't deny it. She could very well be right. "Did you like any of it?"

"Yes, when I wasn't worried to death for you."

"Aw. That's kinda nice to hear." He glanced at her before he had to drag his attention away and concentrate on pulling out into the road behind Jace. "It's been a while since I've had anyone to worry about me."

"I don't believe that."

"Well, Jace cares. Maybe. But I've found he's more likely to smack me in my cracked ribs than show me any sympathy for getting stomped on. No one else though."

"I'm sure there are plenty of females who come watch you ride and worry about you." There was a definite edge to her tone that hadn't been there before.

Hmm, was this her way of fishing for information about his dating life? He didn't mind her little expedition one bit. It could only mean she was interested herself. But she needn't have bothered since he had no social life lately. "There hasn't been a woman to worry about me for a long time. Not since I split with my ex. She hated my riding. So, of course, I used to ride every chance I got to prove a point. Still do now that she's gone. Pretty immature, huh?"

Tuck didn't know what made him tell her all that. He never talked about his ex-wife to other women. Hell, he didn't even like speaking of her to his best friends. But somehow he'd felt compelled to tell Becca. Thankfully, Jace put on his blinker to make a turn and Tucker had to keep his attention on following him and Emma instead of obsessing over his out-of-character confession.

"No. I don't think so. I've got one of those, too—an ex who didn't like half the things I did. But I didn't spend my time riding bulls to prove a point. I mostly sit on my sofa with a pint of ice cream since we broke up. That's going to have to stop, though. I'm afraid I'm starting to get fat."

Tucker risked taking his eyes off the road to glance at Becca. The I'm getting fat statement to get a compliment out of a man was a typical female ploy, but it made him happy she liked him enough to want compliments from him. He'd gladly give her assurance she was perfect just the way she was. "You're not fat."

She screwed up her lips into a pretty pout. "My jeans are getting tight."

"Women should have curves." And Tuck couldn't think of a better way to show those curves off than in tight jeans with a nice heeled cowboy boot that raised her ass up just a bit, like Becca's was tonight.

"I guess the curve theory goes along with your bigger is always better theory." She raised one brow and glanced at him.

"Sometimes. It's all about proportions, you see." He grinned. "But all kidding aside, you look good to me."

"Thank you." It was dark out, but in the dim light of the truck he was sure he saw her blush. God, he loved that about her.

"You're very welcome." As Tuck focused back on the road ahead, Jace cleared a traffic light on yellow. It turned red in front of them. He slowed and then brought the truck to a stop. He glanced at Becca. "It's okay if we lose them. I think I know how to get there."

"It's right up here anyway." She shot him a sideways look. "So you know how you said you haven't had a woman worry about you in a long time?"

"Yeah." Where was this going? Tuck was more than interested to find out.

"Well, I, uh, wanted you to know I haven't been out on a date in literally years—not that this is a date or anything."

She scrambled to add the last part so fast, Tuck had to hide his smile. "I haven't been out or alone with any man except for Jerry, my dickhead ex—in a long while. Which is probably why I'm so bad at it. Being alone with a man, I mean." She sighed, frustration radiating off her.

"Becca, you're not bad at it. Trust me." He smiled.

She got flustered so easily. As uncharacteristic as it was for him, Tuck happened to find that an unbelievably charming trait in her. It was damn nice compared to the women he was used to being around.

He accelerated as the light turned green and considered what Becca had told him. If they were keeping track of official dates, he hadn't been on one for years, either. Not since when he was dating Brenda before they were married. Since the divorce . . . Well, he couldn't call what he'd done to get back on his feet *dating* by any stretch of the imagination. All out angry, rebound, revenge fucking, yes, but definitely not dating.

He was contemplating whether he needed to respond further to her dating confession when she said, "It's right up here."

Seeing the glowing neon sign of the hotel, Tuck steered into the parking lot and parked in a spot in the far corner. He wasn't keen on putting his fairly new truck in danger of getting dinged by squeezing into a spot too near the entrance. He didn't need someone in an SUV full of kids and suitcases opening their doors and crashing into his paint job. But more important, he wanted a minute alone to say something to Becca and he didn't want to risk Emma or Jace walking over, knocking on the window, and interrupting them. Hopefully the other couple would go on in and get a table in the bar and give him and Becca some privacy.

He cut the engine, and the sound of the air-conditioning blower died. He released the seat belt that tugged across his chest and turned in his seat to face her. Reaching out, he leaned his forearm against her seat back and let his fingers trail onto her shoulder. "I haven't exactly been in this situation lately, either. I mean out with a woman. At least not with a woman like you. Not recently anyway. Actually, not for a really, *really* long time."

There he went with the true confessions again. Good thing she was leaving tomorrow. This woman could be dangerous for him if she were staying around for much longer.

"That makes me feel much better." Her gaze dropped from his eyes to his lips.

He wanted to kiss her so badly, it was nearly impossible to keep his own eyes from focusing on her mouth. In fact, he was having a hell of a time keeping his hands off her.

Without realizing how he got there, he found himself leaning closer. Close enough he could hear every one of her rapid breaths perfectly. "Becca?"

"Yes." She released the clasp on her own seat belt and met his stare with a bold one of her own.

That was it. He took it as a signal, whether she'd meant it to be or not. He leaned in and swallowed hard. What had he been planning to ask her again? Oh, yeah, if he could kiss her. That seemed like a moot point now with him hovering so close to her lips. One small move on his part, or on hers, would put them in contact. She drew in a shaky breath that had his gut twisting with need.

It had been a long time since he cared enough to take time kissing a woman. Usually locking lips was simply a necessary means to an end. That end being to get the buckle bunny du jour out of her panties. He'd kissed that string of girls after his divorce not because he'd wanted to, but because it unlocked the pussy he needed to bury his pain and anger inside. Hell, some of them he'd never bothered kissing at all. Becca was different. The urge, the need, to kiss her drove him.

To hell with being appropriate. He closed the distance between them. With one hand cupping her face and the other wrapped around her waist, Tucker took his first kiss from the woman who'd been tempting him for hours. Since the moment he'd first laid eyes on her, looking so out of place in the arena.

He groaned with satisfaction at the first taste of her lips. There was no keeping this kiss chaste. Eyes closed, he tuned out everything surrounding them—the sound of the traffic on the highway, the cool air in the truck rapidly being replaced by summer heat. He concentrated only on her and sank deeper, and still it wasn't enough. Wrapping one arm around her, he hauled her against him. With his hand splayed on her back he felt the thundering of her heart.

This kiss with Becca felt different. Bigger, somehow. Tucker wanted to savor it. To take his time. To test and taste every nuance of this woman. Yeah, he wanted all the rest—all of her—but for now this was perfect. He was happy. He tilted his head, changing the angle and giving him even more possession of her mouth.

The small sound that escaped her throat as she parted her lips to his probing nearly did him in. He growled a response and tightened the grip he had on her with his one hand, while the other plunged deeper beneath the fall of her hair. It was so soft it felt like a curtain of silk against his skin as his fingers cradled her head.

He tasted the beer on her tongue as it tangled with his, and he thanked God he'd chosen not to have a drink at the arena. He didn't want anything, especially not alcohol, clouding this. He'd woken up too many times with only a hazy memory of the girl he'd been with and what had happened the night before. That wouldn't be the case tonight. Tomorrow he'd have crystal-clear memories of every second, of every sensation, sight, and sound.

She sighed against his mouth. It set his pulse racing and his cock throbbing. If just a sigh did this to him, he couldn't imagine what it would be like to hear her come. He wanted her beneath him during a full body-writhing orgasm, but for now, he'd be happy with another pleasure-filled sigh. Tuck drew her closer still, tighter against him, until there was nothing between them but the thickness of the clothes they both wore. She came to him easily. He took advantage of the bench seat and guided her until she straddled him where he sat in the center.

Making out in a truck had its disadvantages, mainly the lack of space and the risk of getting caught, but it had a certain nostalgic charm as well. As a teenager, he'd lost his virginity in the front seat of his first truck. An old clunker that broke down as much as it ran. Damn, he'd loved that old thing. His initiation into the world of sex, with women and not his own hand, was just the first of many good memories associated with the vehicle he'd long ago replaced.

No, Tucker didn't object to being in the truck. He just never thought he'd be in his thirties and making out in the front seat like he was a teenager again. At least now he had a few more skills in his sexual repertoire, not to mention more control of himself than he'd had back then. Though as Becca leaned harder against him and he felt the heat between her legs clear through the denim of his jeans and straight through to his cock, he had to question that control a little bit. If he'd been ten or fifteen years younger, he'd worry he might shoot off right there inside his pants. That's how much her closeness tortured him.

Even so, there was no way in hell he was going to move her. Instead, he planted a palm on each cheek of her ass and held her right where she was. He'd be happy if she stayed pressed against him, just like this, for a very long time.

When she started making small circles against the crotch of his jeans, the seam of which was pressing right into his erection, Tuck drew in a sharp breath through his nose. He wasn't sure how much more he could take before he either flipped her onto her back and took her right there, or actually did end up coming in his pants.

A vibrating in Becca's front pocket pulled his attention away from his wishing both of their clothes would spontaneously disappear so he could plunge into her. He reluctantly pulled back. "I think your jeans are getting a call."

"Sorry." Breathless and adorably apologetic, she leaned back from him just far enough to wrestle her cell phone out of her front pocket. She glanced at the read-out. "It's a text from Emma."

Of course her sister would be looking for her. They'd been right behind Emma and Jace on the drive over, right until the red light he'd been lucky enough to hit had separated them. Still, it shouldn't be taking him and Becca this long to park and go inside to the bar—unless they were occupied doing something else, of course. Tuck noticed Jace wasn't texting him asking where they were. Smart man. He always had been a good wingman. But Emma and Becca were a different story. As much as he hated the interruption, it was right for Emma to worry about her sister and check on her.

"I'm sure they're inside waiting for us." He smothered his disappointment. Inside, where there were lights and people, and where it would be really inappropriate for Becca to straddle him and press her hot-as-hell body against his like she was doing now.

Since she didn't move, Tuck remained where he was as he watched her read the text and then type in what he assumed was a response to her sister. Then she shoved the phone back into her pocket and leaned forward again. With a groan, she wrapped her arms around his neck and zeroed in on his mouth for a kiss deep enough to surprise even him.

He shamelessly took full advantage of the contact, sliding his tongue between her lips, plunging into her mouth the way he'd love to plunge another part of him inside a different part of her. Meanwhile, that other part of him was currently very happy with Becca's close proximity, even if they were still clothed.

He allowed himself a few moments more to enjoy her before, like an idiot, he pulled away and did what he considered to be the right thing. "I guess we should get inside. They're expecting us."

"I texted Emma and told her not to wait for me. Is that okay?" Her words came out soft and a bit hesitant.

Was she really worried he wouldn't want to stay right here and make out with her, rather than go inside to some bar full of strangers watching them? The thought nearly made him laugh. What man wouldn't want to stay here and ravish her?

"Yeah." He smiled and added, "Very okay."

The shyness or insecurity, or whatever had made her sound uncertain before, was completely gone when she leaned in this time. While Becca kissed him, she pressed harder against his belt buckle.

Her kiss got more intense. Her tongue tangled with his as enticing sounds escaped her throat and she ground her pelvis against his. There was no cowboy on earth who wouldn't love getting his buckle polished in this particular way. Tuck was no exception. With her ass held firmly in his hands, he followed her motion against him.

She may have complained she was getting fat and her jeans were too tight, but he enjoyed every beautiful curve on her. Besides, tight jeans could only work to his advantage right now. If hers were torturing her the same way his were him, she felt every move the two of them made together threefold thanks to the denim pressing into her. He decided to help with that.

He ran one hand down the cheek of her ass until he could reach between her legs, then he rubbed the sensitive spot hidden beneath her clothing. She drew in a staggering breath the moment his fingers made contact.

Oh, yeah. He'd have her coming in no time, right through her pants. His only regret would be not being inside her at the time. He repeated the action and rubbed her again. This time she pulled back from the kiss and let out a breathy sound of pleasure that nearly had him coming, too. With more space between them because she'd leaned back, he had more room to operate, and he took full advantage of it. Bringing his hand around, Tucker approached Becca from the front this time.

Her eyes drifted closed as he started to work her in earnest. She began to breathe heavier, and he wished for the hundredth time they were both naked. Or at least she was, so he could give her just a taste of what a man who knew his way around a woman's body could do.

She unfastened the top button of her jeans, and his stroke faltered. He stopped moving all together as she slid her zipper down. The invitation was clear, and who was he to ignore a lady's invite?

His hands were big, and her jeans were tight, but he was nothing if not a problem solver. He slid his palm, fingers first, down the silky skin of her stomach and beneath the waistband of her panties, all the way to her warm, plump lips. Hot and wet, just as he'd hoped, she was ready and waiting to be taken, and he was in the mood to take all she offered.

Just the touch of a fingertip on her clit had her hissing

in a breath. She braced her hands on the seat back on either side of his head. Good. She'd need something to hold on to now he had access to what he needed to drive her crazy. He'd have preferred to use his mouth, but this would have to do. For now.

He worked her until her whole body began to shake and she gave up the attempt to be quiet, letting her cries fill the truck and surround them. He ignored the tingling in the hand he had squeezed into her jeans as it began to fall asleep from lack of circulation. He wasn't going to stop until he had her writhing from his touch.

Luckily, he didn't have long to wait. Her grip moved to each of his shoulders as she held tight and rode his hand. A frown creased her brow and her eyes remained slammed shut as the unmistakable sounds of a woman in orgasm hit him hard. He kept working her until she fell forward against him, gasping for breath. Tuck found he was breathing pretty damn hard himself.

They stayed like that. Becca heavy against him, panting. His hand still inside her pants because she was on his arm and he couldn't move—not that he really wanted to in spite of the pins and needles. Finally, she leaned back again and he pulled his tingling hand out of the happiest place he'd been in quite a while.

With eyes heavily lidded and full of desire, she looked every man's fantasy even before she reached for his belt and began to unfasten the buckle. His pulse raced. A woman only opened a man's pants for one reason, and that was because she was interested in getting to know what was inside a little better. And he sure as hell wanted her to. But damn, here was not the place for what he wanted to do.

He put his hand over hers to stop her before she unleashed the beast and he couldn't control himself.

"I don't want to do this here. Zip up." He patted one

well-shaped ass cheek and leaned his head back as far as he could, away from the temptation of her kisses so he could say what he needed to before he got distracted again. "We're going inside and I'm getting us a room . . . If that's all right with you."

"I don't want you to have to spend the money on a hotel room." Since she kept her hands on his buckle and tantalizingly close to his dick, he didn't think she was coming up with an excuse because she was worried about being alone in a room with him. Her concern really must be the cost.

"If you're honestly worried about me spending the money, don't be. I took second in the bull riding tonight. I went to the payout window right before the autograph signing and now I've got an envelope stuffed full of cash in my gear bag." As well as the strip of condoms Jace had put in there. Damn, he really, really hoped he'd be using some of those tonight. "Now, if you don't want to—"

"That's not it." In the dim light of the truck, she watched him as he tried to read the emotions crossing her face. "If you really are okay paying for it, then I'd like it if we did . . . get a room, I mean." Her gaze dropped away from his, though why she was so shy and insecure he had no clue.

Hell, he'd give a lot more than the cost of a hotel room to be with her. Alone, behind closed doors, and in a cool, comfortable place where they could both stretch out naked on a nice big bed with lots of room to get creative. That was truly priceless.

The thought had his heart beating faster and the pulse throbbing in his erection. "Trust me. It's fine."

"Okay." Ducking her head so it didn't hit the ceiling of the truck, she backed up and managed to turn herself around and sit facing forward in the passenger seat as she refastened her jeans.

He took a steadying breath and dashed the sweat from his forehead. Between the heat of the summer night and the heat between him and Becca, Tuck was even gladder they were going inside to a nice, air-conditioned hotel room. Getting sweaty with a woman after some good sex was one thing, but he'd rather not start out that way.

Opening his door, he got out and stood, stretching his back in the process before he reached behind the seat for his gear bag. Under the guise of getting his payout envelope, he also grabbed the other necessity he'd need for the night, the condoms Jace had supplied him with.

As he shoved both into the pockets of his jeans, he spared barely a thought to what Jace might or might not be doing at the moment with Emma. If Becca wasn't worried about her sister, then he wasn't, either. Jace was a good guy and Tuck knew his friend could definitely take care of himself, and would take good care of Emma, too.

Jace and Emma were probably at that very moment wondering what he and Becca were doing. It was a funny thought. There'd likely be an inquisition in the morning, for both of them.

Lucky for him, tomorrow was hours away. As he walked around the truck to open Becca's door for her, he couldn't care less about the morning. All he had thoughts for was tonight. And her.

Chapter
Eight

"How many nights?" Fingers poised above the computer keyboard, the front desk clerk waited for Tucker's answer.

Meanwhile, Becca stood slightly behind him so the guy behind the counter wouldn't be able to see the guilty expression she was sure was evident on her face—not to mention the flush that was most likely still present from the orgasm she had experienced in the truck. She glanced one more time over her shoulder to make sure Emma or Jace wasn't lurking nearby. She certainly didn't need her sister or Tucker's friend standing here with them while they booked a hotel room for the night so they could have sex.

"Just one." Good thing Tucker answered because Becca wasn't sure she would have been able to get through this whole registering for a hotel room for their one-night stand process if she'd been in charge of the check-in.

One-night stand . . . Jeez, what the hell was she thinking?

A quick review of her life over the past few months squashed that momentary doubt. It was about time she enjoyed herself; that's what she should be thinking. She deserved a little fun after having worked hard her entire life, both in school and in her career. Lot of good that did her.

It had left her with nothing but a written recommendation and a severance check from Vassar—small comfort in the line at the unemployment office, where she'd be if she didn't ace this interview tomorrow.

Then there was her personal life. She'd devoted years to working on her relationship with Jerry. All it had left her with was ten extra pounds on her ass and thighs and scratches in the paint on her door frames from when he'd moved his shit out.

No more. Time for less work and more play, starting tonight. She drew in a deep breath and prayed they'd get to their room before anyone saw them here.

"I have a room with a king-size bed available. Will that be all right?"

"Perfect." Tucker shot her a smirk and she felt her cheeks heat.

How many more embarrassing questions could this desk clerk ask? There couldn't possibly be any more. He'd pretty much covered everything he could to humiliate her.

Yes, only one night. Yes, the bigger the bed the better. Yes, we'll be having lots of sex. Thank you for asking.

"Do you need help with your luggage?"

She nearly choked as the hotel employee managed to come up with one more thing she hadn't even considered.

No, no luggage. Just sex.

"No, thanks. We're good." Cool as a cucumber, as he had been through the entire check-in, Tucker picked up the pen and signed the paper the clerk had pushed toward him.

"We're all set then. Check-out is eleven, and elevators are to your right."

"Great. Thanks." Tucker slid the signed form back and took the keycard from him. After slipping the small piece of plastic into his back pocket, he took her hand in his and turned toward the elevators.

At least that part of the night was over, but even though she couldn't wait to get out of sight of the lobby and the front desk, Tucker moved at his usual pace. Something between an amble and a stroll. It would be very atmospheric in an old Western movie. Here and now, it made the New Yorker in her cringe as she fought the urge to sprint—or at least power-walk—to their destination.

When they finally reached the elevators and were out of earshot of the clerk, she turned to glance at Tucker. "I'm so embarrassed."

He frowned down at her from beneath his ever-present cowboy hat. The bad-girl side of her—the one she hadn't known existed until Emma forced her to go to the rodeo to look for cowboys in the first place—couldn't help wondering if Tucker normally took his hat off to have sex or if he left it on. It was like a fist to the stomach when she realized she'd know one way or the other very soon. Wow.

"Embarrassed about what?" he asked, knocking the image of him, naked except for his hat, out of her spinning brain.

"He must know why we're here. What we're doing." Even though there was no one nearby, Becca kept her voice as low as humanly possible.

"You mean that we're checking in to have *sex*?" He leaned toward her and hissed the last word in an exaggerated whisper tinged with a laugh. "Becca, why would he assume that?"

"Because it's practically the middle of the night." She opened her eyes wide. Jeez. It was so obvious.

"So? We could just as easily be two weary travelers looking for a place to rest on a long journey." The smirk on Tucker's face told Becca he was enjoying this a little too much. She, on the other hand, was not.

She frowned. "We don't look like travelers. We don't even have any luggage."

"You're so cute being embarrassed. Just because we don't have luggage." He smiled and ran one hand up her arm. "If you want, I can go get my gear bag from the truck and carry it past the front desk so he thinks it's our overnight bag."

"No." She rolled her eyes at his suggestion. "That won't work."

"Why not?"

"Because this is Oklahoma, the rodeo state. He'll probably know it's full of bull stuff and think we're doing kinky things upstairs with it or something." She felt the scowl settle on her face at the thought. Best to leave it alone and cut their losses.

"First of all, Oklahoma is the Sooner State, not the rodeo state. But besides that, I'm trying to imagine what kind of kinky things we could possibly do with the *bull stuff* in my gear bag." Tucker raised a brow. "I suppose we could get creative with the tape I use to wrap my wrist. There is the cowbell hanging on my bull rope . . . Although unless you're into some really weird kind of role-playing, that won't be of much use."

He grinned as her cheeks grew hotter. "I know I'm being silly. I felt like he was watching us and, you know, judging. And I'm babbling again. Sorry."

"Don't apologize. Your babbling is adorable. Though I'm definitely looking forward to keeping your mouth otherwise occupied once we're in our room." The elevator door finally swished open in front of them right as he made the suggestion that set Becca's insides fluttering. Acting just as calm and collected as he'd been through this whole harrowing hotel experience, Tucker nodded to the couple who stepped out.

Men.

With her hand still clasped in his much larger one, he tugged her from the spot on the carpet she'd become rooted to and they got on the now empty elevator. After the doors closed they stood for a few seconds, not talking, not moving, Becca feeling shell-shocked. Eventually, Tucker shot her an amused sideways glance and then reached across in front of her. With his left hand, he pushed the button for the fifth floor on the wall panel to her right.

Jeez, she was so flustered she might have stood here waiting to go somewhere for God only knew how long before she realized she hadn't pushed the button. She drew in a deep breath and let it out in a frustrated huff.

As the elevator jolted into action, Tucker gave her fingers a squeeze and turned to face her. He braced his free arm against the wall over her shoulder. With her hand still held in his, she was pretty much pinned in. He stood so close, she had to tilt her head way back to see his face. His blue gaze pinned her just as effectively as the closeness of his body.

"Becca. Don't." His voice was soft and gentle.

She swallowed past the lump in her throat before she dared try to speak. "Don't what?"

"Don't be nervous. I only wanna be with you, and even if we spend the rest of the night doing nothing more than what we already did in the truck, that'll be all right with me."

Her pulse raced at the thought of exactly what they'd done in his truck. More of that kind of foreplay might just kill her. She hadn't had an orgasm that hard or one that lasted that long in . . . forever. Jerry hadn't been so good in that department. He was more of a slide in, get finished, and then turn on the television kind of guy.

Meanwhile Tucker had given and not taken a thing for

himself, yet he was willing to be satisfied with that. His offer was too sweet. Men weren't that selfless. Were they? If
there were men like that, she hadn't met or dated any—at
least not until tonight.

That settled it. She knew Tucker couldn't be as sweet
and selfless as he first appeared. It was unnatural. He must
be hiding something. He was probably a serial killer.

Completely baffled by his offer, she asked, "Really?"

"Really." He let out a short laugh and shook his head.
"Of course, there's no way in hell I'd say no to doing
more. If you're offering it to me, that is."

She smiled, relieved at the assurance he was a normal,
horny, red-blooded male after all. "I wouldn't say no to
more, either."

"That's really good to hear." He dropped his hand from
where it had been braced against the wall and rested it on
her shoulder.

He leaned low and captured her lips in a kiss she let herself get lost in. Eyes closed, she felt nothing but the heat of
his tongue against hers and cared about nothing except how
temptingly close his pelvis was to hers—until the doors
opened again and he took a step back.

He dragged in a big breath. "We better continue this in
private."

No kidding. There were cameras in the elevator and she
and Tucker had probably just made the late crew's night
with their little show.

They definitely needed to get out of the public areas of
the hotel before they made a complete spectacle of themselves. She couldn't keep from glancing down at the erection clearly straining the denim of his jeans. There was no
hiding that. Good thing their floor was deserted when
they stepped off the elevator and into the hall lined with
doors.

Behind one of these doors was their room. The one

with the king-size bed inside. When he stopped their progress in front of a door halfway down the hall and reached for the keycard in his pocket, she knew which. At least it was nowhere near the room she and Emma had booked. That would be all she needed—her sister hearing her and Tucker getting busy. If the actions inside the truck were any indication of events to come, she had a feeling things could get loud. Her heart pounded anew.

He opened the door and reached in to flip on the light switch, illuminating the room and the giant bed that dominated the space. She pulled her gaze away from the mattress as he stepped inside and, still being led by his hold on her hand, Becca followed.

Behind them, the spring-loaded door slammed shut with a definite sound of finality. They were officially alone and she was officially nervous. Her first one-night stand. Her first sex with a complete stranger. Her first—

"Stop thinking so hard, darlin'. You'll get wrinkles from all of your frowning." Tucker leaned low and hovered just shy of her mouth.

She felt her brow crease further at Tucker's ability to read her so well even though they barely knew each other. Not to mention the wrinkle comment. She opened her mouth but didn't get any words out before his lips covered hers. Then, all she could do was sigh as he hoisted her up and braced her back against the wall. She wrapped her legs around his waist and felt the delicious friction of his erection pressing into her.

When she tightened her hold with her thighs and he answered with a moan, the kiss became frenzied. Their tongues tangled as she ground her lower half against him. It felt so good, she wanted more. As heavy as he was breathing, he'd agree, she was sure.

He pulled back from her mouth just a bit. "How'd you feel about getting rid of some of these clothes?"

Her muscles clenched in anticipation. Her insides practically cried out to be filled by him. "How about we get rid of all of them?"

It seemed she'd found her long dormant vixen gene, and Tucker liked it, judging by the crooked smile bowing his lips at her suggestion. She unwrapped her legs from around his waist and he set her down as his gaze swept her body. Becca hadn't had a man look at her like this in a long time. She liked it. It gave her the confidence she needed to reach for the hem of her shirt and pull it off.

Thank goodness she'd worn her nice bra and underwear. As conservative as the plain black lingerie was, at least it wasn't the granny panties she'd left at home in her drawer. That might have been a mood killer. Though seeing Tucker's eyes narrow with desire as he remained totally focused on her told Becca it would take a lot to squash the mood right now.

Tucker took off his cowboy hat and laid it on top of the dresser and then crossed the room to close the curtains. The big question of the night was answered—he did take off his hat for sex.

He ran one hand over his dark hair, but it was so short it didn't even look flattened from the hours spent beneath the hat. She should have expected as much. Tucker was too perfect to get hat head like an average man. It seemed cowboys were immune to that. Although, maybe that was why he kept his hair cropped so closely to his head.

While she obsessed over the state of his hair, he had already unhooked his ornate belt buckle and toed off one boot. She'd just reached for the button on her own jeans when he pulled his shirt out from where it had been tucked tight inside his pants. He yanked the two sides apart and the pearl-covered snaps popped as they released in succession. But it was his sliding the shirt down his arms that showed exactly how wide his shoulders were in comparison to his narrow waist. Not to mention the wash-board that made up his abs, the sight of which stopped Becca in mid-motion.

Wow. Those were some rippling muscles he'd been hid-ing beneath his shirt all night. She'd only seen a man in this good shape on those late-night television ads for home gyms. Definitely not in real life. Just feet from where she stood. In a hotel room with a king-size bed.

When he shoved his jeans down his legs, she found she was having trouble focusing. As he pulled off his socks, she finally remembered to unzip her jeans. She pushed them down her legs, where the hem got stuck on her boot as she tried to step out of them. She reached for the nearest thing as she began to fall, and that happened to be him.

She grabbed his bicep, but she didn't have time to ap-preciate the hard bulging muscles beneath her touch be-fore he scooped her up and carried her to the bed. It was possibly the first time she'd been carried anywhere by any-one since she was a child. To have a man like Tucker swoop her into his arms so effortlessly and lay her on the bed had her feeling as giddy as a child, but in a very wom-anly way.

Standing next to the bed wearing nothing but navy-blue boxer briefs that didn't leave a whole lot to her imag-ination, Tucker pulled off one of her boots. He dropped it to the floor, where it landed with a thud. He moved to her other foot, and that boot followed the first. Then he reached for the waistband of her jeans, which had landed down around her knees when she'd made a complete klutz of herself.

His slow but steady progress undressing her while keep-ing her pinned with his steel-blue gaze had her forgetting her embarrassment. Instead, her need for him was ramped up to the maximum. She raised her feet off the bed as he slid the denim over them, exposing even more of her skin to the cool air in the room. Her pants joined her boots in a pile on the floor, and then he reached for her panties.

She swallowed hard and watched as he hooked two thick, work-roughened fingers beneath the top edge of her underwear and slid the silk down her legs. His expression appreciative, he made quick work of stripping off her socks and then moved on to her bra. He kneeled next to her on the mattress and reached beneath her with hands she'd seen hold on to a ton of bucking bull.

Gentler than he should have been capable of being, he unhooked the clasp and slid the straps from her shoulders until her breasts were bared to him. He took one of her nipples between his lips with a nearly feral growl. Then, without her knowing exactly when it happened because she was so distracted by the pleasure shooting through her, his boxers were on the floor and they were both completely naked. Nothing left between them except for the sexual tension, which was thick enough to cut with a knife. Well that, and his erection, which was also pretty thick and pointing directly toward her. Like a compass arrow and she was true north.

He leaned over and reached for his crumpled jeans on the floor as she tried to remember to keep breathing. It was an effort, but finally Becca managed to wrestle her gaze away from Tucker's cock and on to what he was doing with his hands. It all seemed much more real as he tore open the condom wrapper he'd just pulled from the front pocket of his pants.

Her heart pounded faster as he planted one knee on the mattress and then the other until he was braced over her, kneeling between her legs. He glanced down at her body and his, where he was so close even a small move would have him inside her.

He drew in a sharp breath, releasing it on a groan. "I'm not going to last. How about if the first time is hard and fast and the second go-round we take it nice and slow?"

"The second time?" She might pass out before the first time.

The condom he'd rolled on seemed to stretch to its limit. Tucker was a big man. That excited her as much as it made her nervous.

"Darlin', I've got six condoms and all night." His piercing gaze held hers. "There's going to be a whole lot more than just once. Believe me. I intend on neither one of us being able to walk straight in the morning. You okay with that?"

What he described would be the exact opposite of the kind of sex she was used to having, which made it sound perfect to her.

"Yes."

"Good." He smiled and slid home, hard and deep.

Her breath left her on a gasp. With her head thrown back against the pillow, she closed her eyes at the sensation of being filled by Tucker.

"Did I hurt you?" He tensed over her, his voice sounding strained at the effort to hold still.

She forced her eyes open. "God, no." To reinforce the point, she slid her hands down his body until she reached the tight muscles of his ass. She bent her knees and pulled him in deeper. "Keep going."

Tucker let out a breathless laugh. "My pleasure."

He set a pace that soon had them both breathless. She was so ready for this, for him. Her body coiled around his, tightening, gripping, until she exploded in a release that made the one she'd had earlier in the truck look small.

It wasn't until after she'd stopped throbbing inside, she realized she had a death grip on his ass; he wasn't able to move more than a tiny bit as she held him deep inside her.

She released her hold, and he reared back, plunging into her barely a few times before he surged forward and roared with his own release.

They lay there panting, his weight crushing her, for she didn't know how long. Not that she was going to complain. It was a nice place to be and even better when he pushed up onto his elbows and found her mouth with his. His fading erection still nestled inside her, he tangled his hand in her hair and kissed her.

The tiny circles he made with his hips teased her already sensitive clit, making her want more, until she felt him begin to grow and lengthen. He was getting hard again and she felt it with an intimacy she'd never even imagined, all right inside her.

She let out a moan. They should bottle whatever they fed these cowboys. They could sell it and make a fortune.

He broke the kiss and pulled back so she could see his face. "Ready for the next go-round?"

"Yes."

Chapter
Nine

Bright morning sunlight streamed through the slit between the edges of the curtains when Becca opened her eyes. They must have fallen asleep at some point, though it had to have been very late—or very early that morning—when they finally did. Tucker hadn't been kidding when he'd said the second time would be long and slow. Cowboys had a totally different concept of time than New Yorkers did. Hours different.

She stretched and felt her muscles protest from the workout she'd given them, or rather Tucker had given them. More than just her muscles were sore. She sighed and snuggled deeper beneath the covers as the air conditioner continued to pump cold air into the room. They'd certainly needed the AC last night. He apparently had no issues with working hard enough to get them both sweaty.

The mattress shifted and then the heat of his bare chest pressed against the skin of her back. "Mmm. Good morning, darlin'." His voice was low and husky with sleep.

She could get used to hearing that in the morning. Maybe there were perks to this job in Oklahoma she hadn't initially considered. Cowboys and their *darlin's* were certainly one of them.

"Good morning." She laughed as he used his arm and one leg to reel her in closer to him. Before he got too frisky, she decided she'd better check how late it was. "What time is it?"

"Don't know. Don't care. Text your sister so she doesn't worry, if you want."

"That's not it. I have an appointment to get to." Though it would be easy to forget all about her appointment with him snaking his fingers between her thighs the way he was.

"What time is your appointment?"

"Eleven."

He rolled over to glance at the bedside clock, then rolled back to her. "Mmm. Then we have plenty of time."

"For what?"

"For more. Have I told you how much I like morning sex?"

With his erection clearly wide awake even if he wasn't quite yet, she didn't need him to tell her. "No, but I had already gotten that idea from what's poking me."

"I'll poke you, all right." His finger lazily stroked her clit from the front while the hard length of him pressed into her behind.

She was ready to say to hell with the interview, and the flight home. She could very happily stay in bed with him for another day and night and still not have her fill. She groaned at the idea as well as from the way he was waking her body up. She couldn't resist opening her legs just a bit wider and giving him more access.

He laughed behind her. "I assume you like that?"

"Don't tease me. I've been sexually deprived lately. I had a lot of making up to do."

"You mean since the breakup with your ex?" Tuck somehow managed to carry on a serious conversation, all while never missing a stroke as he teased her body relentlessly.

She let out a short laugh that ended up sounding more

like a moan. "Even before the breakup. My ex . . . well, let's just say he didn't accomplish in years what you did in hours."

"Needed a map to find the clit, did he?" He increased his pressure in that area, as if to prove the point he certainly could find it just fine.

"Mmm, hmm." She had to concentrate extra hard to remember what she'd been about to say. "He'd stumble upon it once in a while, but I think it was by accident."

"Then I suppose he didn't find this spot all that often, either." He rolled her onto her back and slid one finger inside her. He began to rhythmically press on what she could only guess was her G-spot.

"Oh, my God." She hissed a breath in between her teeth. There was a good chance her eyes rolled back in her head as her hips lifted off the bed. "No. Never."

He chuckled. "Then I guess I do have a lot of making up to do. How long did you say you two were together?"

"About two years."

"Hmm, that could add up to hundreds of orgasms. I think that might be a little too ambitious a goal for one night's work."

Becca didn't respond. She wouldn't have been able to find the words even if she had the breath. Tucker had leaned down low. She felt the heat of his mouth on her clit, working it while his fingers rubbed her G-spot. He pushed her right over the edge and into one of those orgasms he'd mentioned.

She was still throbbing when he covered himself with a condom quicker than she'd thought possible and rolled on top of her. She glanced at the clock to make sure she wasn't going to be late for her interview, though at this point, she wasn't sure she would have cared. With her legs wrapped around his waist, she stopped worrying about the time completely as he set a lazy pace. The aftershocks of her climax melded into the slow strokes of the cowboy above her.

Finally, once he rolled off her and they lay panting on the mattress side by side, she remembered her reason for being in Oklahoma. She propped herself up on one elbow and tried to see the clock on his side of the bed. Luckily for her and her career, he didn't last as long this morning as he had last night.

"Relax. I'm keeping an eye on the clock. You still have a few hours." He might say he was watching the time, but he still took advantage of her position as she leaned over him. He pulled her down close enough to draw her nipple into his mouth.

"Stop that." She slapped at his shoulder. "I don't have that long. Not long enough for another one of your long rounds." Becca now knew from experience that even if the first time was fast—if you could call a solid quarter of an hour of muscle-clenching, body-writhing climaxes fast—the next round immediately following could go on for an hour or more.

He let out a dramatic sigh. "Oh, all right. I'll just have to be satisfied with the short round then. I'm gonna shower quick. Don't go anywhere."

"Don't worry. I won't."

"Promise?"

She laughed at that. "Yes. I'm not sure I can walk yet anyway."

The self-satisfied grin he sent her on his way to the bathroom was purely male.

Becca took the time he was in the shower to locate all her scattered clothes. By the time the sound of the water stopped and then the bathroom door opened, she was dressed, but not prepared for what came out.

Tucker wearing nothing but a towel draped low on his hips striding across the room was enough to draw and hold her attention. But when he grabbed his cowboy hat from the dresser and planted it on top of his damp hair, the sight would be enough to make any woman melt. She swallowed hard and tried to wrestle her libido into check and drag her gaze from his torso, glistening with water droplets.

In the light of day she noticed little things about him she hadn't seen last night while in the midst of a sexual frenzy. There were deep bruises on one side of his rib cage. Probably from a bull, if she had to guess, though she hadn't seen him fall last night. But who knew how often he rode . . . and fell. Then just above his left shoulder blade was the tattoo of a cross with something written below it that she couldn't make out.

All tiny details uniquely him. Details she'd probably still remember years from now, because there was no way she'd ever forget this. She thought it best to take her mind off it all—how tempting he looked, how dangerous his job was, how it didn't matter anyway since she'd never see him again. She pocketed that sadness and bent to retrieve the scattered empty condom wrappers from the floor.

"You know, we only used three out of the six. You must be slacking off." She glanced up and saw his brow rise at her comment.

"Skip that meeting of yours and we'll use those and then I'll go out for another box full."

Regret filled her. "I wish I could, but I can't. This meeting is the whole reason I flew out here."

"Next time, then." He walked over, leaned low, and dropped a surprisingly chaste kiss on her forehead.

"Next time," she repeated, knowing as well as he this was a one-time thing. There wouldn't be any next time.

★ ★ ★

"Bye, Becca." Tuck did his best to ignore how hard it was saying good-bye to this woman after only having spent one night with her.

"Good-bye, Tucker. And thank you for everything. Uh, I meant the beer and corn dogs and being so nice at the rodeo. Not the . . ." She glanced at the bed. Watching her cheeks turn pink as she stumbled over her words, he couldn't help smiling. She let out a sigh, apparently giving up on clarifying her thanks. "Anyway, it was really nice meeting you."

"You, too." Out of the blue, he decided he couldn't let her go quite yet. Even though she was already out in the hallway as he held the door open, he reached for her. With one arm around her waist, he dragged her close, angled his head, and gave her one last kiss to remember him by.

When he finally released her, she looked a little unsteady. The muscles in her throat worked as she swallowed. "I should . . ."

"I know." He nodded.

Becca took a step back, putting her farther into the hallway and out of his reach. "Bye."

"See ya." His smile would have been genuine if, as she started walking away, she'd turned back. Said she'd ditch her meeting to spend the rest of the day rolling around with him in bed.

She didn't.

He took small solace in the fact she looked as reluctant to leave as he was to let her go. Tuck watched her walk down the hall until she turned the corner toward the elevators and he couldn't see her any longer.

With an uncharacteristic feeling of loss, he let the door slam. Usually he was the one who couldn't get away fast enough from the women he'd had sex with. It was easier that way. Otherwise the girl might get ideas and think he was the marrying type. Which he wasn't. At least not anymore.

This morning was a rude awakening for him. Now he knew what it felt like to be the one left behind. It sucked.

With a hollow feeling of resolution and a little bit of hunger in his gut, Tuck grabbed his jeans off the floor. He found his cell phone in the pocket and pulled it out. It wasn't so early he couldn't call Jace, and too bad even if it were.

"Dude, about damn time you called." Jace answered on the second ring and didn't bother saying hello.

"I need food. Where are you?" He cut to the chase himself. He wasn't up for small talk. Maybe he'd be less cranky after coffee and eggs, though a full belly still wouldn't make up for his feeling crappy about watching Becca walk away.

"I'm home."

"You're home? Huh . . ." He'd half expected Jace to say he was in Emma's room here at the hotel. "All right. I can be at the diner near your house in twenty minutes."

"I'll see you there."

Of course Jace had agreed right quick. Tuck figured he wanted a report on how he and Becca had spent the night. Too bad for Jace, he wasn't in the mood to give him one.

"All right. See ya there." He disconnected the call, tossed the phone on the rumpled bed coverings, and started to scan the floor for his socks and underwear.

Chapter
Ten

Becca stood outside the room she'd thought she'd be sharing with her sister last night and took out her keycard. What were the chances Emma would still be sleeping? Or even better, out getting breakfast. Even if Emma had encouraged her to go for it with the cowboy, Becca still considered coming home in the morning wearing last night's clothes a walk of shame.

Desperately hoping she'd be able to avoid Emma and her questions, at least until after she'd showered and dressed for her interview, Becca opened the door as quietly as possible. She knew by the bright lights on in the room that Emma was definitely awake.

"Well, well, well. Look what the cat dragged in." Emma was not only up, but dressed and standing, arms crossed, looking too much like their mother.

Becca avoided eye contact, thinking that was the safest course of action. "Morning. I gotta shower and get dressed or I'm going to be late for this interview."

She'd only taken a step toward the bathroom when Emma said, "Oh, no, you don't."

"Don't what?" Playing dumb seemed like a very good plan at the moment.

"Don't you dare think you can walk in here practically glowing, twelve hours after I last left you with a cowboy hot enough to melt ice cubes just by looking at them, and not say a word to me about what happened." Emma planted her fists on her hips.

"I could say the exact same thing. I left you with Jace, didn't I? Are you going to tell me what happened?" She turned the logic back on to her sister. Offense was the best defense, after all.

"No." Emma's face blanched before she recovered. "Besides, that's different."

Interesting. Now Becca was really curious. "Oh, really. I don't see any difference at all." She folded her arms and waited.

Emma let out a huff. "Okay, we'll agree to no details about the guys or our nights."

"Good." Becca spun toward the bathroom.

"But I need to know one thing."

She released a loud, lip-flapping breath and looked back at Emma. "What's that?"

"Just tell me you had a good time." Emma's voice softened, sounding as if she really did want to know Becca was happy. That figured. Her sister always could melt her heart, even while annoying her.

"I had a good time." She indulged Emma with an answer, even if that response was the understatement of the year. Good was so not the adjective she should use. Incredible. Unforgettable. Orgasmic . . . But there was no way she was going to tell her sister about Tucker's unbelievable skills in bed, or her multiple orgasms, or how she'd felt a strange sadness when she'd walked away from him just now. Nope. Not gonna happen.

A wide, satisfied grin settled on Emma's lips. "And?"

"And what?" Becca frowned. She really did need to finish up this chatter and shower.

"And what happened when you said good-bye? Are you going to see him again?"

"You said one thing, and I told you. No more." She had to hide her own smile as Emma frowned and looked totally frustrated she wasn't getting more information. "Besides, I still have to shower, dry my hair, and get dressed so we can check out, drive to Stillwater, and hopefully get something to eat before my interview."

Becca glanced at the clock again. She wasn't kidding. She really did have to get ready, but it was also a good excuse to avoid giving Emma details she'd rather not provide.

Emma pouted, looking more thirteen than thirty. "Fine. Get ready, but we're not done here."

"No, we're not. Fair is fair. I answered your question so you still have to tell me one thing about your night with Jace, and I still have an interview to hopefully not screw up." Now, without Tucker as a distraction, her nerves about the upcoming meeting with the dean at OSU began to kick in full force.

"You'd better not screw it up."

She heard her sister's last bossy order on her way to the bathroom. "I'll do my best."

After she'd taken the quickest shower of her life, Becca tried to ignore the tug of her sex-induced muscle soreness as she stepped over the edge of the tub. When she wiped away the steam from the mirror, she discovered yet another memento when her reflection came into view—the bruise Tucker had left on her throat.

When the hell had that happened?

There apparently would be no forgetting Tucker soon with all the reminders he'd left her. She shook her head at the ridiculousness of the whole situation. A hickey. At her age and on a day she had a huge interview that could mean the difference between her having to take a job checking out customers at her local supermarket or becoming an associate professor, even if it was halfway across the country from everything she knew and loved. No pressure there.

"I'm ironing your blouse for you. It got wrinkled in the suitcase." Emma's voice came through the closed bathroom door, making Becca feel guilty for hiding in there so she didn't have to answer any more questions about last night. Her guilt didn't make her open the door and face her sister, however.

With a huff, she grabbed her makeup bag from the vanity and pawed through to find her cover-up, all while hoping Emma hadn't noticed the mouth-shaped bruise.

"Thank you." Becca swiped a thick layer of makeup over the spot on her neck. She followed it with powder and decided that was the best she could do.

She stared at her reflection in the streaked mirror. There were dark circles beneath her eyes, but at the same time, they'd never looked so bright, and her cheeks were flushed with a healthy glow. One night of crazy sex with a cowboy and she barely recognized herself. As she searched beneath the vanity for the hotel's hair dryer, she tried to decide whether that was a good thing or not.

A knock on the bathroom door made her jump. Ready or not, she reached for the doorknob and found Emma on the other side. "Hey. You need to get in here?"

"No. Take your time. I finished ironing your shirt. I thought you might need it. Though if you went without the blouse under your suit jacket, you might really be a shoo in for the position." Emma smirked.

Becca laughed. She reached for the hanger Emma held out to her, all the while praying the makeup covering her hickey was holding up to the sister scrutiny. "Thanks for this."

"No problem." Emma leaned against the door frame and didn't look like she was going anywhere.

Becca hung the shirt on the towel bar and reached for

the hair dryer. The heat and the noise from a good old blow dryer set on high should hopefully do the trick to drive a nosy sister away.

"Can I ask you something?"

Crap. Emma had snuck her question in before Becca had a chance to even turn the dryer on.

"Um, I guess."

"What are you going to say? If they offer you the job after this interview, will you take it?"

The same question had plagued Becca ever since the call from the dean. A week ago, she hadn't been sure of the answer. Now, however, what she needed to do seemed to be clear. Though foreign and far from everything she'd ever known, Oklahoma seemed nice enough—what little she'd seen of it. And she really was working toward the bottom of her cash savings. And this was an associate professor position, which was what she'd been working toward and never got at Vassar . . .

"If they offer it to me—and remember, there's no guarantee they will—yes, I think I'll accept it." She flipped on the dryer before Emma could comment on her response, but as she reached for the hairbrush, she didn't miss her sister's smug look.

Emma obviously assumed it was the night of hot sex with Tucker that had swayed her decision. Refusing to even think that might be true, Becca frowned at her reflection and began to blow her hair into submission when a folded newspaper landed on the vanity in front of her. She glanced at it, and the many circled listings.

"What's that?" She had to shout over the noise of the dryer, but she wasn't giving Emma the satisfaction of turning it off. Besides, that interview was growing nearer by the moment.

"Apartment listings."

"Em, I don't even know if I have the job yet."

"There're a couple of one-bedrooms for six-hundred dollars a month. Utilities included."

She lowered the dryer. Six hundred? With utilities? Wow. She could actually do this. Move here and live very comfortably. She raised the dryer again and ignored the satisfied expression on Emma's face in the reflection in the mirror. "I'll take a look at it later. I can't be late for this interview if you really want me to get this job."

"Oh, believe me. I do."

And she knew the reason why Emma was extra determined she get this job. His name was Tucker.

Twenty minutes after he had called Jace from the hotel room, Tuck found his best friend in the diner.

Jace glanced up from his cup of coffee. "So? What happened?"

Tuck shook his head and let out a short laugh. "A hello would be nice before you start interrogating me. And you know better than to ask that."

He slid into the booth and eyed the mug in Jace's hand. Wishing coffee would magically appear in his, he looked around for a waitress.

"Why shouldn't I ask?" A deep frown furrowed Jace's brow. "You used to tell me everything about your women all the time. Hell, I was in the same room with you for one of them. I had to pretend I was sleeping while you got all the pussy. Granted I was a little shitfaced after polishing off that bottle of bourbon with you, but I was still there and I heard every damn *Oh, Tuck* all night long." The scowl told Tuck Jace hadn't been too happy about it, either.

Sad, but true. But that was a time in his life that was over now. He drew in a deep breath and blew it out hard. "I know, and I'm sorry about that, but last night was different."

"Oh, really? And why is that, exactly?" Jace looked more smug than interested in what Tuck had to say, as if he already knew the answer.

"Because."

"Because . . ." Jace let the very leading sentence trail off and waited for Tuck to finish it.

He was too tired and hungry to deal with Jace's questions. He probably did need a little bit of self-analysis about last night and this morning with Becca and its lingering effects on him, but he didn't want to do it with Jace. Though there wasn't anyone else he could talk to about this. Jace had been there right up until the post-rodeo activities had begun.

"I guess because Becca's different. She's a lady." Tuck's mamma might have had her hands full raising him and his brother, not to mention his younger sister, but she still got through to him a man needed to treat a lady like a lady. Becca was that.

"You sure that's it?" Jace's brow rose.

"Yes. What else could it be?" Tuck clenched his jaw. Jace was almost making him angry in his attempt to get him to admit something he didn't want to. The truth. That he liked Becca, a lot, and hated that he'd never see her again.

"You sure you don't want to discuss Becca because you actually want more?"

"Of course I want more. Who wouldn't? You saw her." Tuck put him off like it was all about the sex.

Jace shook his head. "Joke all you want, but I think you can see yourself starting something with her. Like a relationship."

What the hell was with Jace, playing therapist all of a sudden?

"A relationship? No. That's ridiculous." He twisted in

his seat and looked behind him. Where was that damn waitress? He needed some coffee and a distraction to get Jace off his back.

"It's been long enough since the divorce, Tuck. Why not a relationship?"

"Why not? Are you kidding me?" Besides the catastrophic end to his last serious relationship and the scars it had left? "For starters, she lives in New York. Even if that weren't a thousand miles and worlds away from Oklahoma, she didn't give me her number. If she'd wanted to contact me, she would have at least asked for my number, and she didn't, which proves it was a one-night thing. For both of us." He added the last part without much sincerity. He definitely wouldn't have minded if it hadn't been only one night.

It sucked watching her leave his room knowing he'd never see her again. Shit. Maybe he did want that serious relationship after all. That was as frightening as it was depressing since, want it or not, he wasn't going to get it.

"She'll find you if she wants to." Jace sipped again on his coffee.

He let out a snort. "Oh, really? How?"

"You're the famous state rodeo champion Tucker Jenkins. One quick search on the Internet and she'll be able to find you."

Tuck laughed, at both the famous comment and that she'd bother to search for him online. "Whatever. Enough about me and my night. What happened with you last night?"

"What do you mean?" Jace donned an overly innocent expression, which only made Tuck more interested.

"Coffee?" Finally, thankfully, a waitress walked over with a coffeepot. Though her timing wasn't great since it interrupted his interrogation of Jace about his evening with Emma.

"Yes, please." He pushed the empty mug sitting on the paper place mat toward her and then refocused on his elusive friend. "You know what I mean. You were at the hotel bar last night with Emma."

"Yes, I was. Where you ditched me without so much as a call or a text or a screw you, buddy."

He splashed cream into his mug and took his first blissful sip of caffeine before answering. "Becca texted Emma."

"And that makes it all right? Humph. Some friend you are." Jace looked away, playing up the role of insulted best friend a little more.

"You're avoiding answering my question, which makes me think absolutely nothing happened with Emma. Which was why you were home, alone, this morning."

"You don't know that."

"Then prove me wrong and tell me what happened," he challenged.

"Hey, like you said. A gentleman doesn't talk about a lady." It sounded to him more like Jace had spent the night alone with his own hand and was jealous Tuck hadn't, but he let it drop when Jace continued, "So, what you got planned for today?"

"I've got a run scheduled at OSU with the cadets."

"A run in this heat?" Jace shook his head. "Better you than me. You wouldn't catch me doing that."

Tuck was sure of that, but he didn't comment. The waitress was back, pad and pen in hand, ready to take their order. There were steak and eggs in his future, which always made the day better. And after the workout he'd had last night, he'd certainly need the protein.

Chapter
Eleven

"Are you sure you're doing all right there in Oklahoma all alone?" Emma's voice conveyed her doubt.

"I'm good. I told you, everything's great." Becca tried to sound as reassuring as possible. Emma was best kept calm, for everyone's benefit. Besides, it was true. Things were going fine so far.

Sure, her off-season clothes were still in big black trash bags waiting to be hung in the closet, but she wouldn't need her winter coats and sweaters for months yet. She'd already unpacked the cardboard boxes full of kitchen stuff she'd moved from home, and she was making good headway on the few other boxes of assorted stuff. She had her favorite mug already in the kitchen cabinet. Her leather-bound Chaucer and Shakespeare collections were arranged on the bookshelf, with the framed pictures of her family scattered between the books. Her toiletries were in the bathroom and her own sheets and comforter were in her bedroom, even if they were on a strange bed.

She had only moved her personal items into the furnished apartment. She'd left everything else, furniture included, in New York. Anything she needed and hadn't brought she could get at the store down the road.

A fresh start. That's what she wanted. What she needed. So far, that's exactly what she'd accomplished.

"Becca . . . are you lying to me?" Emma had that mommy tone in her voice again. She really should just get married and have kids. Then maybe she'd stop mothering Becca.

"Emma, I'm fine. I swear." She laughed, picturing Emma frowning and trying to read between the lines during the long distance phone call.

She meandered to the kitchen and grabbed a diet soda from the fridge. For once, she wasn't just saying what she knew Emma wanted to hear. It was true, but she had to convince Emma, and that could take a while. She popped the tab on the can and prepared for a long conversation. She truly was excited, even a little nervous about starting the new job, but it was all good.

It had been easy, too. Incredibly so. Getting the job offer. Taking it, of course. Renting her condo in New York to an IBM executive who needed a place quick and furnished for the next year meant she had income coming in to cover the mortgage. More important, she didn't need to sell and risk taking a loss, and she didn't have to pay to move her furniture. Knowing she had a place in New York to go back to made moving seem less frightening. A little bit anyway.

Cradling the phone on her shoulder, she grabbed a slice of pizza from the box on the counter and carried it along with her soda and a paper napkin into the living room. She plopped down on the sofa and put the can on the coffee table.

A furnished two-bedroom apartment an incredibly short distance from the OSU campus cost her about a third of what she would pay in New York. Sure, she was surrounded by kids—students who were also renting— but that was kind of nice. It made her feel less alone than if she'd rented in a residential neighborhood full of families. She'd take coeds as neighbors any day over happily married couples reminding her of what she didn't have.

And, also on the plus side, there was certainly no lack of fast food places, all of which delivered. She bit into the slice of cheese pizza. All right, it wasn't New York pizza, but it wasn't bad. They'd acted like she was crazy when she asked if they had fresh spinach as a topping, but still, she could deal with it. Chewing, she waited for Emma's next inevitable question.

"Have you called Mom and Dad yet?"

She swallowed the mouthful of food. "Yes, Emma. I talked to them this morning. And last night, too."

"And . . . have you called anyone else?"

"Like who?" Becca sure as hell wasn't going to call Jerry and tell him anything. Let him wonder how she was. How amusing would that be if he went to the condo and the six-foot plus executive she'd rented to opened the door? If only she could be there to see the expression on Jerry's face then.

That bastard didn't need reassurance she was all right after he'd left her high and dry. Then again, maybe rubbing it in his face how well she was doing would be sweet revenge. She'd have to consider that.

Becca reached for the can to wash down the pizza. She'd need to find a place that made a thinner crust. Too much dough in this one.

"I thought maybe you might have called a certain cowboy," Emma suggested.

In mid-swallow, she choked on the soda bubbles. She cleared her throat. "What?"

"Come on. Don't tell me you haven't thought about calling Tucker."

"Oh, I've thought about it." Becca laughed. "I've thought what a bad idea it would be."

"Why?"

"Emma, he's probably with a different girl every night. Or at least after every rodeo." The way he'd strutted right up to her that night, who was to say he didn't do that at every event? What did Becca know except that a man didn't get that good in bed without a whole lot of practice.

She heard the telltale sound of Emma's fingers on the computer keyboard. "Emma Madison Hart, I swear to God, if you Google him, I will never speak to you again." It had been all she could do to stop herself from searching his name online during the past few weeks. She sure as hell didn't need Emma undermining her resolve and doing it now.

"Becca, come on. What harm could it do to see if he's listed in the local phone book? Ooh, maybe there's a rodeo coming up. You could happen to stop by . . ."

"And see him there with another girl? Great idea, Em. Keep those helpful suggestions coming." She scowled, remembering all the pretty young things hanging around behind the chutes with the riders. They had no problem drooling over Tucker even though he was standing right there with her. They certainly would be on him like flies on bull manure if he were alone.

At that thought, she let out a huff. One night with a cowboy and even her analogies were starting to sound Western.

Through the earpiece, she heard Emma sigh. "All right, but you should really consider giving him a call. Just to let him know you're in town. You're new to Oklahoma. Maybe he could show you around to all the local hot spots."

Any spot where Tucker happened to be would be a hot spot. Becca pushed that errant thought aside. "We don't even know if he's local, Em. You saw the parking lot at the arena. There were license plates from all over the country."

"Tucker's truck had Oklahoma plates on it. So did Jace's."

Crap, when had Emma gotten so observant? "Well, Oklahoma's a big state. He could be from western Oklahoma or something. I still don't think it's a good idea and I don't have his phone number anyway."

"He's probably listed. I could just look it up for you—"

"No!"

"All right. Jeez. You don't have to get loud about it. I'll leave you alone. Anyway, what's on the agenda for your first week of work?"

She seriously doubted Emma would leave this topic of conversation alone for very long, but at least for now there was a change in topic to her new job. This Becca could handle. "I have a meeting with the dean tomorrow, and then he's hosting a faculty mixer in the afternoon to welcome me."

"Aw. That's really nice of him. See, I told you—"

"Yes, you did." She rolled her eyes. "Can we put a date on when you'll stop saying I told you so? You know, so I can put it on my calendar."

"How about, um, I don't know . . . Never?"

"Great." She groaned. She could see it now. They'd be old and gray, living in an assisted living facility somewhere, sitting in matching rocking chairs, and Emma would still be reminding her how she was the one responsible for Becca getting the job.

"Anyway, back to the mixer. What outfit are you going to wear? You'll be meeting your coworkers. First impressions are very important."

Good old predictable Emma—always worried about

fashion. Becca shook her head. "What would you like me to wear?"

Sometimes it was just easier to give in to her sister's bossiness. Besides, she really didn't know what clothes to wear—not that she'd tell Emma that. Did she dress in the typical New York uniform of all black? She had her good black suit. Or should she tone down the formality? Try to look friendly and casual.

Who the hell knew? Certainly not Becca. She wasn't sure of anything anymore, except she wasn't going to go to a rodeo to stalk Tucker. She wasn't even going to Google him so she could call him . . . At least not right now.

Damn it. So much for her resolve.

"Okay, so what to wear . . . What to wear . . . Hmm, what's the weather going to be like there tomorrow? Is it beastly hot? The university should have air-conditioning though, right? But where's the mixer being held? Indoors or outdoors?"

Let the fashion consult begin. She sighed and got up from her comfy seat on the sofa. Knowing Emma, there'd be a lot more questions—some of them might even be about her wardrobe—so she might as well be standing in front of her closet for the discussion.

"So, what do you think of our little school?" Dean Ross steered the car at a crawl past the university's sprawling manicured lawns.

His use of the word had obviously been tongue-in-cheek. Becca laughed. "I wouldn't exactly call it little, but it certainly is beautiful."

The place was huge—like five hundred buildings and who knew how many acres huge—but lovely. Much more so than she'd expected. From the university's original building dating from the 1890s, to the Georgian styling of the library, student union, and the formal garden he'd shown her, it had all been a pleasant surprise. She hadn't seen much more than one administration building when she'd blown into her interview, cutting it close and almost late, the morning after . . . She stifled the thought of what that had been after.

Dean Ross's smile beamed with pride. "It can be a bit overwhelming, I know. Our student union is the largest in the world, but you'll get the lay of the land soon enough."

Becca made a mental note to allow herself lots of time, and comfortable shoes, to explore the student union. "Thank you. I'm sure I will."

She glanced sideways at the man while he concentrated on a group of students crossing the road in front of the car. He'd worn a suit for her interview last month, but he'd gone for the casual look today—khaki pants with a blue button-down shirt and a slightly off-kilter red tie. No jacket.

It was nice to have a boss who wasn't old and stuffy. Pretty much the opposite of Vassar, and right now anything different was good. She made a note of all the details about Dean Ross and his fashion choices, down to the fact there was no ring on his finger. Emma would most likely quiz her relentlessly on the phone later about everyone and every little thing.

Maybe she should turn the tables on Emma—invite her here for a visit and introduce her to Dean Ross. That would teach Emma to stop meddling in Becca's love life. Though her sister dating her boss could be problematic. Or maybe it could help her career.

Hmm, this was something she'd have to consider later, because he'd turned toward her now. "So, are you ready for the mixer?"

"As ready as I'll ever be."

Now was as good a time as any to meet her new co-workers, she supposed. She had on the outfit she and Emma had compromised on last night—the black pants and jacket from the suit Becca wanted to wear, but with a periwinkle blue tank top underneath for a pop of color and a more casual feel to go along with the open toe shoes Emma had insisted on.

She could hear her sister now. *You want to look professional, but you also have to appear friendly, and a little bit sexy wouldn't hurt, either.* Becca shook her head at the memory. Sexy, at a faculty mixer. What was she doing taking career fashion advice for her new job from Emma anyway? The woman worked as a graphic designer, not an English professor.

Too late now. She stared out the car window through her sunglasses as the dean parked the car. Two men dressed in camouflage from head to toe caught her eye as they walked down the path and toward the door of the building.

"Are those soldiers?" Becca frowned. She turned to the dean as the two men disappeared down the path and around the corner of the building. "Are we under attack or something?"

It was only partly a joke.

He laughed. "No, we're perfectly safe. There's an ROTC program on campus." At her blank stare he continued, "Military studies . . . army officer training."

"Oh." Nodding, she tried to look like she had some clue as to what he was talking about, all while attempting to work out the letters in the acronym.

The officer training part fit the O and T, but she gave up on the task of deciphering the rest when what the R and the C could possibly stand for eluded her. Good thing she wasn't in a cryptology military studies course. She'd fail.

"In fact, I expect they're on their way to our mixer. The head of the program's a friend of mine. I invited him and told him to bring whomever he wanted. I hope that's all right." With one finger, he pushed his wire-rimmed glasses higher onto the bridge of his nose.

She smiled at the dean. "Sure. The more the merrier."

So Dean Ross hadn't just invited the English department faculty. Hmm. Becca kind of liked the idea. A mixer that included the English and the military science departments. That certainly would be interesting.

Soldiers, in uniform, at her little mixer. And she'd dressed in her sexy yet professional outfit for it. Emma would approve.

Good thing she wasn't here to play matchmaker. If history were any guide, if Emma had been here prodding her to do things she wasn't sure she wanted to do, there'd be a very real risk of Becca waking up in the morning in a bed with combat boots beneath it.

She shook her head at the thought and released her seat belt as Dean Ross did the same. Time to face the troops. Literally.

Chapter
Twelve

Tuck shot the man walking at his side a less than happy look. "There are a thousand faculty members at this campus. Tell me again why I have to attend this tea party or whatever the hell it is?"

Logan Hunt, head of the OSU ROTC program and theoretically—all right, officially—Tuck's boss, glanced over. His dark brows rose. "It's not a tea party. It's a mixer and I'm told they'll be serving wine—"

"Wine. Oh, great. Will there be sherry, too? Or perhaps a nice port? Should I run home and get my smoking jacket and my—"

"—*and* you're attending because I asked you, nicely, to come with me." Logan continued as if Tuck hadn't been speaking . . . or bitching. Whichever.

Asked him to. Sure. As if Tuck could have said no. Logan was his friend, yes. He had been for years, since way back when they'd grown up together, long before they'd both joined up. But Logan was his superior officer as well as a friend, and he'd done Tuck a huge favor during the crash and eventual burn of his marriage.

When Tuck's deployment ended, Logan used every military connection he had and pulled all the strings he could to get Tuck assigned the billet in the ROTC program on campus.

Tuck had needed to be here in familiar territory, around people and places he knew, not in Germany, or Italy, or deployed again where his head not being in the game could cost lives. His own, or worse, those of the men around him.

He owed Logan plenty for that. When he'd joined up all those years ago, he'd never in his wildest imagination thought he'd end up being a teacher, even if it was as an instructor in OSU's ROTC program. But he really never thought owing Logan a favor would mean having to sip wine with a bunch of librarians. Boss trumped friend today. Hell, probably any day. But an English department wine mixer? What the devil did this have to do with work?

He drew in a deep breath of hot summer air. "I don't see why you have to go at all, with or without me. This has nothing to do with our department."

"Mark asked me to come," Logan answered.

"Mark Ross? The dean I met at your poker game that one time I sat in as fourth?"

"Yup."

They continued toward the building where this wine party was being held. It was a hell of a hike in the August heat to be walking clear across campus for no good reason, while wearing his army combat uniform to boot. Maybe if there were a nice cold longneck waiting for him it would be a different story, or if the mixer part referred to cola to mix with a bottle of bourbon, Tuck's feelings might be changed.

In any case, he knew he could bitch about the mixer, but he didn't dare complain about the walk or the heat. If he did, Logan would probably make him run the campus with a full pack like he was a damn cadet. Army strong and all that. A soldier could complain about being forced to mingle at a party with some pansy-asses, but he'd better not complain about anything even closely resembling PT.

Even if the T-shirt under his ACU would be soaked with sweat by the time they reached this shindig.

Maybe subjecting his new professor to two sweaty soldiers would teach this friend of Logan's from the English department not to invite the military science crew to a fancy wine mixer.

Tuck considered why they were invited in the first place and still couldn't come up with a good reason. "You know, just because you guys play poker together every week still doesn't give me any reason why you have to go to this English mixer thing."

"He wanted a big turnout for his new professor. She just moved all the way from New York and doesn't know anybody, so he thought it would be nice. She's supposedly smoking hot, if that helps ease the burden on you any." Logan shot him a sideways glance.

New York. That's where Becca was from. He swallowed away the dryness in his throat. His body still reacted viscerally at just the thought of Becca. If he didn't watch it, he'd have a hard-on walking into this party.

He drew in a deep breath and let it out slowly, focusing again on the conversation before his memories ran away from him. "I seriously doubt she's hot, and even if she is, I don't exactly think English professors are my type. Or that I'm theirs. The only books I own are *The Art of War* and Schwarzkopf's autobiography."

"So? I thought that bio was a good read."

Tuck frowned so deeply he could see the brim of his watch cap lower from the action. "Yeah, it was. And what do you think the chances are little miss professor has read it? I'll tell you, slim to none."

Logan laughed. "You never know. Besides, opposites attract and all that."

He let out a snort. "You can't get much more opposite

than a soldier and bull rider from Oklahoma and an English professor from New York."

"Don't sell yourself short. You're on equal footing here. You're both faculty at a damned good university. Just because you're usually teaching military operations and tactics and she teaches—hell, I don't know—poetry or whatever, doesn't mean you're not on the same level."

What was this big push by all his friends to make him keep associating with random women from New York? First Jace at the rodeo—not that he regretted that, except for all the sleep he'd lost over Becca since then. But now Logan was in on the act, too, by making him go to this party.

He frowned at Logan. "You're single. Why are you trying to push this woman off on me? What about you? You can just as easily compare military biographies with her as I can."

"If that's how you feel, fine." Logan shrugged. "Just thought it was about time you got back on the horse. You know, started to get out and meet people. Mingle a little. It's been a year since the divorce."

What, did all his friends have the anniversary of his divorce marked on their calendars? "I'm fine, thanks. I don't want to meet any new people. And I've recently been back on the horse, thank you very much."

The only thing admitting the truth to Logan did was make Tuck miss that ride, and regret never seeing again one particular filly with bright blue eyes and hips a man could hold on to all night long. Crap, he was definitely going to get a full-blown hard-on if he didn't redirect his thoughts. And how had he let this conversation turn to sex?

"Oh, really?" Logan actually stopped walking and turned to face Tuck. "When?"

He kept walking and said over his shoulder, "I'm not talking about it."

"Fine." Logan's long strides brought him even with Tucker again in no time.

Meanwhile, he had taken a moment to consider this mysterious guest they were going to meet and what Logan had said about her. His frown deepened. "Wait a minute—the dean of her department is going around telling people his new hire is hot? That's pretty unprofessional. He's lucky if he doesn't lose his position and get his ass sued for shit like that."

Tuck should know. They'd all had to sit through more than their share of sexual harassment seminars in the military.

"It wasn't Mark. One of the cadets told me. He was on line behind her when she was getting her photo ID yesterday. He heard everything. She was telling the clerk she'd just got hired in the English department. That she moved from New York. Has to be her." Logan shrugged.

"Hmm. Guess so."

"The kid compared her to some actress I never heard of but all the guys apparently think is smoking." Logan pulled open the door to the building and held it while Tuck let that information soak in.

An English professor who was hot enough for a still wet-behind-the-ears cadet to notice. Hmm. Too bad Tuck wasn't interested. Hot women were nothing but trouble. Take his ex-wife for example. And Becca—one night with her had left him waking up in the middle of the night hard and unhappy for weeks now.

He followed Logan down the hallway of the air-conditioned building, happy at least to be out of the sun. Maybe some of that wine wouldn't sit so badly after all—if it was cold.

Once inside the room, he decided he might need more than wine to endure this event. He stifled a groan and then glanced at Logan, unhappier about this than before. It was even worse than he'd imagined.

One old man who looked freakishly like Santa Claus was stationed next to the cheese platter, where it looked like he was trying to eat enough so he wouldn't need dinner. There were two women of indeterminate ages, heads bent low as they whispered to each other. They were both dressed in sweaters even though it was August. The pinched expressions on their faces made the mean librarian from Tuck's high school look warm and fuzzy.

He swiped his patrol cap from his head and shoved it into one of the pockets in his pants as he looked around at the other attendees. At first glance, they seemed no better than cheese guy and the two conspiratorial librarians.

"Uh, Logan, how long do we have to stay?" It was like a nursing home in here, which made the reports of the new English professor being hot even more ludicrous.

"At least until the guest of honor gets here and Mark sees me."

Ha! Judging by his tone and that answer, he could tell Logan was no happier to be here than he was. Good to know, since misery loved company. Misery also loved alcohol. "I'm getting a drink. You want one?"

Logan let out a snort of a laugh. "Oh, yeah."

"Be right back."

He forgot to ask Logan what he wanted, but when he got to the table with the ice and glasses set up, there wasn't much of a selection anyway. It looked like some sort of fancy bottled water and wine were the only options. Well then, that made the choice easier, except for whether to get white or red.

Tuck made the decision all on his own to get the white wine since it seemed closer to the beer he really wanted and he was still hot from the walk. He'd get Logan the same. It wasn't as if either of them knew or cared anything about wine anyway.

Hell, while he was there, he grabbed two bottles of water for them, too, and shoved them both in the crook of his arm. Double-fisting wasn't considered bad party manners if one was nonalcoholic. Right? Besides, the importance of keeping hydrated was a lesson troops learned well during any deployment to a hot region in summer.

Hands and arms full, he headed back to Logan and handed him his half of the refreshments. Logan would have to go up and get the cheese his own damn self if he wanted any. Tuck wasn't about to wrestle Santa for it.

"They're late." He glanced around the room one more time, hoping to see Ross and the guest of honor so they could say their hellos and good-byes and get the hell out of there.

"No, we're early."

Great. Nothing like arriving early at a party he didn't want to go to in the first place. "So you mean some more new and exciting guests might still show up? I don't know if I can handle any more excitement than this."

"We could stay for the whole thing . . ." Logan's veiled threat put a gag on all future smart-ass remarks.

For lack of anything better to do, Tuck chugged the bottle of water in one go and then tossed the empty into the nearby recycling can set up next to the trash. One down, one to go. The excitement never ended around this place. He raised the wine to his lips and was about to take the first sip to determine if it was even worth drinking, when he saw her walk in the door.

He had to stare to make sure he was really seeing who he thought he was seeing. But staring didn't change a thing. It was her. "Holy crap."

"What's wrong?" Logan laid a hand on his shoulder when he didn't respond. "Tuck? You all right? You look like you've seen a ghost."

A short laugh escaped Tuck at that comment. Seeing Becca here and now when he'd figured he'd never see her again was almost like seeing a ghost. His focus never strayed from the doorway, where Becca smiled and shook hands with whomever Mark Ross was introducing her to.

"Tucker." Logan's voice knocked Tuck out of his shocked silence.

"Yeah. I'm fine." He finally remembered to respond to Logan. "Uh, do you happen to know the name of this new English professor from New York?"

"I think Rebecca something. Why?"

Close enough. While he considered exactly how to go about explaining the situation to Logan, his friend had already followed the direction of his gaze.

Now Logan was staring at the doorway as well. "There's Mark. And that must be her. Phew. Now I know why you look like you're in a trance. The kid wasn't wrong. She is smoking. Judging by your uh, shall we say, reaction, you agree." Logan glanced at him. "So, you still not interested in meeting her?"

Tuck let out a snort. "You're way too late for that."

He knew the moment Becca saw him. She frowned, looking almost as if she couldn't place him. Even if she did recognize him, the uniform and his being here at the university would have thrown her. It didn't fit her memory of him in chaps and his cowboy hat at the rodeo. Or later on of him naked and in bed.

After a few seconds recognition must have hit her. Her eyes opened wide. Her boss had to touch her arm to get her attention, but even when she did manage to shake hands with the woman he was now introducing her to, she kept glancing in Tuck's direction.

"Tuck, what's going on?" Logan asked.

How should he put this? "Um, you know how I told you I'd gotten back on the horse recently? Well . . ." Tuck cocked his head in Becca's direction.

"Her?" Eyes wide, Logan couldn't have looked more shocked if he'd tried.

"Yep."

"When?"

"Couple of weeks ago."

"Since it looks like I'm going to have to drag every word out of you, I'll move on to my next two questions. How and where?"

"They were in the audience at the rodeo back in July. She and her sister were here from New York for a couple of days. She said she had some meeting." Tuck let out a laugh as it all started to click in his head.

The important meeting Becca couldn't miss—it had to have been about this job. So the entire time they were together she knew there was a chance she'd be moving to Oklahoma, if she hadn't already been hired by then. Yet she never told him. Didn't give him her number. Didn't ask for his. Never said a damn word. Like there was no chance she'd ever want to see him again even if she was living in spitting distance from him. That made Tuck feel pretty damn shitty.

"Wow." Logan's gaze was back on Becca as he shook his head.

Wow was as good a word as any for his surprise at not only seeing her but finding out all she'd kept from him after the kind of time they'd had together. Apparently he'd been good enough for Becca for one night, but she wasn't interested in a repeat. If she had been, she would have told him about the job. They would have exchanged phone numbers. He would have been meeting her for dinner, not at this damn wine mixer.

"You gonna be okay?" Logan glanced at him again. "You're not looking too good."

"Oh, I'll be fine." He downed the wine before the thin plastic cup became the victim of his clenched fist.

This was going to be one hell of an introduction, and judging by the beeline Ross was making in their direction, it was happening sooner rather than later. Jaw set, he lobbed the empty cup into the garbage and turned back for the big introduction. Widening his stance, he folded his arms and braced himself.

"Logan, glad you could make it." A smiling Mark Ross grasped and shook Logan's hand, then turned to Becca. "Dr. Rebecca Hart. This is Lieutenant Colonel Logan Hunt, battalion commander of our ROTC program. He's the military science department head and a good friend of mine."

As she extended her hand, Becca's gaze shot to Tuck before she dragged it back to Logan. "Nice to meet you."

"Pleasure's all mine, ma'am." Logan glanced sideways at Tuck.

In a normal situation, it would be polite for Logan to make the introductions between him and the new arrival since it was doubtful Ross remembered Tuck's name from the one night they'd played poker. But there was nothing normal about this situation. Logan looked a little lost as to how to proceed, and Becca looked like she'd rather be anywhere else but here, under Tuck's scrutiny. The bitter, spiteful side of his personality took great pleasure in Becca's obvious discomfort.

"Mark, you remember my friend Staff Sergeant Tucker Jenkins?" Logan turned to include Tuck in the happy group.

"Of course. Nice to see you again, Sergeant. Glad you could make it. Let me introduce you to Dr. Rebecca Hart."

Becca had a frigging doctorate. She had really been slumming with him that night. This just got better and better.

"Doctor." He extended his hand and waited to see what she'd do, but he'd be damned if he'd say *"nice to meet you."* Forget about that crap. They'd done way more than *meet* that night in July.

"Sergeant." The tension in her voice was clear to him. It might even be evident to Logan now he knew. Her boss, however, blissfully ignorant of the situation, looked happy as a clam they were all getting to know each other.

The muscles in her throat worked as she swallowed hard and extended her arm. Becca's hand in his was as small and soft as he remembered it. That night he'd loved every second he'd held her hand. But to hold it again now, knowing what he knew about her and that night, hurt.

Damn, that was a surprise. Sure, he expected his pride to sting from her slight, but this? This felt like more. It felt like sadness. Regret. Pain.

Crap. He should have stuck to bending buckle bunnies over the bumper of his truck. It was too soon to be with a woman he'd actually wanted to spend more time with. A woman he had really liked.

Damn Jace and his pushing. He'd forced Tuck into it. It was his fault. Logan's, too. All that *get back on the horse* talk was about one more friend trying to push him into something he wasn't ready for. Getting on the horse was a damn good way to get knocked back down to the ground and trampled on, if you asked him.

He realized he'd been holding Becca's hand for far too long and dropped it. He finally brought himself to look her in the eye and found her watching him, but when their gazes collided, she yanked hers away.

"Logan, are you going to hang around for a little bit? I have a few more folks I'd like Rebecca to meet, but I wanted to talk to you about next week's game. I might have a scheduling conflict."

Ross had directed the question to Logan, but all Tuck could hear was that he and Logan would be sticking around here longer, when he would really rather not.

"Sure. No problem." Logan nodded to Becca. "Nice meeting you, ma'am."

"Uh, you, too." Her gaze cut to Tuck before her boss steered her off toward cheese man, who'd now moved on to the cut fruit display.

"You can stay, but I'm not." He glared at Logan while yanking his cap out of his pocket.

Logan pinned Tuck with a stare. "Yes, you are."

What the hell? This was ridiculous. "Why do I have to stay?"

"Why do you want to leave?" Logan cocked a brow.

"Because it's obvious the guest of honor isn't interested in socializing with me. Jeez, she nearly fainted when she recognized me. She didn't even admit we knew each other." Forget about how they knew each other in the biblical way.

"Yeah, you're right." Logan bobbed his head. "But that's a good thing actually. With the non-fraternization rule and all."

That got his attention. What kind of shit was Logan trying to pull here? "The what?"

"Non-fraternization rule," he repeated.

Tuck's brows rose. "Uh, you do know Becca's a civilian. I don't think the military's rules about fraternization apply in this case."

"Oh, so she's *Becca* to you, huh?"

Tuck shot Logan a look that said he might just get punched if he continued on that tangent.

"Okay, moving on." Logan cleared his throat. "I'm not talking about military rules. I'm talking about OSU rules.

Didn't you read the notebook human resources gave you when you got hired?"

"Um, I skimmed it." Tuck hoped that lie didn't show. He had opened it, but only to see what days they had off for holidays and school breaks. "That rule is in there?"

"Yeah. Something to the effect of no faculty member may engage in a personal or inappropriate relationship with a student or another member of the faculty."

Tuck's forehead creased in a frown of disbelief. "What? That's ridiculous. I mean the student part, that's fine, but with each other? We're adults. It's archaic."

"Yeah, but you're forgetting OSU was founded way back in the eighteen ninetics. Folks were a little more Victorian in their thinking then."

"Well Jesus, Logan. The university could update the rules every century or so, don't you think?" He scowled.

"Sounds to me like you're interested in engaging in a personal and or inappropriate relationship with Becca. So why do you want to leave?" Logan's gaze was once again more intense than Tuck was comfortable with. Like the man could read his thoughts.

Maybe Logan was right. He might have pursued a relationship, rules be damned, if she were into him, too. Which she obviously wasn't. "Do I need to repeat myself, Logan? She's not interested."

"You could have fooled me."

Frustrated and ready to be done with this conversation as well as this party, Tuck let out a sigh. "You don't know what you're talking about."

"Maybe I don't." Logan shrugged. "And maybe she hasn't stopped looking this way since Mark dragged her off. Of course, she could be interested in me and that's why I keep catching her staring in this direction."

Logan's smirk had Tuck frowning. Real nice friend he had. Nothing like a little teasing to rub salt in the wound.

If Becca was looking his way, it was probably because she was afraid he'd go spreading tales about their night together and ruin her reputation. As if he would ever do that. She really didn't know him at all, which made his gut twist a little more.

He let out a huff of breath. "You really won't let me leave?"

"Nope." Logan shook his head but looked a little too amused for Tuck's taste.

"Is that an order?"

"Does it have to be?"

This whole situation was getting more and more unbelievable. He glared at Logan. "Why are you trying to make me miserable?"

"It's fun."

"Great. Thanks. Glad I can be of service amusing you, but since there's that rule and all, I think I'd better leave. Don't want to get nailed for fraternizing or anything. You wouldn't want me getting fired right before the big training retreat." Tuck grasped at straws. Anything to get out of being in the same room with Becca. It was as good an excuse as any, and it wasn't even a lie. They'd definitely *fraternized,* a few times.

"Oh, I think it probably wouldn't count since she hadn't officially started work yet. Besides, how could you have known, right? Nope, you can stay." Logan continued to look amused. "You want another wine?"

Yes, with a beer chaser and some bourbon on the side. Tuck let out a snort. "Sure. What the hell."

"Great, I'll take one, too, while you're there." Logan grinned and waited, not moving.

Tuck shook his head and pivoted toward the bar . . . where he saw Becca standing. Now he had no way to avoid walking past her, and he would bet next month's pay that had been his supposed friend's plan.

He glanced back at Logan. "You know, you can be a real bastard sometimes, *sir.*"

He'd made sure to emphasize the *sir*. Logan deserved the dig. Pulling rank to make him stay at a damn party that had nothing to do with ROTC or anything else remotely related to their department or the army.

Logan laughed. Apparently there was nothing like torturing a man to raise another man's spirits. With a huff, Tuck headed for the table where the wine was set up. Hell, maybe he would just grab a bottle and a few cups. That would cut his in and out time considerably.

Luckily, Ross was doing a good job keeping Becca occupied. Good man. He rose a notch or two higher in Tuck's esteem. Her boss currently had Becca bogged down with the mean-looking librarian ladies. He might just get out of this thing without having to talk to her again, because if he did have to and they weren't surrounded by a bunch of her coworkers, he might be tempted to give her a piece of his mind. He wasn't sure Miss English professor could handle what he was thinking right now.

The problem was, what he was really thinking—and had been since that morning he'd said good-bye to her—was how they'd not only had one hell of a good night but they'd also gotten along great. And if she hadn't left for New York, that night could have been repeated many times over. He'd liked her. A lot. Enough to want to see her again, both in and out of bed.

What a load of crap that notion had been. It was obviously not what she wanted. *He* wasn't what she wanted. Apparently, when it came to dating, Oklahoma rodeo cowboys weren't good enough for hoity-toity East Coast English professors with doctorate degrees.

The wine splashed out of the cup and onto the tablecloth. He ignored it and planted the glass bottle down with a thud. He grabbed the tiny cups, thinking one of those nice pint-size plastic ones would be much more fitting to his current mood than these flimsy, thimble-size pieces of garbage.

"Tucker."

Crap. He tried to ignore the small voice behind him and make his getaway, but her hand on his arm stopped him in mid-step. How had she gotten away from talking with the nasty sisters so quick?

Too late to speculate, because now she had him in her clutches, literally. He stayed put, making Becca walk around to the front of him.

"Wine?" He thrust one cup at her. Let Logan get his own. This was his damn fault anyway.

"Sure." She took it and raised the cup to her lips, which only made him remember the taste and feel of her kisses.

He shook that vision from his mind and remembered he was mad at her. "So, I was surprised to see you. You know, here. In Oklahoma. When I thought you'd be in New York."

"You were surprised to see me? How about me seeing you? What are you doing here?" She kept her voice low, but what it lacked in volume, it made up for in intensity.

He shrugged, trying to look more casual than he felt about this conversation. "I've been working here for a year. What are *you* doing here?"

"You know why I'm here. I got hired as an associate professor. What I didn't know is you work here, too. Why didn't you tell me?" Her narrowed gaze swept him from head to toe. "And you're in the army? You seemed to have neglected to mention that, too."

She was actually mad at *him* for keeping secrets? That was ironic.

"You didn't ask." He raised the cup to his lips and nearly drained it in one swallow. When she was still looking at him like he was a liar, he repeated. "What? You never once asked what I did for work."

"That's because I thought you rode bulls for a living." A frown creased the brow between her perfectly shaped eyebrows.

He forced his focus away from her looks and back to the subject at hand. "Becca, there aren't very many riders who can earn a living just from riding bulls. Not at that level of competition anyway."

"How was I supposed to know that? You said you had an envelope full of cash just from coming in second that night." She ditched her cup on the table and crossed her arms over her chest.

Tuck let out a laugh. "Yeah, I had an envelope full of twenties. Not hundreds. It wasn't like I competed in and won the national finals in Vegas, Becca. There'd be a lot of extra zeroes added to the prize money if I had. All I did was take second in one event in a little local rodeo."

"I don't know that kind of stuff. I'm a New Yorker. There's no rodeo there."

He cocked a brow. "Actually, there are rodeos there, and I hate to correct a professor, but you're no longer in New York. Now it seems you live in Oklahoma, doesn't it? You see, darlin', the blame swings both ways. You never told me what you were doing here."

"It didn't come up."

"Actually it did. That morning, when I asked you to spend the day with me. Remember your answer? You said you had a meeting. An important one. That it was the whole reason you'd flown here to begin with."

"That's all true."

"I'm sure it is, but that might have been a nice time to mention this meeting was an interview at OSU for a position that if you got it would mean you would no longer be living a thousand miles away in New York, but instead just a few miles down the road from where you and I spent the night sweating up the sheets."

The sheets comment had her looking horrified. He didn't care.

"You wanna know what I think, darlin'?" Tuck didn't wait for the answer. Now he'd gotten started, he was on a roll. And as pansy ass as this white wine was, it had been a long time since he'd eaten lunch and the second cupful he'd downed in one gulp had gone to his head enough to loosen his tongue. "I think I was good enough to scratch your itch for a night, but that's it, because you think I'm not good enough for you."

Her eyes opened wide before they narrowed. He watched her nostrils flare. Phew, she looked even hotter when she got angry. "Let me tell you something . . . I could say the same thing about you. Did the thought of us seeing each other again even once cross your mind that night? No, more important than that, since that night have you even given me a second thought while you're strutting around in your tight little jeans and assless leather chaps in front of all those perky young girls behind the chutes? Huh?"

Well, now. This was an interesting turn of events. Was Becca jealous? Still, it didn't make him pull his punches when he said, "You don't know me near as well as you think you do, darlin'."

He had thought of her. Every damn day, and worse, every night. It had cost him hours of sleep he couldn't stand to lose with his overly filled ROTC and rodeo schedule.

"Well, you . . . you . . ." She struggled for words. "You don't know me, either."

Tuck laughed. "Yeah. That's become more than obvious. Excuse me. I need to get . . . somewhere."

He was done with this conversation. He turned away from her and made a beeline through the sparse crowd to

Logan. Orders or not, he had to get out of here. He needed to cool off was what he needed to do. Get away from her and all the emotions she riled up. Get alone to consider this new revelation. Jealousy was the last thing he'd expected from Becca.

Of course, it could just be the typical female reaction. The hellcat rising up inside her. She didn't want him, but she didn't like the thought of anyone else being with him, either. Then again, he'd noticed an insecure side to her that night. Maybe she did think he was a player and she was just a notch in his belt.

It was all too much for him to deal with here and now, under the watchful eye of both his boss and hers.

He paused just long enough to say to Logan, "I'm out of here."

"Where's my wine?" Logan's gaze dropped to Tuck's hand, where he held one empty plastic cup.

"I drank it." Tuck waited to be dismissed.

His superior took his sweet time answering, but finally he nodded. "All right. You can go. I'll see you tomorrow morning at PT. Zero-six-hundred."

"Yes, sir." Even a pre-breakfast workout sounded better to Tuck than spending one more minute here second-guessing himself and obsessing over Becca, his feelings, hers, that night . . .

Watch cap planted on his head, Tuck strode out of the room, and out of the building. The heat beating on his back was a welcome change after being trapped inside that room. Hell, maybe he'd even run back to his building. He could sure use the diversion.

Chapter
Thirteen

"Everything all right?"

Becca glanced up, but the man in the uniform standing in front of her pouring himself a cupful of wine wasn't the one who had her heart pounding. What was his rank again? His last name was written on his chest, but that didn't do her much good since she was pretty sure she couldn't call him mister.

"Um. Yes. Fine, Lieutenant." She tried not to cringe as she heard the doubt in her own voice when she took a shot at remembering his rank.

"You can call me Logan, Doctor." He smiled. "It's only the cadets who have to call me Lieutenant Colonel or sir."

"All right." She nodded. "And please, call me Becca."

She'd worked hard to get her doctorate, but she still felt strange being called doctor by anyone other than a student. It wasn't like she was a medical doctor or curing cancer or something.

"Becca." Logan returned her nod.

She'd seen Logan and Tucker talking. She could only imagine what that conversation had been about. Her. Them. That night. Still, Becca couldn't stop herself from saying, "So I see your friend had to leave."

Logan's brows rose. "Yeah, he did. But he's never too far away. If he's not here on campus with the cadets, he's at home alone in his apartment just off campus. Then of course, sometimes you can find him on the back of a bull at the rodeo."

The way he was watching for her reaction after that rodeo comment told Becca he knew something. She opened her mouth but couldn't figure out what to say, so she closed it again.

Logan smiled. "I've known Tuck for a long, long time. Not just since his billet here in the ROTC program. We grew up next door to each other. As a kid, he was in my house as often as he was home. He went through school in the same grade as my little brother. I've got a few years on them both, but I can't remember a day the two of them weren't getting under my feet, or getting into some sort of trouble."

His casual friendly grin put her at ease, and the chance to get inside information about Tuck, even if he had acted like a jerk today, was too tempting to resist. She smiled. "You do know him well."

"That I do. And I know even though he can be a real smart ass sometimes, there's not a bad bone in that man."

Again, she found herself taken off guard by Logan's comment. She swallowed. "That's good to hear."

"So, you settled in after the move?"

"Mostly. I still have a few more boxes to unpack, but moving was actually less stressful than I thought it would be." This she could handle. She'd been fielding this question for days now from family back home and people she'd just met here.

"Good. I'm glad. And there's a staff directory with contact info for everyone who works here. In case you need anything, everyone is just a phone call away. You know who's really good at unpacking boxes?"

"Who?"

"Anyone who's in the military. Moving. Organizing. All

that kind of stuff. It kind of comes with being in the army. Lots of moving around. Tuck and I are pretty much both experts at moving. You should give Tuck a call to help you."

Becca couldn't help her bitter laugh. "I'm sure he has plenty of other things he'd rather be doing." Things. Girls.

"I wouldn't be so sure about that." Logan was sure doing his best to convince her Tuck was a good guy.

She let out a sigh. After how he'd acted, and how she'd reacted, she didn't think she could bring herself to call him. Good thing Emma wasn't here, exerting undo influence over her again, or Tuck's number would already be dialed.

"It's good to see you mingling." A smiling Dean Ross appeared at her elbow.

She quickly reviewed the tail end of her conversation with Logan to make sure the dean hadn't heard anything he shouldn't have. As surreal as seeing Tucker here had been, Logan's pushing her to call him was equally strange. She had heard people comment fate had led them to a current boyfriend or girlfriend, but after the past few weeks she had to wonder if maybe it hadn't been fate or any other mysterious force in the universe at all, but simply meddling friends and family.

"Yes, I've been making the rounds, and just now the lieutenant colonel and I were discussing the dreaded chore of unpacking."

Logan grinned knowingly. "Yes, we sure were. I was offering my world-class advice on the best way to get that unpacking accomplished."

The way Logan said the word, she got the sense somehow *unpacking* had become a euphemism for her getting in touch with, and probably doing so much more with, Tucker.

"Good. Good to hear." Dean Ross slapped the other

man on the back. "Logan and I have been getting together for a weekly poker game since he took over the ROTC program."

She couldn't imagine anything odder than the studious English department dean with his slightly wrinkled pleated pants and tie, and the lieutenant colonel in his combat boots and stiff camouflage uniform being friends. She was pretty sure there must be a good story to go along with the formation of that odd couple, but she didn't feel up to asking about it now. She needed to get out of here and regroup after the shock of seeing Tucker.

Becca saw her opportunity to escape. She suddenly had the urge to call Emma. As amazing as it seemed, she needed her sister's advice, which was a testament in itself as to how much this surprise encounter with Tucker had thrown her off balance.

"Ah, yes. Poker, the manliest of card games." Grasping her last semblance of calm, she donned a smile and tried to look normal, as if a ghost from her very recent past hadn't just stomped his combat boots right out the door of her welcome mixer.

She glanced around the room. She'd met and spoken to everyone here, and it seemed less crowded than before, so people had obviously begun to leave. That could have something to do with the waning cheese plate, which was down to not much more than the mangled rind from the Brie and a few crackers. Of course the room could feel emptier just from the absence of Tucker's looming presence.

"If it's all right with you, Dean Ross, I'm going to sneak out and get back to that unpacking we were discussing. Leave you men to discuss your cards."

"Of course. You must have so much still to get done. I probably should have planned this little gathering for after you'd settled in more."

"No, not at all. I'm very happy to have met everyone sooner rather than later."

Wasn't that the truth. If Tucker was this pissed off now, she couldn't even imagine how mad he would have been after finding out she'd been on campus teaching for a while. She pushed that thought out of her head, torn between feeling guilty she hadn't told him the night they'd met that she might be moving to Oklahoma and being angry he had the nerve to be mad at her about the oversight.

"That's exactly what I was hoping." Dean Ross nodded. "Never too early to make new acquaintances."

Or reunite with old ones . . . "Yes, you're right. It was a lovely mixer. Thank you so much for arranging it. I feel very welcome here."

"That's the idea. Glad you liked it, and I hope the department has you here for many, many more years to come."

"Thank you, Dean Ross." She glanced from her boss to Tucker's friend. "Pleasure talking to you."

"The pleasure was all mine." Logan treated her to another knowing smile. "Good luck with that unpacking."

Meaning good luck with calling Tucker. She'd have to think long and hard about that advice from Logan. She still wasn't sure whether she'd be taking it or not, or what reaction she'd get from the pissed-off cowboy slash soldier slash military science instructor slash former one-night stand. Her head spun with all Tucker encompassed.

"Thank you." With a nod to the two men, she gratefully took her leave and headed toward the door.

Once Tucker had left and the strange conversation with Logan was interrupted by Dean Ross's return, she felt the definite need to be out of that room and away from the scrutiny of both men.

She fled out the nearest exit and into the brilliant sunlight, only to realize that though the dean had parked right outside this door, her car was in the lot all the way on the other side of the building. She obviously wasn't thinking clearly or she would have gone out the other exit, the one closer to her car, and avoided the long walk in the August heat. It seemed Tucker had the ability to strip her of all good sense. He had since the moment she'd met him . . . She couldn't forget that wasn't all he'd done that night. He'd also stripped her of her clothes and her inhibitions.

It was too late now to do anything about her night spent with Tucker or about being what seemed like a mile from her car because she wasn't going back inside, walking past the open door of the party she'd just abandoned to go out the other side of the building.

Becca peeled off the suit jacket and draped it over one arm. Good thing Emma had made her wear this tank top. The sun warmed her shoulders as she prepared for the hike around to the car. She pulled her sunglasses out of her bag and slid them on.

She followed the path that cut through the manicured lawn and led around the building, but all the while she couldn't stop glancing up, expecting to see Tucker at every turn. After the shock of seeing him standing, in uniform, in the last possible place she'd ever expected to see him, nothing would surprise her now.

The whole situation was crazy. She needed to talk to someone about it. She found her cell phone and hit the button that brought up her recent calls, and of course, Emma's number was right at the top. Becca hit the button to dial.

"About time you called me." Emma answered on the first ring.

Becca didn't bother explaining how she couldn't have called earlier since she'd been on the campus tour with the dean and then at the mixer until just now. Soothing her sister wasn't the purpose of this call. Quite the opposite. If anyone needed some soothing, it was Becca.

She swallowed away the dryness in her throat and said, "He's here."

"Who's there?"

"Tucker Jenkins, that's who." Now she'd said it out loud, and to the only other person on earth who knew the full impact of what that statement meant, her pulse began to pound.

"Your bull rider? Wait, here's where? You mean in Stillwater? Did you see him somewhere in town? You saw him and didn't call me right away?" The tone of Emma's voice went from sounding surprised to curious to insulted and accusing, all in the matter of seconds.

"I mean he's right here at OSU. He was a guest at the welcome mixer I just this minute left. He's a member of the faculty."

"Your cowboy is a teacher?" Her sister's pitch rose high.

"Apparently, and wait. There's more. He's a soldier, not a bull rider. Like an active-duty, head-to-toe camouflage, combat-boot-wearing kind of an army soldier."

"What?" Emma sounded about as shocked as Becca had been when she'd walked in and spotted him there—uniform and all. "Wait. You're confusing me. You have to start from the beginning."

Emma thought *she* was confused. Ha! She should have been in Becca's place for the unexpected reunion. Seeing him nearly knocked her off the casual yet professional open-toed, high-heeled sandals Emma had told her to wear.

The fast pace she'd set toward her car, as well as the pounding of her heart and her head, had Becca breathless and woozy. Her head had started to hurt the moment she'd seen Tucker again, and now the ache had gotten worse.

She consciously slowed both her speed and her breathing and launched into the entire story, beginning with when she'd first spotted two men in uniform from the dean's car. It was a riveting enough tale that even Emma remained quiet and listened to her talk without interruption until the end, and that was saying something.

Becca wrapped it up with, "So that's it. I got out of there as fast as I could without being rude and making the dean suspicious, but the last thing his friend Logan hinted to me right before I left was that I should call Tucker."

Emma let out an audible breath. "Wow. So what are you going to do?"

"Good question. I have no idea. What do you think I should do?" She juggled her jacket to dig the car key out of the pocket now that her car was in sight.

Hot, sweaty, and mentally exhausted, she realized how desperate her state was if she was willingly asking her sister for advice on her love life.

Love life. Ugh. Love was the last thing she wanted to pursue right now. Not on the heels of the recent demise of her two-year relationship with Jerry, and in the midst of building a career and a new life in Oklahoma.

Then again, flashing back to that night with Tucker, the sheer pleasure and reckless abandon, the incredible sex, maybe that was exactly what she needed.

Becca picked up her cell phone, then put it back down on the table. Staring at it wasn't going to magically resolve the situation with Tucker. Though calling him might not do that, either. He'd seemed pretty angry with her at the party.

She let out a huff, wishing Emma were here to dial the phone, then hand it to her once he'd answered and it was too late to hang up, like she'd done when Becca was too chicken to call and invite Billy Beckley to the junior prom. That had worked out pretty well back then. Billy had said yes, but unlike her prom date, Tucker wasn't seventeen. He hadn't spent the entire eleventh grade sitting next to her in English class asking her to help him with his essays.

Then again, she'd shared much more of herself with Tucker than she ever had with Billy.

Her laptop was out on the table, the staff directory on screen and scrolled to the page listing the staff members with the last name beginning with J.

J for Jenkins. J for jerk, too, at least today. Maybe she was to blame for not telling him about the interview at OSU. Probably more than he was for not telling her he was only a part-time bull rider but a full-time soldier and teacher, also, as coincidence would have it, at OSU.

Neither of them was at fault, really. There had been a lot of sex that night, but not all that much discussion. Though there had been enough talking for her to know she really did like him. Enough to regret they had nothing in common—or so she'd thought. A bull-riding cowboy surrounded by sexy young girls all the time, and a recently scorned and still insecure English professor from New York—of course she'd thought they had no future together. Who could blame her?

But he wasn't only a bull-riding cowboy. He was faculty, like she was. And now she lived in Oklahoma, like he did.

Damn, it was a hell of a coincidence. If there was such a thing as fate, what was it trying to tell them? That they should be friends? They should be together? They should have more casual sex?

Who the hell knew? Fate should learn to be more specific. Then again, God helped those who helped themselves. She grabbed the phone, punched in the number, and didn't let herself think or she might second-guess the decision.

"Hello." The deep tenor of his voice, funneled directly into her ear from the cell phone's earpiece, sent a shiver down her spine.

Memories of that night cascaded over her. "Hi. It's Becca."

The dead air on the line during his agonizingly long pause didn't bode well for the success of this call. "Oh. That's why I didn't recognize the area code."

Small talk. Okay, that was fine.

"It's a New York area code. Dutchess County, actually. That's about seventy miles north of Manhattan." And now she was babbling, and that wasn't going to get her what she wanted. "Um, have you eaten dinner yet?"

There was another long pause. Was that a cowboy trait or an army trait, this thinking before you spoke? Maybe she should try it herself some time. Finally, he said, "No. You?"

"I grabbed some cheese at the mixer."

The sound of his laugh surprised her. "That couldn't have been much, since cheese guy planted himself there until the tray was empty."

Relieved the conversation had lightened up a bit, she happily jumped on the topic. "Oh, my God, did you see that? I think he might have had a plastic bag in his pocket he was stashing cheddar in."

"I wouldn't doubt it," he responded, and then there was silence. Again.

He wasn't making this easy for her. She steeled her nerves. "There's a pizza place not far from here that isn't too bad. Maybe if you wanted to come over, I could order a pie and have it delivered."

"You want me to come over there?"

She could hear in his voice, Tucker wasn't sure of her. "Yes. Unless you have other plans."

"No. No other plans."

"I can give you my address." Or he could laugh at her for even asking him to come over. She felt like a shy teenager again. Didn't that life stage ever end?

"I don't need it. Your address is listed in the faculty directory."

What did this mean? He was coming over? And wait, had he been looking her up in the directory to call her just as she had been looking him up? This uncertainty was agonizing. "So, I'll call the pizza place and order a delivery?"

"Forget the pizza. I can do way better than that. I'll be over in about thirty minutes."

"Oh, okay. Great. See you then." Her heart began to race as she heard him disconnect the call.

Things were still far from better, judging by their stilted, awkward conversation. He hadn't exactly been warm and fuzzy, but he was coming over and that was a good start.

And he'd be here in thirty minutes. She had half an hour to get herself and the apartment ready. She turned from the mug she'd left on the coffee table that morning, to the suit jacket tossed on the back of the sofa. And crap, she remembered her pajamas were still draped on the towel rack in the bathroom, and she'd never gotten around to making the bed.

There was too much to do. She flipped the laptop shut and held it to her chest, and her head spun. Getting it all done was going to be a challenge, especially since she couldn't seem to focus on one task. Maybe it would take her mind off her nerves, because right now, she was shaking.

Tucker was coming here. The man she'd had one incredible night with was on his way. Strangely, her biggest concern at the moment was what she should wear. Emma must be wearing off on her.

Chapter
Fourteen

Tuck blew out a frustrated breath and ran his palm along the back of his neck, wondering if he'd lost his mind.

In one hand he held a take-out bag from the local barbecue place. In front of him stood Becca's closed apartment door. And it felt like there was a ten-pound lead weight in his gut as he considered what the hell he was doing here.

One short phone call from Becca was all it had taken to break down his resolve to steer clear of her. Oh, he was still mad as hell at how she'd kept the Oklahoma State job from him, but as his dick remembered the feel of her and twitched inside his jeans, he realized his bruised ego apparently didn't matter all that much in this situation.

Maybe this was a good thing. Maybe it had been just sex with her. Nothing more. Nothing deeper. Nothing emotional. That would be good. Sex, he could handle.

Too bad all the evidence told him it wasn't. If it had been just physical, he wouldn't have been nearly as pissed or hurt that she had waltzed away from him that morning. And without a second glance or a word about her impending move to his own damn town.

The food in the bag was getting cold, and if he knew anything at all, it was that delaying this little reunion wouldn't make it any easier. Though maybe a little more procrastination wouldn't hurt. After all, ribs were still pretty damn tasty at room temperature . . .

Crap. A man shouldn't have this many thoughts in his head. That's why he liked bull riding—get a clear head, get in the chute, try not to get bucked off. Easy. Bull riding was simple, but women? Women were not. He should have said no to her invite. A smart man would have.

He obviously was not a smart man. He raised his fist and knocked on the wooden door hard enough to make his knuckles sting.

She opened the door before he had a chance to change his mind and run away. At this point seeing Becca face to face was both a blessing and a curse. Much as he dreaded it, he needed to face her. It sure didn't help she looked so damn good and smelled even better. That figured.

"Hi." Becca's one tentative-sounding word carried the weight of far more.

"Hi." He shifted his weight from one booted foot to the other in the awkward silence, before raising the bag for her to see. "I got dinner."

"Thank you. Come on in." She took a step back from the door, and he followed her lead, entering the apartment.

He glanced around the space, which looked like most apartments around campus, only with a hell of a lot more books. "Nice place."

"Thanks. I still have some to do. Unpacking. Hanging some things on the walls." She closed the door behind him and flipped both locks.

He watched with a raised brow. He was all for safety, especially when a woman lived alone, but did she really think anyone was getting past him? With all of his training, he could take a man down with his bare hands, even without the folding knife he kept stashed in his jeans pocket.

Then again, Becca didn't know that. He supposed he should be happy she was double-locking the door with him on the inside and not on the outside. That had to be a good sign.

He remembered the food and put the bag on the island between the kitchen and the living area. "Not a problem. There's a take-out menu in the bag so you're not stuck ordering only campus pizza every night."

"Thank you. So, I guess I'll get us forks and plates."

"Knives, too, if you've got any. There's a rack of ribs and some brisket. Though they smoke the meat all day so you can pretty much cut it with a fork."

"Mmm. It smells great."

All he could smell was her. What was that light scent that assaulted his nose and made parts lower harden? Soap? Perfume? Just Becca? And she was wearing jeans. In the black suit she'd worn to the party he might have been able to resist her. But in bottom-hugging denim that reminded him so much of watching her peel her jeans off that night, he was fading fast. Not to mention that little blue tank top that accentuated her assets so nicely.

He watched her move around the island and pull open one drawer and then another.

She glanced up and cringed. "I'm still trying to figure out where I finally put things. First I put the utensils in the drawer closest to the island, where I'll be using them most, but then I thought they should probably go near the dishwasher."

Becca looked at him once more, and then away, concentrating overly hard on counting out two of everything for them to eat with. She was nervous. He could tell by the way she rambled. It was her tell, talking too much and a little too fast . . . And wasn't it insane he knew that about her after just one night together?

Tuck pushed that thought aside and shrugged. "It takes time to get used to a new place."

"I guess. Oh, I haven't offered you anything to drink. I have soda, but it's diet . . ." There was that cringe again. "I have red wine, but no beer. Sorry. I should have run out and—"

"Don't worry." He held up one hand to stop her apology. "Water is fine for me." Better actually. He didn't need his already wobbly judgment affected by alcohol.

"Water, I have." She smiled and then frowned at the cabinets. "The glasses are . . . Above the sink, I think."

Dammit, why was she so adorable? The girl couldn't even find where she'd put her own stuff, and it was making it really hard to stay mad at her. "I'll get it."

He stepped around the island and toward the cabinet, which would have been way too high over her head for her to reach anything anyway. It was a dumb place to put everyday glassware in his opinion. She moved in the same direction he did, and they crashed against each other hard enough to knock his breath out of him with an oomph.

He reached out to steady her.

"I'm sorr—" Becca never quite finished the word. Her eyes went soft as they gazed into his, and Tuck found his hands were no longer safely on her arms but now down holding on to her hips. Those round, beautiful hips he'd held on to for dear life while plunging into her in the hotel.

Tuck swallowed hard and found it hard to breathe. The situation only got worse when she took a single step closer, putting her dangerously near the rising erection in his jeans. He drew in a deep breath, which filled him again with her scent. It was all too much.

There was no fighting this attraction. Tuck dipped his

head low and claimed Becca's mouth with his own. When her lips parted for his tongue, he knew their dinner was definitely going to get cold, and he couldn't have cared less.

He pulled her hips tighter against him, knowing she could feel him outlined in his jeans. She moaned low and sexy in her throat and pressed closer. He wanted her as much as he had that first night, and by all indications, she felt the same . . . And he didn't have a condom. He pulled his mouth away.

"Crap." With a loud sigh, he took one giant step back.

"What's wrong?" Becca's voice broke on the question.

He let out a short, sad laugh. "Nothing you did, darlin'. No condoms. I came expecting to eat barbecue. Not to . . ." He bowed his head and spread his hands to indicate the space now separating them.

Becca took a step forward and narrowed the distance. "I'm on the pill, if that helps any."

They didn't have to worry about a condom for disease prevention. He was pretty sure Becca wasn't the type to sleep around. That night with him had been the exception, not the rule. He'd used protection every time he'd been with anyone since his divorce, and the army required he be tested every six months. He could slide into her and have nothing between them. Her revelation nearly destroyed his last bit of control.

"Yeah, it helps." He groaned and took another step toward her until his thigh was cradled between hers.

The birth control issue settled, he thrust his hands into Becca's thick hair and crashed against her mouth again. It felt so good to kiss this woman. That's what made it even crazier when a niggling thought broke into his pleasure. A thought that had him pulling away. "Wait. Were you on the pill the last time?"

"Yes."

He frowned. "Why didn't you tell me then?"

And why the hell was he talking now?

Because he needed to know, which was insane. But it seemed Becca had kept quite a few things from him. He'd had a woman like that in his life already. In fact, he was still sending her monthly spousal support checks and would be for the next year.

"I didn't tell you that night because I didn't really know you then, and we had all those condoms so it wasn't an issue."

It made sense. He could understand that, but one question remained. "You think you know me better now?"

"Yes, I think I do."

This could lead to a whole long conversation, but he didn't want talk. He wanted Becca. Her excuse was good enough—for now. Tuck ran his hands up and down her arms, his suspicious mind satisfied enough to allow him to listen to his dick for a little while. If things continued as they were he'd have her very soon, and that thought alone broke the last semblance of his control.

He scooped her into his arms. She let out a squeal when her feet left the floor.

"Bedroom?" His growled word came out sounding more like an order than a question.

She bit her lip and looked at him even more enticingly than she had in his many dreams about her. "To the right of the front door."

He angled both of their bodies past the island and reached the bedroom doorway with a few long strides. The bed wasn't king-size like the one they'd enjoyed in the hotel, but it was still plenty big enough for his purposes. He dropped her on top of the covers, following her down until his weight pressed her into the mattress. Tuck slanted his lips over hers, sinking his tongue into her mouth.

The clothing between them was more than he could take. Rolling to one side, he reached down and yanked at the button at Becca's waist. At the same time, she pulled the hem of his T-shirt out of his jeans. Pawing at her like he was a horny teenager about to get lucky, he abandoned the tight denim for the moment and pushed the hem of her tank up over her tits. The lace of her bra was no barrier. He pushed that down and latched on to one nipple with his mouth.

She arched her back and pressed up. He took advantage of that move to reach beneath her to unhook the bra's back clasp. At the same time, she helped his quest to have her naked when she pulled her tank top the rest of the way off and tossed it to the floor next to the bed. She moved on to his belt buckle. He should probably have helped her with that, but instead he was too busy enjoying a mouthful of Becca. He scraped his teeth across her nipple. She hissed in a breath and ramped up his need to have the rest of her.

"Oh, God." Tuck hissed in a breath of his own.

He had forgotten how much her tiny sounds got to him. He wanted her naked. He needed to be inside her. She must have shared that desire since she was yanking the zipper of his jeans down. He agreed. They both still wore too many clothes.

Tuck rolled off Becca and stood next to the bed. He shoved his pants down his legs, cursing when he realized he still had his boots on. With a few clumsy steps, he managed to kick off both boots and jeans without falling over. He shoved his underwear down to the floor as well, along with his socks.

Reaching out, he grabbed Becca's hand. She came to him easily, until she was standing next to the bed and staring up with heavily lidded eyes. He ran his hands over the bare skin of her torso, then down to the jeans she still wore. His mouth followed the path of his hands, kissing down her stomach as he unzipped her pants.

They worked as a team. She kicked off her slip-on sandals and he pushed the denim down her thighs. He did the same with her underwear, the heat of her bare skin warming his palms as he did. She turned toward the bed. Bending at the waist, she reached for the top edge of the comforter. He supposed she was planning to pull it down so they could get under the covers together.

He wasn't in a bed kind of mood. Not with Becca's heart-shaped ass poised so invitingly in front of him. Definitely not while he was still nursing the mad he'd been holding on to since the party. A pride-fueled anger he hadn't quite managed to tamp down just yet.

Nope, this wasn't going to be the "snuggle under the covers and spoon afterward" kind of lovin'. He was in the mood for some good hard and fast sex. If that didn't scare her off, they could get to the snuggling-in-bed part later, when he was more in the mood for the tender stuff.

Stepping up behind her, he grabbed her hips and angled his cock at her entrance. One thrust seated him firmly inside. She was that wet, and he'd be lying if he didn't admit it was a total turn-on.

His eyes slammed shut at the feel of her. He couldn't see her or the room around them, but he clearly felt the sensation of being engulfed by her heat. Clearly heard her intake of breath as he sank deeper.

A shiver ran through him. He'd forgotten how good it felt to be inside her, and to be uncovered and inside—it was enough to make him lose control. Tonight was going to be one more thing that would make it impossible to stay away from her—not that he'd done a great job of it so far. He glanced down to where they were joined and watched his cock slide into her.

Nope. There was no way in hell he'd be able to stay away from her after this.

She made one of those little noises that made him want to take a bite out of her, and he realized he was in real danger with this girl. And not only because of how good it felt to slide into her. No, it was everything from how she couldn't find the silverware in her own kitchen to the adorable way she bit her lip.

Shit. He was not going to get soft over this woman. Time to take back some semblance of control of this situation. Bracing one hand between her shoulder blades, he pushed her torso lower, which raised her ass higher. Perfect. He widened his stance, grabbed her hips, and pounded into her until he hit the point of no return.

Tuck had intended to be selfish this time. To only concentrate on himself and his own needs. He thought it was what he needed to do to get rid of his hurt and anger, and protect his heart. As it turned out, it proved impossible to block Becca out. He couldn't do it. She invaded his every sense, from the feel of her surrounding him, to the sound of her breaths as they quickened, to the look in her eyes when she glanced over her shoulder just before the orgasm hit him.

Coming inside her took him off his feet. Tuck felt his knees buckle. He wrapped his arms around her and had them both crashing head-first onto the bed.

Becca, crushed between his weight and the mattress, gasped for breath beneath him. With his face buried in her hair, he was having a hell of a time catching his own breath. He rolled them both onto their sides and rested his head above hers. They lay there for a while, until he went slack inside her, but he still didn't move. Neither did she. But just because his body wasn't moving didn't mean his mind wasn't racing.

All this thinking about a woman was surely not a good sign. Finally, he couldn't take it anymore. "Why didn't you tell me that first night about the position at OSU?"

"I honestly never even thought about it."

It shouldn't matter to him, but it did. They'd just had great sex. Well, he had; it probably hadn't been all that great for her, but still, sex should be enough for him. It wasn't. He might be less pissed now after the bout they'd just had, but he still wanted answers.

"Why not?" He hated the tension he heard in his own tone.

"Honestly?"

"No, I want you to lie." He rolled his eyes even though in their current positions she couldn't see. "Yes. Honestly. Please."

He wondered if he'd regret saying that.

She turned in his arms and looked at him. "Because I figured it didn't matter even if I did get the job and move to Oklahoma, because I thought you traveled the country riding bulls for a living. Different city every night. Different girl every night."

Becca shrugged as if it didn't matter, but he could tell from how she wouldn't meet his eyes it did.

"I don't." His heart and his voice softened toward her. "I mostly ride right here in Oklahoma. Sometimes in Texas, but that's it. No traveling the country. I'm right here in Stillwater almost all the time, working or working out with the cadets, or helping to coach the rodeo team."

"I didn't know that."

"I know. And as for the rest—no, there isn't a different girl every night. Not lately anyway. I won't lie to you, Becca. I went through a bad time and a lot of women right after the divorce, but that's all in the past. Things haven't been like that for a long time now." He brushed a hair off her face. "You okay with that?"

She bit her lip and then nodded. "Yes."

"So, is that the only reason you kept your moving here from me? Because you thought I was working my way through every buckle bunny on the rodeo circuit? Honestly."

She glanced at him, then away again. "That's not everything. I'm fresh out of a two-year relationship. I'm not ready to start anything new."

Tuck nodded. He was about a year ahead of her in the healing and moving on department. That was fine. He could wait. Hell, he should wait because after his divorce, he wasn't ready for the deep water yet, either. Dipping a toe into the shallow end was enough for now. "Understood."

"And . . ." Becca winced. "Emma wanted me to look you up and call, but I was afraid we didn't have anything in common. I mean, we're so different. From such different places. We're good at this, but—"

"But sex isn't everything." Sad but true. If having good sex together had been enough to build a relationship upon, his ex wouldn't have been catting around with other men while he was deployed and he'd still be married."

"Right." She let out a huff of air.

"Okay, so I guess I can see how you could think a city professor and a country cowboy wouldn't have anything in common, but I do have one thing to tell you about the nothing in common part. My ex-wife and I had pretty much everything in common. Same hometown. Same interests. Same education right down to the same teachers all through school . . . You'll notice something, though. In spite of all that common ground, she's still my *ex*-wife now."

She paused a beat, then nodded. "I'll keep that in mind."

"You do that." He couldn't let Miss English Professor

think she was right all the time, because in this case, he knew from personal experience she was dead wrong. They'd spent hours that night at the rodeo, talking, laughing, enjoying the time together. The differences weren't as big a deal as she'd assumed. Not when all the rest was so good.

"Do you think we could start over? Be friends?" An adorable crinkle appeared between her eyebrows as she frowned, looking concerned.

Crap. She'd just told him she wanted to be friends. He wasn't ready for the kind of serious hold this woman could easily get on him. Yet in spite of all that, he couldn't stop thinking how cute she looked or how good she felt, either. "We could do that—be friends—or we could be slightly more than friends. Friends with benefits would be nice."

He shouldn't have suggested that. Hell, he shouldn't even be thinking it. Even so, his gaze dropped down her body. He reached out and laid his hand low on her belly.

Becca glanced down at his hand. "I think we already are."

"Yeah, I guess we do kinda have that part covered." He leaned closer, about to kiss her, before he held back. Tuck pulled away one more time. "You don't have anything else to tell me, do you? Anything at all. Kids? More job interviews? A husband? Prison record?"

Might as well cover all bases and start this thing, whatever the hell it was, with a clean slate.

She smiled. "No, I don't think so."

"Good." He didn't want any more surprises from the new friend he was hoping to get very friendly with again in the next few minutes. He owed her an orgasm. No time like the present.

Becca's hand on his chest stopped his downward descent toward her mouth. "Hold on a minute. What about you? Any other surprises for me, *Sergeant*?" She cocked a brow.

"Surprises?" He smiled and moved his hand down her belly, heading for a spot he was anxious to get to. "Yeah, I may have a few more tricks left up my sleeve, but don't worry, because I'm about to show them all to you right now."

Chapter
Fifteen

The phone rang way too early in the morning considering how late she'd been up having sex with Tucker the night before. Becca slapped at the nightstand until she found her cell. She managed to answer it through the hazy remnants of sleep. "Hello?"

"You're still in bed?"

"Emma, I'm in a different time zone." Maybe one day her sister would remember that.

She glanced at the closed bedroom blinds. Okay, so the sun was up, but that didn't mean she had to be. She threw one arm over her eyes. Good thing she hadn't moved to the West Coast, or Emma would be calling her at four in the morning and wondering why she wasn't awake yet.

"It's still pretty late there, even with the one hour time difference, and you didn't call me or respond to the text I sent you last night. I was worried."

She remembered hearing a text come through. It was about the time Tuck had wrapped her legs around his waist, hoisted her off the bed, and carried her to the bathroom. Thank goodness that curtain rod was good and sturdy, because at one point she'd been hanging on to it while they did things she'd never even thought of doing in the shower.

"Sorry, I was, uh, busy." Becca's belly let out a rumble.

She was awake, and hungry. Might as well get all the way up and see what was in the kitchen. She and Tucker had managed to eat at one point last night, in between . . . other things, but she remembered him shoving take-out containers of leftovers into her fridge. Since Becca's morning laziness knew no bounds and it would be all she could do to manage to brew a cup of tea in her current state this morning, she figured that tasty side of macaroni and cheese he'd brought over with the barbecue would make a good breakfast reheated.

"Oh, my God. You saw him!" Emma's accusation woke Becca up more than her morning tea would have.

"What?" How the hell did Emma know that? They'd barely said a handful of words to each other.

"Tucker. You saw him again. Were you out with him last night? Is that why you didn't call me back? Or, wow . . . was he there? *Is* he there right now? Is *that* why you're so tired?"

"Okay, hang on. He's not here. But yes, I saw him." She was too tired to even bother trying to lie as she stumbled barefooted onto the cool kitchen floor.

"Oh, my God! Tell me everything."

"Emma, please, you have to dial it down a notch until I get some caffeine in me." She glanced at the clock on the stove as she set the kettle on the burner. Seven. Poor Tuck had been at some sort of workout with the ROTC people since six. She couldn't even imagine. The most physical activity she was planning today was maybe some more unpacking followed by a shower and a nice nap. She had to take advantage of the free time she had before the new semester of classes started in just days.

"Excuse me for being excited for you. If you were a normal woman, you'd be excited, too. Jeez, another night with that hot cowboy—do you know how many women wish they could be in your situation?"

That would be a clear case of *be careful what you wish for,* because her situation was kind of messed up. She wasn't sure she was ready for a boyfriend right now. Not one who'd been divorced for only a year. Especially not one whom the army could probably send away at any second. She'd have to research this ROTC thing better and see if these guys got shipped off to war. And who knew what Tucker wanted? Sure, it was obvious he was as interested in sex as she was, but they hadn't talked about having a relationship. Last night could have been simply a booty call with barbecue. Not a bad thing by any means, but she definitely had to make sure to remember that was the extent of it. Falling for a booty call would be bad.

"Well . . ." Nothing clever came to mind, so she gave up and wrapped up with, "those women should think again."

"Why? What happened?"

"Nothing happened." Well, nothing but some sex on the bed, and then some sex in the shower, followed by some creative after-play on the bed again—she'd never forget the vision of opening her eyes, glancing down, and seeing Tuck looking up at her from between her thighs. Her belly twisted at the memory. She was in deep trouble.

"Rebecca!"

"What?" God that had come out sounding whiny, but Emma was being too demanding for this early in the morning.

"Tell me what happened."

If Becca knew her sister at all, she was wearing a deep frown and breathing heavily right about now. She enjoyed that image.

The water in the teakettle started to make bubbling sounds. That was promising. She managed to get her mug out of the cabinet without dropping it, which also boded well for her hope there would be caffeine in her near future.

"I called him. He came over with takeout. We decided to be friends." Friends with benefits. Very, very nice benefits. She smiled at the memory of exactly how nice and grabbed a teabag out of the box in the cabinet.

"Just friends? Are you crazy—" Emma's rant was cut off by the beeping of another call coming in on Becca's phone.

"Hang on. I got another call." She certainly was a popular person this morning. After dropping the teabag into the mug, she pulled the phone away from her ear and looked at the caller ID; the number she saw stopped her dead in her tracks. Finally knocking herself out of the shock, Becca brought the phone back up to her head. "Em, I gotta go. I'll call you back later."

Emma had begun to protest when Becca hit the button and switched to the incoming call. "Hello."

"Hey there. I didn't wake you, did I?" Tucker's deep, sexy voice filled her ear.

"No, I was awake. Just making some tea."

"You find your tea cup all right?"

She laughed. "Yes, smart ass. I know where that is. Right next to the stove, where it should be."

"Of course. Because that's where the hot water is. On the stove."

"Exactly. See, there is a method to my madness." She smiled. "How are you this morning? You get up in time for your workout?"

"Yeah. Just finished that. It was just a run . . . well, a run in full combat uniform including our packs, but it was only five miles so not so bad."

Her eyes opened wide. "Oh, sure. That's nothing. I do at least that every morning, you know, before tea."

He laughed. "I'm sure. So, what are you doing today?"

"I don't know. No big plans. You?"

"I was thinking it might be my duty, as your friend and all, to show you around town. Someone needs to teach you where all the good bars and restaurants are so you don't keep thinking there's nothing more around here than those take-out places down the street from you. It may be a college town, but there is more than takeout in Stillwater, you know."

"That would be nice. I am getting tired of eating like I'm living in a frat house."

He let out a chuckle. "I bet you are. So, I can be over at, like, ten. We can explore a little, then have lunch if you want."

"That sounds great." Just two friends, hanging out . . . Sure. Her heart had started to pound the moment she'd heard his voice. "I'll see you then."

"See you then." He disconnected and she spun toward the teakettle, willing it to whistle already. She had to shower, figure out what to wear, blow-dry her hair, put on makeup, avoid talking to Emma, and make the bed . . . just in case.

Her pulse pounded harder. Just friends, her ass.

Chapter
Sixteen

"And there is the bank I use." Tuck pointed out the side window of the truck. "The university will set up direct deposit for your checks if you ask them."

Listening to himself drone on, he had to stifle a groan. Could his tour of Stillwater be any more boring? He was really making an effort to honor Becca's *can we be friends* request, even though he had taken advantage of the friends' benefits package more than once last night in her apartment.

She followed his gaze and then turned back. "I guess I'll have to open an account."

"Do you want to do that now? They're open."

Her stomach grumbled, deep and loud. Her eyes opened wide as she covered her belly with her hand.

"Or we could stop for an early lunch. I could definitely eat." He laughed.

He pushed aside naughty thoughts about the parts of Becca he'd like to nibble on and realized after his workout with the cadets this morning he was more than ready for some food. Another dose of caffeine, too, come to think of it.

"You wouldn't mind if we ate?" She glanced at the dashboard clock and cringed. "It's barely eleven."

"Yup. It is, and I've been up since zero-five-thirty so no, I won't mind. Not one bit. I'm ready for lunch. You in any rush to get home?"

"Nope. Nothing planned for the rest of the day."

"Good." Though with Becca sitting next to him in a sundress that would make any man stand up and salute, he was ready for more than lunch. He was ready to head back to her place, but that would have to wait until later. "There's a place I know that makes the best smoke sauce and jalapeño hush puppies you've ever tasted."

He checked the mirrors and swung the truck into a wide turn, heading for the road out of town toward a spot he knew. It was in Drumright, which was a bit of a drive, but it had great food. And since it was so far out of town, there was little chance of someone from the university seeing Becca and him on what might look like a date.

It was bad enough he'd spent a considerable amount of time breaking the school's non-fraternization rules with her last night. They'd probably break those rules again later today if he had anything to say about it. But he didn't think he should push his luck by taking her to lunch someplace where a slew of OSU people—either faculty or students—were likely to be.

He looked over and saw Becca glancing at him and smiling. Tuck narrowed his eyes. "You laughing at me, woman?"

"Never. It's just . . ." She shrugged. "Besides the fact I don't even know what a hush puppy is, forget about having ever had one to compare these to . . . I'm finding it kind of nice having somebody to show me around. Take charge of little decisions like where to eat so I don't have to."

If that's what she liked, he could take charge, all right. Not a problem at all. After all, the military had trained him

to be a leader. He could lead her to good chow. He could also lead her straight to the bedroom.

He couldn't help his own smile. "I'm glad you're having a good time."

"I am. Thank you—" The ringing of her phone interrupted her. Becca stared at her purse but didn't make a move.

"Aren't you going to answer that?"

"Nope."

"Why not?"

"It's probably Emma."

"And?"

"And she's going to grill me about you."

Tuck grinned and extended his hand. "Give me."

"What are you going to do?" Her voice squeaked with panic.

"Let me handle your sister."

She looked hesitant but finally handed over the phone. He glanced down and hit the button to answer. "Hey there, darlin'."

He glanced over and saw Becca's jaw drop at that, which was only slightly less amusing to him than Emma's stuttering on the other end of the phone line.

"Um, I, uh was calling my sister?"

"You got her phone. Don't you worry." He couldn't help laughing.

"Um, is she there?"

It was too much fun to tease these city girls. "She is, but we're fixin' to grab a quick lunch and then do a few . . . other things after. Is it okay if she talks to you later? But it may be much, much later, if you get my drift."

As Emma seemed speechless on the other end of the line, Tuck grinned when Becca covered her eyes with her hand. Silly girl. As if that would do anything to block

her from hearing him. "Anything else I can do for you, Emma?"

"Uh, no. Just tell Becca I will definitely be talking to her. Later."

He had no doubt about that. "Will do. Have a great day." He disconnected the call and handed the phone back to Becca. "There. All taken care of. See how easy that was?"

"Easy for you, maybe. I'm going to get the third degree when she calls back later."

If she wanted a take-charge kind of guy, he'd be one. "If I'm still with you, I'll answer then, too. I do have rodeo practice tonight with the team, though, but that'll only take a few hours at most."

"Army workout in the morning. Rodeo practice at night." She shook her head. "You sure have a full life, Tucker Jenkins."

"Don't forget *be Becca's tour guide* in the afternoon. That's as important as the rest of my day." And much more fun. He smiled and sent her a sideways glance before checking his mirrors and changing lanes.

"Thank you." She blushed prettily at his comment.

"You're welcome." Though if she were really intent on thanking him, he'd come up with a few ideas of how she could . . . later, in private.

He navigated the truck onto the highway that would lead them to Joseph's Fine Foods. The country station on the radio filled the silence between them, until he glanced over and saw Becca smirking. "What's tickled you so now?"

"Are you listening to the lyrics of this song?"

He had been too busy salivating over thoughts of what he'd be ordering for lunch and thinking about what Becca could provide him later for dessert to be listening to the damn song. "No. Not really. Not a fan of country music?"

"I can't say I've had much exposure to it."

"Well, you will here in Oklahoma. That's for sure. You can change the station if you want."

"No. It's okay. I'm going for the full immersion experience now I'm here."

He'd like to immerse something into her. He kept that thought to himself. "Good for you."

Tuck opened his mouth to ask if she'd like to come to his rodeo team practice as part of her Oklahoma culture indoctrination, then closed it again. He couldn't be seen bringing Becca, the new English professor, to the OSU rodeo team practice. There was no reason for her to be there. Damn non-fraternization rule.

He got off the exit and drove down the street to the restaurant, where he parked easily enough. It was well before noon, so the place wasn't packed with the usual lunch crowd yet. That was good. It would afford them privacy and cut down on the chances of being seen by anyone from the university taking the hike to get some of Joseph's signature smoke sauce.

The hostess seated them at a back table, also good for privacy, and handed them menus. Two needs dominated him when he glanced over the menu at Becca, looking adorable across the table—food and sex. Since he wasn't sure he should be talking about sex so early in the day, he figured he'd better stick to the other topic occupying his thoughts. Food.

"I'm not letting you leave here without having your very first hush puppy. We're definitely ordering those. So besides that, let's see what else looks good."

She frowned down at the menu. "There's a lot on here."

"Not all that much." He smiled at her. She most likely meant there was a lot of food on this menu she'd never had, and some she'd likely never heard of. "Want me to help you choose?"

Becca folded her menu and laid it on the table. "That would be good. I'll eat anything except the fried smoked bologna sandwich."

He couldn't help laughing at that. "All right."

"What's so funny?"

"That's my favorite."

"Fried bologna?" Her eyes opened wider. "You're kidding, right?"

"Nope. Love it. Get it near every time I come here. It's an Oklahoma barbecue tradition. Hickory smoked and deep fried with melted cheddar on top and a side of steak fries."

Her expression had him laughing out loud as she reached for the menu she'd put down. "I think I've changed my mind about you ordering for me. I'd better pick my own."

"Stop. I won't order you that. Promise." He glanced down at the listings. The stacked sandwich with beef, sausage, and coleslaw piled high would probably send her running for the door, but he couldn't let her leave here without at least trying some of the smoked beef served with smoke sauce. "How do you feel about the brisket?"

Becca pursed her lips and finally nodded. "Okay."

"Good." When she didn't put down her menu right away, he reached out and took it away from her. "Stop. I know you're looking at the chicken Caesar salad or something equally safe, but you can't eat in an Oklahoma landmark famous for its special sauce and smoked meats and order something you could get anywhere in New York. As your tour guide, I won't let you do it."

She finally relinquished her hold on the menu. "All right. Since you're my tour guide, and since you're not making me eat the deep-fried bologna thing, I'll listen to you."

"Oh, I won't make you order the bologna, but you're sure as hell gonna take a bite of mine." That came out a bit more suggestively than he'd intended, but she didn't seem to mind.

"Oh, really. Is that a fact?" Becca leaned in, her voice low and sultry, and his gaze dropped to her tempting lips.

"Yes, it is." He noticed his own voice had dipped lower.

"*If* I do, I certainly hope it lives up to expectations." Her eyes narrowed.

He let out a snort. "Oh, it will. Believe me."

And now he had a raging hard-on from talking about fried bologna sandwiches. Though not really, because somewhere along the way, this conversation had taken a severe left turn.

They definitely weren't talking about sandwiches any-more. As hungry as he had been for food, he was hungrier for Becca. All he could think of now was her lips wrapped around him. He was ready to say forget it and forgo eat-ing. Get back in the truck, find a private road, and do with her what he'd dreamed about so many times.

"Have you decided?" The waitress, pad in hand, stood by waiting for their order and putting the kibosh on his fantasy plan.

"Oh, yeah. I'm good and ready." With any luck they'd order, get their food before the lunch rush arrived, and be in and out of here fast. After that conversation, he wasn't going to be satisfied no matter how many fried bologna sandwiches he ate.

Chapter
Seventeen

Becca unlocked the door and had just turned the knob when Tucker grabbed the back of her head, spun her around, and crashed his mouth into hers. As he kissed her silly, he backed her into the apartment, kicking the door shut behind him. He didn't stop until they'd hit the kitchen island.

She broke away from the kiss, a little breathless, but she still managed to ask, "What got you all . . ."

"Horny?" he suggested before he latched on to her earlobe with his teeth and tugged.

That proved so distracting she had to struggle to maintain her train of thought. "Not exactly my choice of words, but yes. That. You've been looking at me strangely since the restaurant."

"The bologna sandwich conversation got to me." He growled his answer near her ear and then nipped the skin of her neck.

A tingle ran down her spine, even as she pulled back. "Are you serious? Bologna sandwiches got you turned on?"

"Oh, yeah." The dark, overt sexual desire she saw in his eyes now, and to a lesser extent every time he'd looked over at her in his passenger seat, was proof he wasn't lying.

His raw need was more than enough to make Becca's

insides heat. She supposed it was a good thing they'd made it through lunch at all. At this rate, they could both waste away to nothing, because sex with Tucker was much more enticing than food.

He lifted her as if she weighed nothing and set her on the kitchen island. With a near feral growl he bit her neck while his hands settled on her thighs.

"What are you—" She didn't have to finish the question, not that she could have since his mouth had found hers again. The answer was more than obvious when he pushed the hem of her sundress up her legs. She leaned back. "Tucker! Oh, my God. Here?"

"Mmm, hmm." He smiled as he spread her thighs and stepped between them.

"But the bedroom is right there—"

"I know very well where your bedroom is. If I'd wanted to take you there, I would have."

"But—"

"Live a little dangerously, darlin'. You might like it." His smile looked devilish. "You will if I have anything to say about it."

This did seem dangerous, all right. She was pretty high up, sitting there on the island. One wrong move and she could fall off, break a tailbone or something. It was almost as scary as when he'd tried to pick her up in the shower last night and she wouldn't let him. Slips and falls in the shower were a very real danger. How would she have explained that in the emergency room?

"Stop thinking so hard or I'll be forced to do something to distract you." He issued that order just before he leaned over her.

He slipped the tip of one finger beneath the elastic of her panties. That was certainly distracting. He plunged his other hand beneath her hair and held her head captive as he claimed her lips again. After a few heat-filled moments, he pulled back, but the clenching need low in her belly didn't stop just because the kissing had.

"Mmm, you keep any honey in this place for that tea you're always making?" He spoke so close to her ear, the warmth of his breath sent another tingle of desire through her.

"Yes."

"You remember which cabinet it's in?" There was laughter in his question.

Maybe. She wasn't sure she could think right now with what he was doing to her. "Next to the stove, where the cups and tea are. Why?"

"We didn't have any dessert, but I'm thinking we can come up with something both of us will enjoy." He leaned back and raised his eyebrows. "If you're game."

Her cell phone rang on the counter inside her purse. He reached for it and glanced at the readout. She watched as he answered and said, "She'll have to call you back, Emma. She's busy. Bye."

"Tuck!"

He hit the button and tossed it back into her bag. "What? I didn't tell her what you were busy doing."

"You have to stop answering my phone." Her eyes opened wide to reinforce her point.

"Why? It's always your sister. You don't want to talk to her right now while we're together, so instead of being rude and ignoring her, I answered." He shrugged.

"But . . ." She frowned because his logic was . . . well, logical. "What if I started to answer your phone?"

"Go ahead." He pulled it out of his pocket and put it on the counter. "It'll be either Jace or Logan. Possibly my parents or my brother or sister, but not usually since I call them once a week."

"You're serious. You really wouldn't care?" She found

his offer intriguing enough to pursue, even if his thumbs were currently making tantalizing circles on the skin of her inner thighs.

"Nope." He shook his head and looked pretty certain about his answer.

"What if it was a girl calling you? What then?"

He laughed. "It wouldn't be a girl. You are the only female who has my phone number, besides my mother and sister." He thought for a second. "All right, correction. The students do have my number, and we have a few female cadets, but kids nowadays don't call. They text. So no, no girls will call who aren't related to me. Feel free to answer away."

She tried to come up with some response but was having trouble.

"What's the matter, darlin'? Run out of things to say?" A sly smile bowed Tucker's tempting lips.

Hating to admit he was right, she frowned. "Maybe."

"Good, because I've got a better idea for that pretty little mouth of yours." He ran a finger along her lower lip and grinned. "Let's find that honey."

Tucker found the correct cabinet on the first try and reached up for her plastic honey bear. He returned and planted the bear on the counter next to her. "Squeeze bottle. Convenient."

"What are you going to do with it?" She was starting to get an inkling of what he might have in mind, which only made the flutter of desire inside her grow.

"You'll see. Come on. Time for the bedroom." He set her down on the floor with ease.

"The bedroom. Now?" She had a suspicion they were about to get very creative—and sticky—with that honey. Of all times they should be having any sort of sex in the kitchen, it seemed like now would be a good one. "Won't that be . . . messy?"

"If we're both careful and lick it all off real good, it won't be."

Oh, boy. "Oh. Okay."

"Besides, we need a bed for what I have in mind." He continued, as if unaware what his words were doing to her imagination. He grabbed the honey bear with one hand and her with the other. "Come on. Don't dawdle. I only have a few hours before I gotta leave here for practice. We definitely don't want to have to rush this."

"Rush?" A few *hours* of honey-filled sex would be rushing it? She swallowed hard as she realized exactly how boring her sex life had been before the night she'd met Tucker.

He shot her a grin over his shoulder. "I tend to last for an extra-long time doing what we're about to do."

An extra-long time? Longer than usual? Wow. She glanced back at the fridge, wondering if she should grab a few bottles of water before the marathon, but she was already being pulled halfway across the living room. "And what exactly are we about to do."

"Don't worry, darlin'. You'll see soon enough."

Tuck turned much too fast into the gravel lot at the practice arena. He hit the brakes and the truck skidded to a stop. Judging by the number of vehicles already parked and all the activity, he was among the last to arrive. But considering he'd been enjoying Becca's company until just moments ago, he couldn't feel too bad about it, even though he probably should.

It would take a stronger man than he was to leave when Becca's gorgeous lips were wrapped around his honey-coated cock. The thought of watching the pink tip of her tongue poking out to tease the length of him was enough to have him getting hard again. He had to stop thinking about it, as if that were possible when he still had the taste of Becca mixed with honey on his own tongue.

Damn.

Tuck decided they'd have to repeat today's bedroom exercise real soon, but right now he had to talk down his hard-on. He wasn't exactly late for the four o'clock practice, but he sure wasn't half an hour early like usual. He liked to be there to make sure the kids and the stock were all okay and didn't need any help.

He'd just stepped down out of his truck and onto the ground when Jace was beside him. "Hey. Where the hell you been lately?"

"Busy." Tuck spun toward the arena, walking as he talked to make up time. Jace matched his step. He glanced at his friend. "Thanks for coming. I appreciate the help this week."

"No problem at all. Always happy to help guide the youth of America." Jace grinned.

"Yeah, I'm sure." Tuck was also sure it was the case of beer he'd promised to buy Jace for helping with rodeo team practice that added to his enthusiasm.

"So tell me the schedule for this week again?"

"Do you listen to me at all when I talk to you?" Tuck frowned.

"Yeah. Mostly. I just don't want to screw it up."

He blew out a breath of frustration and launched into what was happening this week for the second time. "Tomorrow's team practice is while I'm away camping with the cadets, so you'll be here to take my place to help with the bull riders. B & N Rodeo Stock brings the bulls in, so you don't have to do anything with that. The two owners are Ben and Ned and they handle the stock. Just be there to make sure the kids don't get hurt and give them advice on what they're doing wrong."

"Gotcha." Jace glanced around. "I don't see any bulls."

"That's because today's practice is for barrels and roping. I told you that on the phone." Tuck shook his head. "You better pay attention tonight so you'll know what the hell you're doing when I'm gone tomorrow, because there are no cell phones allowed on the ROTC retreat."

"No cell phones?" Jace's expression was one of absolute horror. "What if you need something?"

He had a feeling Jace was thinking more what if *he* needed something and couldn't call Tuck to get it. "We lock the phones in the vehicles. We can get to them if we need them but that's it, so don't bother calling to ask me any questions. Got it?"

"I'll be totally alone?" Jace looked like he was regretting agreeing to step in as coach in Tuck's absence.

"No. My assistant coach will be there to help. I'm going to introduce you to her. She should be here already."

"She?" Jace visibly perked up.

"Jace . . ." His voice dipped low, carrying the weight of his warning. "Stay away from her."

"Well, how can I work with her if I stay away from her?" He cocked a brow and though he may have been trying to look innocent, it wasn't working.

"You had better act like a professional. Promise me." Crap. Tuck was starting to rethink this decision, but he really had no choice. He couldn't be two places at once. With the OSU rodeo team practicing three days a week, and the ROTC cadets' retreat falling on the same day as one of the practices, he needed help.

"I promise." Now they'd reached the rails of the practice arena, Jace's gaze scanned the action. "Which one is she? Your assistant coach?"

"Jace, I swear to God." He spoke through clenched teeth. "Hands off her and, for heaven's sake, don't even look twice at the female students."

Maybe he should call Dillon McMann. He hated to take the kid away from his wife and new baby daughter for a three- or four-hour practice, but . . .

"Tuck, relax, will ya? It'll be fine. I'll be good. I'm just cuttin' up with you. Jeez." Jace rolled his eyes. "So what's the deal? Do we do some exercises with the ropers while the barrel racers are using the arena?"

Jace seemed sincere so Tuck forced himself to try to relax, just a little bit. Hoping he wouldn't regret the decision tomorrow, he tilted his head toward the action. "Let me introduce you to Carla and the team first; then I'll run through procedures."

An hour later, Tuck felt a little better about the situation. He watched Jace inside the arena, his brow creased as he concentrated on showing one of the ropers what he thought was the proper way to tie a piggin' string. If nothing else, Jace liked to be a know-it-all, and this position as stand-in coach allowed him to do just that. The man had even gotten on a horse to show a student the proper way to dismount when going after a calf.

He came back to Tuck dirty and breathing heavy, but looking happier than he had in a while. "The kid was adding a good three seconds to his time tying the calf like that."

"Well then it's a damn good thing you showed him the right way to do it." Tuck grinned.

"You ain't kidding." Jace brushed the dirt from the knees of his jeans. "So, you wanna get a few beers after this is done?"

Tuck made a face. "I probably should get home and go to bed."

"What? Are you joking?" Jace stared at him like he'd grown antlers.

"I have to be up before dawn tomorrow morning." And he hadn't gotten a whole lot of sleep last night.

"What's going on with you this week?" Jace turned to fully face Tuck, his back to the arena now. "Half the time I call you, you don't answer the phone. You'd rather go to bed than out for a beer. What the hell?"

"I'm tired. Sorry." Tuck shrugged, keeping his attention on the action behind Jace as another calf was released from the chute and the next horse and rider left the box.

Jace's eyes opened wide. "Oh, my God. You've met a woman, haven't you?"

"Uh . . ." Tell the truth or lie? Tuck debated the best course of action here. Maybe he might want that beer. This could be a long story.

"You have, haven't you? Holy sh—"

"Language," Tuck warned, eyeing the nearest students.

"I never thought I'd see the day." Jace shook his head. "I mean when you didn't get the phone number of that hottie from New York you spent the—"

"Jeez, Jace. Please. Shut it." He ran his hand over his face. If he didn't watch out, the entire team would know all of his personal business thanks to his friend's big mouth.

"It's just—" Jace took a step closer and lowered his voice. Tuck was more than grateful for that, though he'd rather they drop the subject all together. "I thought you weren't ready to date or get serious."

"I'm not getting serious."

"But you are seeing someone." When Tuck didn't respond, Jace blew out a frustrated sigh. "Come on, bro. Give me something."

"All right, but I swear, you give me any crap . . ."

"No crap. Cross my heart. Now spill."

"Well, you obviously remember Becca from the rodeo last month."

"Yeah, so what? Did she look you up? You two sexting long distance?"

"Jace . . ." After that warning, Tuck waited to see if his friend would stay quiet, then drew in a deep breath and continued. "She got a job at OSU. We frigging work together."

"No!" Jace's eyes opened wide. "Are you serious?"

"As a heart attack."

"Holy sh— cow." Jace corrected himself with a sideways glance at the students nearest to him. "That's crazy."

"Tell me about it. And that's not all." Tuck figured he'd already started, so he might as well spill it all. "There's a non-fraternization rule for the faculty."

"So you two can't even . . . you know." Jace waggled his eyebrows.

He ignored Jace's insinuation. What happened in Becca's bedroom was going to stay in her bedroom. Didn't matter whether the person asking was a friend or not.

"As faculty we're not supposed to date or interact in any way that's not professional, but I figure it should be okay since we're not dating. We had dinner last night and lunch today . . ." Crap, that sounded an awful lot like dating when he said it out loud. He added, ". . . as friends."

"You're more than just friends, you dog." Jace grinned wide. "I can see it in your face. You're getting laid."

"Shut up, Jace." He shook his head. "I shouldn't have told you anything."

"No. I'm glad you did. It explains so much. So, so much."

"What are you talking about? *So, so much.*" He mimicked Jace with a scowl.

"You're in a mood today and I think it's because of her. I think you like her too much, and it scares the hell out of you."

"What? Stop. It doesn't. I'm not scared. It's just . . . the situation is confusing. Working together and sh— stuff."

He glanced at the group of students nearby. Luckily all their attention seemed to be focused on the roper in the arena.

This conversation should definitely not be happening here among the team. Not only because talking to Jace made Tuck want to cuss like a sailor, but because it was an inappropriate damn subject to be discussing in front of them—for so many reasons.

Jace folded his arms and ignored the crowd around them. "It's confusing because you *like* her."

Tuck fully expected Jace to break into a schoolyard chant and start skipping circles around him, he was acting like such a child about this. "You're a fool."

"Oh, no. If anyone is being a fool, it's you. You can't even face it yourself."

"Face what?"

"That you're attracted to this woman but you're afraid to take a chance on a relationship after the last one. Why don't you just give in and start dating her? See how it works out."

Tuck let out a huff and shook his head. "You're not listening again. I'm not allowed to date her."

"And yet you just told me you two had dinner last night and lunch together today."

"I was only showing her around town today. Help her get familiar with Stillwater." *All the way to Drumright.* Tuck kept that part to himself. "And last night's dinner was just to welcome her to town. I mean it's only proper I be neighborly."

"Neighborly. Yup. I know what you mean. And if I know anything else at all, it's how you look when you're getting laid. You've got that look now, so don't you try to tell me there's nothing going on."

"I'm not discussing this here." He focused on the rider

in the arena, hoping against hope Jace would disappear, or at least shut the hell up.

"That's okay. We don't have to talk about it now. I'm sure she'll be around for a good long while. Plenty of time. In fact, maybe I'll get to see some more of that cute sister of hers now you two are an item. Is she coming out to visit soon?"

Tuck shook his head and took a step forward, putting his friend and, he hoped, this conversation behind him. He drew in a deep breath and called out, "Looking good, Lucas. Watch that barrier, though."

Jace meandered up to stand beside him again, all the while smiling in his annoying know-it-all way. "Yup, a judge in competition would have given a penalty for that run."

Tuck knew damn well Jace's smile had nothing to do with the roper and the calf, and everything to do with the city girl who'd roped him.

Chapter
Eighteen

The phone vibrating in Becca's pocket nearly had her dropping the heavy, leather-bound volumes stacked in her arms.

It shouldn't be Emma calling. She'd already talked to her sister today and been put through the ringer as to every detail of her day with Tucker—the G-rated parts anyway. She glanced around. The campus library was silent as a tomb this time of night since the new semester wasn't in full swing yet. She was at the opposite end of the building from the few others who were there, so she figured it was safe to answer without disturbing anyone.

Becca jostled the books a bit and finally managed to pull her phone out of her pocket. She smiled at the name in the display. "Hello."

"Hi there. Where are you?" Tucker's smooth, sensual voice had her cradling the phone closer. She had it bad. He'd only left her apartment a few hours ago.

"I'm in the library." But she could definitely leave if he had other plans for them. She remembered their time spent alone together earlier that day and made a mental note to pick up some more honey at the store.

"The library?" The long silence after he'd repeated the location told her he was confused. "On campus?"

She laughed. "Yes, Tuck. The library on campus. That big building full of books. I'm sure you've heard of it."

"Hey, now. No need to get snippy about it."

"I didn't mean to be snippy. I'm sorry." She felt bad. That had sounded as if she were calling him a dumb cowboy who'd never heard of a library, and that wasn't what she'd intended at all. "I only meant I'm not sure why you're so shocked I'm in the library. Classes start soon. I'm an English professor. Books are kind of the tools of my trade."

"I know that. But do English professors always go visiting their tools at twenty-one-hundred hours?"

If their day had been taken up by lunch and very creative sex, followed by a nap, they might. And what was he talking about? Twenty-one-hundred hours? "And it's not that late." She glanced at the clock on the wall. "It's nine p.m."

The sound of his laugh came through the phone. "That's what I said . . . never mind. Anyway, I'm done with practice. I already went home, showered, and grabbed a bite. Stay there. I'll meet you."

She glanced at the rows and rows of books in front of her, suddenly no longer as inspired to look through them all as she had been. "Don't bother coming here. I can finish this tomorrow. Why don't you meet me at my place? The key is under the potted plant outside to the right of the door."

"What?" A long string of foul language followed, before she heard him draw in a deep breath. "You leave a key under a plant outside?"

"Yes, so I don't lock myself out." She no longer had Emma right down the road to drive over with a spare key.

"But you triple locked me inside with the dead bolt and the chain last night."

Why he was still sputtering about this topic, she didn't understand. "Well, of course. When I'm inside I use the dead bolt and the chain. A single woman living alone can't be too careful."

"But somebody could use the key to get in when you're not home and be hiding . . ." He let out a big breath of air. "Never mind. We'll discuss this key situation later. Just stay where you are now. I'm on my way. I don't want you wandering around campus alone this late at night."

"I'm sure it's perfectly safe. I'm not parked very far."

"Becca. The semester hasn't officially started yet. When there are twenty thousand students there and the security patrols aren't still on a summer schedule, yeah, I'd agree with you that it's safe. But the campus is a ghost town right now and I don't want you walking to your car this late at night, so please just stop arguing with me and stay there until I come get you. Okay?"

That was quite an impressive rant from a man who'd rarely spoken more than a few words at once during all the time they'd spent together. "Okay. I'm in the stacks by the Chaucer."

He laughed again. "Yeah. Okay. I'll call when I get inside and maybe you can come up with some better directions than that."

"All right. I'll work on it." She smiled.

Becca hung up and stashed the phone back in her pocket so she could re-shelve the books she'd pulled out to look through. The library did have a decent collection, and it was an impressively big building. There were probably books here she'd never had access to at Vassar.

When Tucker finally appeared at the end of the row of shelves, she couldn't help thinking he was something else she hadn't had access to back home. She smiled. "Hey. I thought you were going to call for directions."

"Since I can guide a platoon using nothing but the stars

as a reference, all while the bad guys are out to get us, I figured I could find Chaucer."

"I'm very impressed."

"Then I probably shouldn't tell you I asked at the front desk and the librarian told me which number shelves to go to." He smiled and took a step forward.

She laughed and moved into his arms. "That does make it seem a bit less impressive."

"Sorry. Just being honest."

"Don't apologize. Honesty is good."

"Then maybe I should continue and tell you, as inappropriate as it is, I'm getting turned on." He pulled her closer and she felt the bulge in his jeans. "I never knew books were so sexy."

"You got turned on today by a bologna sandwich, too." She wrapped her arms around his waist. "I don't think it's the books."

"You're right. Maybe it's not the books or the bologna." He leaned lower.

"Maybe it's not." She rose up on her tiptoes, closer to his tempting mouth.

He groaned and closed the small distance between them, backing her up against the shelves as his lips covered hers. He kissed her until she was off balance, when he finally broke away. She blew out a breath but didn't dare let go of him yet. He stayed where he was, keeping her nestled between his body and the books, which was good since the man could take her breath away with just a kiss.

His gaze moved to the volumes behind her head. "Ah, there's my buddy Chaucer now. Just who I was looking for." Tuck grinned down at her.

"I'm sure." She rolled her eyes. "Can we go now?"

"Yeah. I'll see you to your apartment—crap, I can't even believe I'm saying this but then I'm going to have to go home."

"You can't stay? Why?"

"The cadets are rallying at zero-four-thirty."

That sounded awfully early, even in military time. "In the morning? That's before the sun is up."

He laughed. "Believe me, I know. It's an overnight camping retreat, so I won't be back until the day after tomorrow."

"Oh. Okay." Crazy as it seemed, she didn't like the thought of not seeing him for two whole days.

Still pressed close to her, he shook his head. "Maybe I could hang out at your place for just an hour or two."

"No, Tuck. Stop. You got hardly any sleep last night. You should be in bed sleeping already now. I'll let you walk me to my car and watch me drive safely away, but that's it. You're going home and getting some rest for this retreat thing."

After a moment's pause during which she could almost see the battle going on inside him, he nodded. "Okay." He glanced left and right before his hands dipped lower until he cupped her butt cheeks in his large palms. "You better kiss me good night here so no one sees in the parking lot."

"Good plan." Becca had gone through many, many years of schooling in her life. She'd spent more hours in libraries than she could begin to calculate. Yet this was the first time she'd ever made out in one. As he claimed her mouth for the second time against the volumes of Chaucer, she realized all she'd missed out on in the past.

When the pull of desire got her so wound up she was pretty sure she wouldn't be getting any sleep tonight, she pulled away. "Come on. Time to go."

His eyes twinkled. "Good idea."

"I meant time for me to leave so you can go home and get to sleep."

"Oh, all right." He gave her one last squeeze and stepped back, sighing as he dropped his hold on her.

They couldn't exactly walk past the front desk holding hands. The librarian might get suspicious as to what they'd really been doing in the stacks, but knowing Tucker, she suspected that's exactly what he'd like to do.

He glanced at her as they walked. "By the way, there are no cell phones allowed on the retreat, so I won't be able to call or answer."

"No cell phone for two days?" That was a frightening concept. She stared at him. "What if there's an emergency?"

"You and Jace been comparing notes?" He laughed.

"No, why?" She frowned.

"No reason." He shook his head. "And we have phones on site, we just can't use them except in an emergency."

"Okay. Good." That made her feel a little better. Who knew what could happen on an overnight camping trip. There could be bears, or wolves, or murderers hiding in the woods from the authorities. Someone tripping on a tree root and spraining an ankle might be more likely, but either way, Becca and her overactive imagination would feel much better knowing Tucker had a way to call for help if he needed to.

He gave the librarian a nod on the way past and pushed the exit door open for Becca. When they were outside on the sidewalk, he asked, "You worried about me, darlin'?"

"No. Of course not. You can take care of yourself," she lied, and turned to lead him toward her car. "I'm parked this way."

"Good, because I've been taking care of myself for a while now." He followed her until they were standing at her driver's side door. "You take care of *your*self while I'm gone. Okay?"

"I will."

"Logan's number is in the faculty directory. Call his phone if you need anything."

"Won't he be camping with you?"

"Yes, but since he's in charge, he'll have his phone on him. I won't. And if for any reason he doesn't answer and you need anything, Jace's home number is listed in the local book. Jace Mills. Can you remember his last name? Never mind, I'll just text both numbers to you when I get home so you have them."

"Tuck, if there's an emergency I'll call the police. If there's not, it can wait until you're back."

"All right. I just hate leaving you with no one—"

"There's always Dean Ross."

"That's right. Call Ross if you need something. That's good."

"You are a big worrier." She was beginning to realize that about him. It was incredibly endearing how concerned he was for her.

"Not usually."

"Then why now?"

"Good question." He let out a snort. "Now get in and get going before I don't let you leave."

Tucker reached behind her and opened the door. He dropped the quickest kiss on her lips she'd ever had from him, then stepped back, his hand on the door frame as he waited for her to step inside so he could close her door. He must be really determined to not stay the night.

"All right. Have a good night. Get some sleep. Have fun camping, but be careful."

"Now who's the worrier?" He grinned. "And will do, to all of the above. Night, Becca."

"Night, Tucker." She bit her lip to stop from saying what she was feeling. How much she'd miss him.

Chapter
Nineteen

"You're quiet this morning." Tuck shifted the weight of the near seventy-or-so-pound pack on his back. The sound of his boots hitting the dirt in the dim morning light melded with those of the cadets ahead, and Logan's beside him.

"Yup." Logan's one-word response had Tuck glancing sideways at him.

"Something wrong?"

"Nope."

"All righty." This was going to be one hell of a retreat if this conversation set the tone for the next two days.

Logan's pace slowed. Not enough for the cadets hiking ahead of them to notice, but enough for Tuck to. There was no way Logan was winded. First, this walk was a piece of cake. Second, Logan would never fall out of a march, even if he were exhausted and near collapse. It would set a bad example for the cadets. His hanging back must mean he wanted privacy.

Tuck matched Logan's slower stride as the distance between them and the line of cadets ahead increased. "What's up?" he asked.

"You tell me."

"Um, all right. Can you give me some direction as to what I'm supposed to be telling you?"

"Forget it." Logan shook his head. "I shouldn't even be fucking asking you this, because as your superior officer I truly don't want to know if you're openly flaunting the university's fraternization rules."

Tuck's boot hit a loose rock on the path, and he stumbled before catching himself. This was about Becca? Both of his friends—Logan and Jace—needed to get a life if all they could do was worry about his. He let out a snort. "That rule is archaic, but even so, I'm not openly flaunting it, as you say."

"What about behind closed doors?"

"Well . . ." Tuck tilted his head and grimaced. "You're right. You'd better not ask if you don't want to know."

"Okay, I get the idea."

"You disappointed in me?" He glanced sideways at Logan and kept walking.

"Hell, no." Logan laughed. "I'd be disappointed in you if you let that opportunity pass you by. That's me speaking as your friend and surrogate big brother. As your commander, however . . ."

"I know, I know. Let's just keep it *don't ask, don't tell.*"

Logan let out a snort. "That former policy wasn't instituted for this particular kind of situation, but I guess it'll work. Just be careful. Okay? And that's both your friend and your commander talking."

"Understood." Tuck nodded.

One of the kids up ahead slowed, then turned and waited for Logan and Tuck to catch up.

"Something I can do for you, cadet?"

"No, sir. I just wanted to thank the sergeant for the recommendation of that restaurant in Drumright. Me and a few of the other guys drove out there yesterday. You're right. Best smoked bologna sandwich in Oklahoma."

Tuck's heart skipped. "Oh, good. Glad you liked it."

"We loved it, sir. Were you there yesterday, too? I think we just missed you. I saw your truck pulling out right as we were pulling in." The kid's question sounded innocent enough, but Tuck still felt his pulse racing.

He tried to remember that they couldn't have seen inside his truck if they weren't sure it was him. His brain spun with the question, lie or tell the truth? Sticking as close to the truth as possible was always the best way to lie, so under the watchful eye of Logan—who had to be wondering what the hell was taking Tuck so long to respond to a simple question—he answered.

"Yeah, I was there. Had the bologna myself. Hush puppies, too. You ever try those?" He tried to swing the conversation away from his being there, and who might have possibly been in the truck with him, by concentrating on food, figuring about now the cadets should be starting to get hungry.

"Oh, yeah. I love those things. You ever try the big stack? That sandwich where they pile up all that brisket and sausage and coleslaw?"

Tuck nodded, relieved the kid seemed way more interested in beef than in Becca. "Yup. I've had it. Good stuff."

Logan shot Tuck a look that said he knew there was more to the story, but they had put the don't ask, don't tell policy in place, so Tuck ignored it and let the kid keep babbling about barbecue. Silently though, he made a vow to himself he and Becca would start to be much more careful. From now on takeout only. Which, considering how much he enjoyed the time they spent alone together in her apartment, wouldn't be a bad thing.

Thoughts of Becca occupied him throughout the rest of the march. Even through setting up the campsite. He kept how much she occupied his mind to himself. What choice did he have? Logan didn't want to know. Correction, his friend Logan wanted to know. It was safer for all involved if his boss, battalion leader LTC Logan Hunt, didn't know.

Stupid frigging non-fraternization rules.

As Tuck sat beside the campfire, he had too much time to think. Think about what it would be like between Becca and him if those rules didn't exist. Then again, those rules he was beginning to despise might just save him. Those rules forced him to take things slow with Becca, at least as far as the public was concerned. They sure as hell hadn't taken things slow in the bedroom.

But the deep scars from his ex-wife's betrayal were just starting to heal, so it was better that the first woman he was interested in being with for more than a night since then couldn't be his public girlfriend. That way if things went south, at least the public humiliation of the breakup would be eliminated. Not the private pain, though.

Maybe he should just stop all this thinking. He and Becca were having fun together. That was enough. For now.

As the sun dropped lower toward the horizon over Lake McMurtry, it turned the dim hues of blue in the sky to mottled streaks of pink and orange. Tuck took a sip of the hot coffee in his cup and thought how beautiful Becca would look in this light. How nice it would be to roll out his sleeping bag and make love to her right there on the ground next to the fire.

What the hell? He wasn't supposed to be thinking of shit like this during an ROTC training while surrounded by the entire cadre.

He tore into his MRE. Maybe food would distract him. Nothing like one of Uncle Sam's Meals-Ready-to-Eat to remind a man where he was and what he was doing.

This MRE was supposed to be a tasty *Southwest style beef and black beans with sauce.* At least that's what the label on the package said. You could have fooled Tuck. He swallowed a mouthful and longed for a sandwich from Joseph's Fine Foods.

The thought only made him more dissatisfied with his current meal and brought to mind Becca and the look on her face as she bit into her first ever hush puppy. That led to him thinking about how he couldn't wait to see her again tomorrow night when he finally got home from this retreat. He could shower and then pick up some takeout and be at her house by dinnertime. He could sleep over so they'd have the whole night together and still be up early enough to work out with the cadets in the morning.

He stopped his fork halfway to his mouth when the full impact of what he was thinking hit him. This thing with Becca was a slippery slope. He'd willingly spend every waking moment he could with her if that were possible. The last woman he'd felt this way about was now his ex-wife. The thought scared the shit out of him.

This OSU no dating rule wasn't so bad after all. He lowered his gaze and lifted his fork, specifically not wondering whether Becca was noticing at that very moment how gorgeous tonight's sunset was.

He tried to distract himself. Tomorrow's repelling and climbing exercise should keep his mind occupied, even if today's land navigation training course had not. Though he had a feeling it would take much more than basic survival training to knock thoughts of Becca from his brain. In fact, an actual insurgent attack like the ones he'd lived through in Afghanistan might not even do it at this point.

Chapter
Twenty

Tuck's cell phone rang just as the steam began to fill the bathroom from the hot water. The only thing that could tempt him to delay the pleasure of a much-needed shower after a two-day retreat would be Becca, and since he'd just gotten home and hadn't talked to her yet, the call could very well be her.

He flipped the water off and reached for the phone lying on top of the heap of camouflage on the floor. The display spelled out LOGAN, and he nearly dumped the phone back onto the floor and let him wait. Logan had had him at his beck and call for the past two days. Why the hell was he bothering Tuck now when he'd just barely walked in the door? Couldn't a man even take a shower in peace?

Hitting the button to answer, he decided to give Logan a piece of his mind. "Jeez, man. I just left you a few minutes ago. What could you possibly need—"

"I need you to get into my office. *Now.*" Logan, obviously in full commander mode, interrupted Tuck's bitching.

Tuck let out a huff of air. Something must have happened with one of the cadets and Logan wanted Tuck to deal with it. They'd only had the juniors and seniors with them on the retreat. God only knew what kind of trouble the new crop of incoming freshmen and sophomores could have gotten into over the past two days while he was gone. "Fine. I'll be there as soon as I shower."

"No. Now."

"Logan, I've got two days' worth of campsite dirt and stink—"

"Tucker. Now." When Logan used that tone of voice, he meant business.

"All right. I'll be right there." But he'd be there in a dirty uniform. That's what Logan got for not giving him time to shower, forget about do laundry.

Annoyed, Tuck walked into the military studies office with an attitude, but one look at Logan's face dispelled it. "What happened?"

"Shut the door."

Shit. This couldn't be good. Tuck did as asked, then moved to sit in the chair on his side of Logan's big head-of-the-department desk. Then he waited.

Logan hit a few keys on his laptop, then spun it to face Tuck. The video was a grainy, black-and-white image typical of surveillance tapes. It took him a second to place where it had been taken, but once his brain registered that those dark, close-set walls were shelves of books, his heart rate doubled. Tuck swallowed hard and watched the two forms on the video. Watched the larger of the two back the smaller one up against the shelves and start kissing her.

He finally wrestled his focus away from the screen to look at Logan. His mouth open even though he was speechless, Tuck shook his head, not knowing what to ask first.

Logan's brows rose. "This is what you call being discreet?"

"How did you get this?" That question seemed as good as any to begin with.

"I'm the one who got the guy who watches the security cameras all night his job."

Tuck glanced back at the images on screen. He and Becca were really getting into it, but still, it was nearly impossible to tell who the people in the video were. If he hadn't been the one with his hands and mouth all over Becca, he probably wouldn't have been able to identify them. "How did he know it was me? Or know to bring this to you?"

"There's a nice clear shot of your face when you finally stop mauling her and turn to leave. He recognized you as one of mine."

"Oh." Not much more Tuck could say to that, except to ask, "What now? What does this mean?"

Logan's answer would determine not only his future, but also Becca's. He was more worried about her than himself. He might lose this billet and get shipped back overseas, but they wouldn't kick him out of the army for something like this. Could they? He wasn't so sure.

Either way, Becca shouldn't be punished and lose her job because of his inability to control himself. He'd do whatever was necessary to ensure that.

The delay in Logan's answer only served to ramp up Tuck's anxiety. Of course, that was probably the intent. Finally, Logan said, "Nothing."

"Nothing?" Tuck repeated him, afraid to believe it was true.

"My friend in security broke the rules, put his own job in jeopardy, and gave me the only copy of the tape."

"Why would he do that for me?" He didn't even know this guy.

"He didn't do it for you. He did it for me. You see, when he retired from the military with such severe PTSD he was afraid to even drive a car because the street noise could send him mentally back to the war zone, I got him a good job where he could sit in a nice, quiet room and watch monitors."

Tuck dropped his chin and closed his eyes, trying to fully absorb exactly how lucky he and Becca both were, thanks to Logan. He finally looked up. "Thank you. I owe you." More than he could ever repay.

"You sure as hell do owe me, and starting right now things are going to change."

His attention snapped to Logan's words. Tuck's fear of what he was implying made his mouth go dry. "What do you want me to do?"

Logan shook his head and let out a curse. "Dammit, Tuck. Couldn't you have found a girl who wasn't a professor here?"

"I didn't know when I met her in July—"

"I know." Logan cut him off. "And that's one reason I'm not telling you never to see her again."

"You're not?"

"But I swear to God, if you don't start being more discreet . . . What the hell were you thinking? Taking her out to eat at a restaurant you recommend to the cadets? Practically having sex in the library?"

"I know. I was stupid. It was risky. None of that will happen again."

"Make sure it doesn't."

He nodded and sat, waiting, not sure if this well-deserved reprimand was over or not.

Logan glared at him for a long, uncomfortable moment. In his decade in the military, Tuck had been glared at by the best of them. This was different, though, because Logan was a friend. More, he was like a big brother, and Tuck had disappointed him. There was nothing Logan could say or do to him that would outweigh the feeling of disappointment he had in himself.

"Get out of here."

"Yes, sir." He rose, his head spinning so he didn't even remember opening the door and leaving the office. The next thing he knew he was outside the building, staring at his cell phone in his hand. He didn't know what to do, to tell Becca or not, but he needed to hear her voice.

She picked up on the second ring. "Hey, are you back home now?"

"Yup. Well, I'm still on campus actually, but I'm on my way home."

"That's good. So what did you do on your camping trip? Or is it top secret, military-type stuff?" She sounded so cheerful and upbeat, how could he possibly lay the weight of what he'd found out from Logan on her?

He decided to make small talk and stall while he considered the situation. "No. Not top secret at all. We had a paintball game. Did some climbing. Land nav. You know, basic survival stuff."

"Ah, of course." Her tone told him she had no idea what land nav or basic survival training was, but she was pretending she did anyway.

Even as ill as he felt over the situation, he couldn't help smiling at how damn cute she could be. "What did you do while I was gone?"

"Oh, I did exciting stuff. I finished unpacking the last of the boxes. I jostled some money between the new zero percent interest credit card I just opened and the outstanding balance on my old card. I can use the interest I'm going to save each month to help pay the rent here."

He frowned. "I didn't know money was that tight for you."

"Being out of work for a few months ate up my savings. Then the cost of flying out here for the interview went on my credit card. And to move I had to rent a trailer. Pay for gas for the drive from New York to Oklahoma, which with today's prices is a small fortune. Then I had to lay out a security deposit and a month's rent for the apartment. It all adds up." She paused. "There's nothing to be worried about. I'll be fine once I start getting my paychecks from OSU. Now, if I *hadn't* gotten this job, then that would have been something to worry about."

Her laugh was light and casual, but he felt anything but. Becca needed this job. Badly. If she lost it because of him, he'd never forgive himself. He wasn't going to let that happen.

"So, what are your plans for tonight?" There was a suggestive lilt to her voice. Before his visit with Logan, that would have sent Tuck running to her apartment. Now, not so much.

Thoughts of her apartment had him facing a harsh reality. She lived just off campus. Her neighbors were mostly students. It was amazing he hadn't already been spotted sneaking out of her place in the middle of the night. Hell, maybe he had and that other shoe was about to drop.

And his truck . . . it stood out like a sore thumb. Not just because it was big, which was true of most trucks in this area, but the ARMY STRONG bumper sticker and the ARMY emblem on the back window screamed it was his.

He couldn't go to her place. It was a risk they couldn't take. "Actually, I'm kind of beat. All I want to do is shower and fall into bed."

"Okay." That one word conveyed how disappointed she was.

"It's just that after two days of hiking and a night of sleeping on the ground . . ."

"I understand."

He steeled his resolve. He couldn't give in and go there. Not when he had so many things to figure out. Knowing her relationship with him could cost her a job she desperately needed put a whole new perspective on whatever this thing was between them. Still, he had to give her something to dispel that insecurity he heard creeping into her voice. "I'll call you tomorrow."

"All right."

"Night, Becca."

"Good night, Tucker."

He hung up the phone feeling like absolute crap and wanting nothing more than to drive directly to her place.

Shit. What the hell was he going to do?

Chapter
Twenty-one

"What's going on with tall, dark, and handsome?"
Emma's daily phone interrogation shouldn't have
surprised Becca, but today she really wasn't in the mood
for it.

Becca let out a short, humorless laugh. "I wish I knew."

"What's wrong?"

Since her sister's question had actually sounded sincere,
she answered. "I don't know. It feels like something's up.
He calls me. He's sweet on the phone. He asks me about
my day and tells me about his. On the surface it seems like
everything is fine . . ."

"Except?"

Except before this weirdness started she wouldn't have
been talking to Tucker on the phone. She would have
been under him in her bed. "We make polite small talk but
that's it. And it feels like he's avoiding seeing me. He hasn't
come over in a week."

"Why would he be avoiding you?"

She let out a huff. "I have no idea."

"Here's my opinion. If he wasn't calling you at all, I
would think he was maybe seeing someone else . . ."

"Thanks for putting that image in my head." She
scowled.

"Oh, please. As if you haven't thought that yourself.

What I'm saying is, he doesn't sound as if he's dumping you. It has to be something else."

"Something else, like his secret wife and baby are back in town and he can't get away?"

"You've been watching too many of those cheesy made-for-television movies."

"Have not." Becca reached quietly for the remote control and muted the current movie on screen.

"Classes just started this week, right? Maybe there's something going on at work, and he's busy or having a tough time."

"I don't know."

"Well, let me ask you this, have you asked him what's going on?"

"No."

"Becca, you need to. Jeez, just ask him. For a woman who makes a living out of words, you really are a horrible communicator."

Only her sister would say something like that to her. "I communicate just fine, thank you."

"Then call him right now and ask him what's wrong."

"But—"

"But what?"

She couldn't voice aloud what she was thinking. What if he wasn't alone? What if he wanted to dump her and was trying to be nice about it?

"Becca, if you don't call him, I will."

"You don't have his number." She sneered at Emma's threat.

"I can get it."

She couldn't deny that. Her sister, Internet guru, definitely could. "Fine. I'll call."

"Good. Then call me right back."

"All right."

"Promise?"

"Yes, I promise. Now let me go so I can call him."

"Okay. Bye."

"Bye." Nothing worse than a nosy, computer-savvy sister with no life of her own. Becca steeled her nerves and hit Tucker's number.

"Hey, there." There was no *darlin'* in his greeting, but at least he had answered.

That she'd half expected him not to and let her call go to voice mail proved exactly how insecure she was about their relationship right now. Which was kind of funny, because to both herself and her sister, she kept denying there was any kind of relationship.

He wasn't her boyfriend. They were just friends. Friends who used to have sex until he'd started to avoid her.

"Hi." Her heart pounded so hard it vibrated her body. "Can we talk?"

He hesitated. "Yeah. I think that's a good idea."

The tone of his voice was more serious, sounded more ominous, than she'd ever imagined it could. A sick feeling settled in her stomach. This was a clear case of be careful what you wished for, and it was all Emma's fault. If she hadn't asked him to talk, things could have kept going just as they were and she wouldn't be facing him dumping her now.

"Um, okay. Do you want to come over here?" Just what she needed, bad memories in her new apartment, but what choice did she have? She wasn't going to let him get away with ending their friendship, and whatever else they were to each other, on the phone. He'd just have to do it face to face.

Again there was that pause. At least this seemed to be hard on him. It would really suck if it were easy.

"Do you think you could come to my place? Is that all right?" he asked.

"Sure." Why not? Maybe then she could look for clues.

Some sign of why he was ending things. Evidence of another woman, such as tampons under the bathroom sink or diet soda in the fridge.

"Let me give you directions."

"No need. I have GPS." And the online faculty directory bookmarked to the page with Tucker's information. "I'll be right over."

"I'm on campus still. I had a meeting with Logan. Can you give me an hour? Then I'll meet you at my place."

"That's fine. See you then." An hour. She pressed a hand to her roiling stomach. Plenty of time for her to be sick, fix herself up, and get to Tucker's.

Tuck disconnected the call with Becca and opened the door to Logan's office. He went back to the chair he'd been occupying before Becca's call had vibrated the cell phone in his pocket and he'd excused himself to take it outside.

He dared to glance at Logan, seated across the desk from him. "Sorry."

Logan drew in a deep breath. "Tuck, are you sure about this?"

"Yup. The wheels are already in motion." He really didn't need anyone putting doubts in his mind at this point. The decision had been made.

"Those wheels can be stopped. Things can change hourly in the military. You know that."

"I don't want to change the plan. It's best if I go. Besides, I'll be back before you know it. Six months is nothing. It's just one semester."

"The rest of this semester and the first two months of next, during which I'll have to get a replacement for all your classes."

"Is that what's really bothering you? Getting a replacement for the program?"

"Do you have any idea what you're getting yourself into?"

He took that as a *no* and that Logan had more of an issue with where he was going than his leaving. "Sure. I've been to Afghanistan before."

Logan let out a humorless laugh. "You were at a forward operating base. FOBs are nothing like the outposts or the firebases you'll be going to. The border regions are an entirely different place."

"I can handle it." Tuck was many things, some good, some bad, but he wasn't a pansy or a coward. Whatever was thrown at him where he was going, he'd deal with.

"You being tough enough to handle it is not the point."

"Then what is the point?" Of all people, he had expected Logan to support this decision. It would give him the space and perspective he needed right now when things with Becca were moving too fast and getting far too complicated.

"Hell, I don't know. All I do know is this woman shows up here and you haven't been the same since. Maybe that right there is my point."

That was funny coming from Logan, the guy who'd said Tuck should get back on the horse. "You're the one who forced me to go to that damn wine mixer for her to begin with."

Of course, Logan hadn't known at the time he and Becca already had a past—however brief. Or that Tuck would be incapable of keeping his hands off her once they were reunited.

"I didn't think you'd blatantly flout the damn rules. Taking her out in public. Smooching against the Shakespeare section in the campus library. Are you insane?"

Actually, if they were going for alliteration, it would be more accurate to say there'd nearly been *coitus in front of the*

Chaucer collection since Tuck hadn't noticed any Shake-speare behind Becca when he'd been grinding against her, but he didn't dare correct Logan. "I know, Logan. It was crazy, which is why I'm leaving."

"My point exactly." Logan spread his hands wide while shaking his head. "Giving up the ROTC billet and volunteering to go to a battalion in Afghanistan is not a normal reaction to the situation. Couldn't you just be more careful from now on?"

"You're not making a whole lot of sense." This conversation was starting to make Tuck's head hurt. In one breath Logan was yelling at him for being with Becca, and in the next he was encouraging him to be with her.

"Neither does your decision to volunteer to go to Kunar for six months. I talked to a guy who's been where you're going. Men come out of there changed. He said if the hundred-and-thirty-degree heat and tarantulas didn't get to you in the summer, the sheer boredom in the winter would. Then there are the IEDs . . ." He let the sentence trail off, obviously aware Tuck knew exactly what happened when soldiers got hit with one of the insurgents' improvised explosive devices.

"The platoon currently there is nine months into a fifteen-month tour. They needed some new blood to rotate in for the last leg of it. I've got combat experience and I needed a change. It's a perfect match." Tuck shrugged.

Yes, the IEDs were a real danger, but heat and spiders? Seriously? That's what Logan was using to try to dissuade Tuck from going? Hell, Logan should try sleeping in a horse trailer after it had been sitting in the sun all day the way Tuck had on a few occasions while rodeoing with Jace full-time.

"I don't know what to say to you to change your mind." Logan shook his head and let out a breath that sounded filled with frustration.

"I'm not changing my mind, Logan. Just tell me what you need me to do before I leave to help with the transition to a new instructor, so I can get out of here." He glanced at his watch, remembering Becca would be at his place in less than an hour.

"Why? You got a hot date tonight?" Logan's tone showed exactly how unhappy he was with Tuck at the moment.

"No, and I'm not supposed to tell you even if I did. You don't want to know, remember?" He raised a brow in challenge.

No hot date, but he did have a woman to . . . To what? Say good-bye to? Break up with? Not that they'd been dating in the first place. It was more like he was going away for a little while. Just taking a break from their being together.

He wanted Becca, but he sure as hell didn't *want* to want her. Not this much, this soon. And who knew if she wanted more from him? Then there were the rules and the risk they were taking breaking them. A risk to her career she couldn't afford to take.

Compared to women, war seemed exquisitely simple and uncomplicated. Maybe after six months of blowing shit up, he could come home with a clear head and know exactly what he wanted and what to do about getting it. But right now, things with Becca were about as clear as mud.

Chapter
Twenty-two

Tucker was just getting out of his truck when Becca pulled her car in behind him, her heart pounding, her mouth dry.

This was it. The beginning of the end. It wasn't lost on her that though she'd insisted they weren't dating, both to herself and to Emma, she was awfully fearful he'd break up with her. She'd freely admit this situation—their situation together—was confusing, but that didn't mean she wanted it to end.

Maybe this was the time to stop being a sissy and take a chance. Actually commit to a relationship again. Just because Jerry was a dick of a boyfriend didn't mean Tucker would be. And it really did seem as if he didn't roam the country riding both bulls and babes as she'd originally feared. Most days he worked from sunup until sundown with the ROTC and the rodeo students.

She realized she'd sat in her car procrastinating, avoiding getting out, for long enough. Too long considering Tucker was standing in the driveway waiting for her. In fact, she'd taken so long, he was now moving toward her. Gentleman that he was, he reached out and opened the door for her.

A hot guy capable of amazing sex, who was polite and

had a good job with benefits—why had she not wanted to commit to a relationship with him?

Because she was afraid he might not want her, that's why.

The little voice in her head that consistently undermined her rational thoughts whispered again, planting doubt where just seconds ago there was none.

She glanced up at him as he reached to help her out of the car. "Hi."

"Hi." He smiled but it had a strangely sad look to it. "Come on in."

He dropped his hold on her hand and turned to lead the way inside.

Becca didn't know a lot right now—things had gotten very strange very fast—but if she knew anything, it was that Tucker was a hand-holder. He had been from the very moment they'd met, even before they'd had sex. That he'd released his hold on her now was not a good sign.

As the voice of doubt got louder in her head, she braced herself for the big brush-off. The I-think-we-should-just-be-friends speech. Or maybe the I've-met-someone-else excuse. Following him to the door, she realized the blame lay squarely on her own shoulders. She couldn't even blame Emma for putting her in the current situation. At least not totally.

Sure, Emma had bought those rodeo tickets and practically thrown her at Tucker that night, but what happened after the rodeo, and after their unexpected reunion at OSU—that was all on Becca. She'd picked up that phone and asked him over. She'd kissed him more than willingly when he'd barely put down the take-out food bag in her kitchen. And ultimately, she'd said let's just be friends— friends with benefits.

This mess was all Becca's, and following Tucker through

the door of his house she prepared herself to clean up the pieces of her pride after he shattered it. She refused to admit, even to herself, that her heart was going to be pretty well bruised along with her ego after the impending dumping.

The condo was cool and dark as the air conditioner pumped cold air and the window blinds kept out the heat of the day. He pulled off his camouflage hat and tossed it onto a table right inside the door.

When he flipped on a wrought-iron table lamp, it illuminated a space that was all male. If testosterone was a decorating style, this would be what it looked like, but not necessarily in a bad way. A Native American print blanket hung on the back of the distressed brown leather sofa. A nubby tweed reclining chair, cowhide rug, and a rustic wooden coffee table piled with books on war completed the seating area.

"This is nice." Her gaze cut to a row of hooks on the wall that held his cowboy hat, chaps, and some distinctly cowboy-looking ropes.

A Manhattan decorator would have hung those things to enhance the rustic Western style of the room, but she knew good and well from having seen that stuff in use, he was simply storing his gear there between rodeos. He was an intriguing, complex man. She probably should have appreciated that more when she had him.

The corner of his mouth pulled up in a crooked smile. "You don't have to be kind and say you like it."

"I wasn't. Really, I'm serious. It's perfect." She glanced around the room again. "It looks like . . . you."

"Yeah, I guess that was the point when I bought all this stuff. But I sure ran up a hell of a lot on my credit card the month I moved out of the house."

Ah, a post-breakup shopping spree. Maybe men and women weren't so different after all, though she'd been too depressed to leave the house so she did her shopping online, and her purchases comprised more purses and jewelry than furnishings.

Through an open doorway she saw a tiny galley kitchen, and there was a closed door off the living room. The bedroom most likely. Judging by how far away he was standing, and the absence of his usual lip lock the moment they were alone, she wouldn't be seeing that room.

She swallowed hard and turned back to him. "Well, you did a good job."

"Thanks." He delivered his thank-you along with a nod. "Want a beer?"

A beer? They were definitely in the *just friends* mode now. Maybe there was a game on TV and they could kick back and eat nachos or something, like they were old buddies. She decided it was time to get this dumping going. "Do I need one?"

One of his brows cocked up. "I don't know. That's up to you."

Since he looked as if he wasn't going to offer anything willingly, she pushed him further. "What's going on? Things are different between us and if you don't want to see me or be friends anymore, I'd rather you just tell me than—"

He strode to her so fast, it seemed as if she'd blinked and he was there, gripping her arms in those big, rough hands that never failed to let her know she was truly being held. "Don't ever think I don't want you. That's not it."

She believed him. He might not be the best communicator lately, but she'd never known him to be a liar. "Then what?"

Tucker drew in and released a long, deep breath. "I'm deploying to Afghanistan."

"What?" She shouldn't have been so surprised at his announcement. He was standing in front of her in uniform.

The twin tapes on his chest, right at her eye level, spelled out his name on one side and his branch of service on the other, yet she was as shocked as if he'd just announced he'd booked a flight on the next space shuttle. "When?"

"Soon. Real soon actually." His regret showed clearly in the tense way he held himself and the sadness in his eyes.

She shook her head, still having trouble wrapping her brain around the concept. "How long have you known?"

"It all happened pretty fast. I haven't known it was definite for very long."

She took a steadying breath and moved on to the next question, not sure she wanted to know the answer. "How long will you be gone?"

"Things change a lot in the military, and in that region particularly, but it shouldn't be much more than six months. Seven, maybe."

Six or seven months? Whole lives could change in that amount of time. Hers certainly had done a one-eighty from where she'd been six months ago.

"I'm sorry, Becca."

That statement surprised her more than the news of the deployment had. "Sorry for what?"

A shadow clouded his features. He looked like he wanted to say something, then changed his mind. He shrugged. "That I'm leaving."

She frowned. "It's not your fault. You can't help where the army sends you."

"Yeah, well, still. I'm sorry." For the first time since the confession, he pulled back and dropped his hold on her.

Becca stepped closer, into the safety of his arms. Now of all times, knowing she wouldn't have him around anymore, she needed him close. It didn't take long before he drew her tight against him, his thick arms encasing her. Even with her face buried in the stiff fabric of the utilitarian uniform, she felt better. Safe. Held.

He was a good hugger, and it seemed now he'd confessed what had been bothering him, the ban on touching had come to an end. Not that it would do Becca any good for very long, because soon he'd be gone.

She hated to ask it, but forced herself. "When exactly do you have to leave? Can you tell me? Do you know?"

"Yeah." He swallowed hard. The motion moved his chest beneath her cheek. "I fly out next week. But . . . my mom isn't handling my leaving as well as I'd hoped. I promised I'd go home and spend as much time with the family as I can before I leave."

Surprised, she looked up at him. That was sooner than she'd imagined, and now he was telling her he wouldn't even be around until he left? She felt a little nauseated hearing it. "How far away do they live?"

"It's still in Oklahoma but it's a few hours' drive. This is a big state." He looked so apologetic, she couldn't be upset—or at least she shouldn't be.

"Oh." Squelching the sick feeling in her gut that this could be the last time she saw him, she pulled back enough to make eye contact. She squeezed her arms around his waist a bit harder. "Then we'd better not waste a minute of tonight."

The surprise was clear in his features. Good to know she could throw him off kilter as easily as he could her. "Ah, Becca. You're amazing. Do you know that?"

She glanced at what she hoped was the bedroom door. "I think I might need you to show me."

It was different, their good-bye sex. It felt like the end. She had no doubt he sensed it, too. They'd only been together a handful of times, but she knew how sex with Tucker usually was, and it was nothing like this.

Gone was the always playful, sometimes adventurous, and usually naughty lover she'd grown accustomed to. In his place was a tender, gentle, reflective man. It was as if he were trying to sear the image of their last time together into his mind. He ran his hands over her body as if committing every curve to memory.

He watched her face while loving her, until she could almost physically feel the intensity of his stare. And after he'd shuddered within her, he collapsed and stayed there for what seemed like forever, his face pressed into her hair, his breathing unsteady, his heart pounding against her chest.

Finally, he asked, "Did you eat dinner?"

"No." Her response was muffled beneath him.

"Are you hungry?"

"No." The sick feeling in her belly returned every time she thought of him going to a war zone he might not return from.

"Can you stay a little longer?" His question was so soft, so hesitant, it almost didn't sound like him.

"I can stay as long as you want me to."

"Good."

Chapter
Twenty-three

"He's going to Afghanistan." Becca's voice broke as she announced that horrifying reality into the phone.

"Huh? What? Who?" Emma sounded as if she was about one cup of coffee into the day. Awake, moderately alert, but don't throw anything too heavy at her, such as the word *Afghanistan*.

Becca drew in a shaky breath and tried to steady herself. "Tucker. That's why he's been avoiding me and acting differently. He's being deployed."

"Jeez." Emma paused, obviously taking a moment to absorb the news that had probably sounded as crazy to her as it had to Becca just last night. "But at least he didn't have another girlfriend or want to break up with you, right?"

"Emma, he's going to Afghanistan!"

"All right. I hear you. Well, you did say he was in the army. But I'm confused. I thought he was a teacher now."

"I don't know. I don't understand it, either." She'd thought about it all night as Tuck held her in his bed, and yet she still couldn't fully grasp it. "He explained a little bit about it, but he was talking about billets and battalions and I don't understand this stuff. I never knew a soldier before. How am I supposed to know what he's talking about?"

"We can probably look it up online." Emma threw out her usual solution to everything.

"I'm afraid to." She didn't watch a whole lot of news broadcasts, but when she did, there was always some sort of bad stuff happening in Afghanistan. And now, Tucker was going to be there.

"Becca, try not to worry. Things aren't as bad over there as they were at the start of the war."

"You don't know that." Becca frowned.

She'd love it to be true, but how could Emma know so much about everything? From rodeos to war. Did the woman sit online all day and read? Actually, knowing Emma and her job, she probably did. Maybe it was true. Maybe things were quieting down over there.

"Sure, I do. Why else would the president have called for troop reductions in that region?"

"H . . . he did?" Becca stuttered. Troop reductions? She really needed to pay more attention to current events now that she had a very personal stake in them.

"Yes, he did. Didn't you hear that on the news?"

"No." She hated to admit she'd rather watch one of the morning talk shows and see what new movies were releasing and which celebrities were getting into trouble. Emma, for some reason, was a news hound. "I'll start watching."

"No! Don't do that. Now is definitely not the time for you to take a sudden interest in international news. It's best if you don't see or hear anything else about the war until Tucker is back home and safe. When will that be?"

"Six or seven months." She had been much calmer before saying it out loud. Hearing it now, it seemed like a very long time.

"That's not so bad." Emma put on her coddling voice. The one she saved for when Becca needed . . . well, coddling. "You'll come home to New York for Thanksgiving and the long break between semesters. You'll stay here with me. We can spend the holidays at Mom and Dad's. Then before you know it, he'll be home, safe and sound."

The school year always did seem to fly by, especially leading up to Christmas. There never seemed to be as much time as she wanted or needed to get all her shopping and decorating done. Hopefully that would hold true for this year and the months would speed past until they were well into the new year and Tucker was back.

"All right." She eyed the clock. "I have to get ready for my classes."

She hadn't even showered yet. She'd come directly home from Tucker's as the sun was rising and called her sister the moment she was in the apartment. Thank God for the one-hour time difference. It was only early in New York, not insanely early.

"Wait, don't hang up yet. One more question."

"Okay." She didn't know if she could handle one more when the subject was Tucker's leaving for war.

"When does he have to leave?"

"Next week, but he's spending the rest of his time with his family." She swallowed the sick feeling away. "Last night was our last together. We . . . we said our good-byes this morning." And she'd barely made it to her car before the tears started to fall.

"Oh, Becs. I'm sorry. That really, really sucks."

Yes, it did.

"Jeez, Tuck. Afghanistan again?" Jace put down the coffee mug he'd just lifted halfway to his mouth. "It feels like you just got back."

"I've been back for a while." Long enough to find out his wife had been cheating on him, finalize the divorce, and get on with his life. That all had taken a good bit of time.

"I guess, but I thought you'd be home for a little while

longer before they sent you back over there. Especially now you have the job at OSU."

"Eh, you know the military." Tuck shrugged, feeling bad for not telling Jace the full truth. That he'd volunteered to go. "Ain't no telling where or when they'll decide to ship you out to next."

"I guess so. And on such short notice, too. Damn. Glad I'm my own boss." Jace grinned. "Ain't nobody can tell me what to do."

"That's true. You're lucky," he agreed, and figured this was as good a time as any to broach another subject. The other reason he'd asked Jace to breakfast. "That brings up another thing I wanted to talk to you about. My assistant coach is gonna be taking over the rodeo team practices all on her own, but since you're your own boss and all, you think maybe you could help her out once in a while?"

"Help out that cute young thing? Oh, yeah. Not a problem."

"Jace . . ."

"I know, I know. Hands off. Just yanking your chain. I'd be happy to help. I wanna see if that one roper has been following my advice anyway. Did he get his time down any since I worked with him?"

"He has, actually. You did good." He smiled at Jace's enthusiasm.

"Eh, it wasn't exactly rocket science showing him a quicker way to complete that tie-down, but I did what I could."

"You helped a lot and I appreciate it." Tuck felt a little better about leaving.

Jace, even with all his joking around, was basically a responsible guy. And the man practically breathed rodeo. Tuck had no doubt Jace would fill the gap left in the coaching staff just fine. As far as the gap he'd be leaving in the ROTC program, Logan, in spite of all his bitching, would have no problem covering Tuck's duties there, either. A local guy in the Army Reserves was interested in the position and willing to take over until Tuck returned.

The only thing left that still bothered him was leaving Becca, but unlike ROTC and the rodeo team, that wasn't such an easy fix. Tuck wouldn't find a replacement to fill the hole he'd be leaving in Becca's life even if he could. Though it scared the hell out of him, she might just find one on her own.

And that was exactly why he needed to go. He was too damned attached to her already. Well on the way to feeling for a woman the way he'd thought he never would again after the disastrous end to his marriage. If he stayed, he'd get more attached. They'd end up getting careless and eventually get caught, and she'd be fired.

"You're okay with going, aren't you?"

He glanced up and encountered Jace's intense stare. "I'm fine with it. Why?"

"You just looked . . ." Jace hesitated. "I don't know, worried, I guess. You've been there before. It'll be just like that, right?"

"Yeah. It'll be fine. I got a lot of loose ends to tie up before I go. And I'm leaving for my parents' house tonight, so I needed to get everything OSU related out of the way now. That's all." He hated hearing himself say those words. *Loose ends*. Becca was many things to him, but that was not one of them.

"Well, I'm here for you. Whatever you need. And don't worry about the rodeo team. That loose end's been tied good and tight."

Good and tight—just like the knots saying good-bye to Becca this morning had tied in his gut. He'd thought it would be easier on them both to say their final good-byes this morning, after spending the night together, than it would have been later on today when he was busy getting ready to leave. It hadn't been. For the last few hours, he felt as if he'd been punched, and the feeling didn't seem to be going away any time soon.

Chapter
Twenty-four

The Kunar Province, Afghanistan

All of the early-morning workouts with the cadets hadn't prepared him for this. When—if—he ever got back to the States, he'd give Logan a piece of his mind about the ROTC training. Because even though Tuck had been deployed to Kandahar, and had kept himself battle ready during his year on the faculty at OSU, nothing had prepared him for what he found here in the mountainous region that lay between Eastern Afghanistan and Pakistan.

These mountains broke both men and machinery. Make that American men and machinery, because it seemed the locals had long ago figured out how to use the terrain to their advantage. The proof was in the numbers. The company he'd joined had a disproportionately high percentage of both contact and casualties compared to elsewhere. One reason they were happy to take Tuck. They had to rotate in new men to replace those sent home either wounded or, sadly, in body bags.

And today was supposed to be a fairly easy assignment. Tuck and his team were hiking into position to provide overwatch for a foot patrol. But for a man not used to these conditions, the simple mission felt more like climbing Mount Everest.

Pain seared through his lungs, and he had to wonder if it had been the mountain or the enemy that had gotten to all those men.

The weight of all he carried had long ago made various body parts go numb. Water, food, weapons, ammo, first aid kit, body armor—it all added up to nearly half his body weight. At one point during the five-hour hike, Tuck got so hot he started to feel icy cold. Yet he kept going. To fall out would put all of them in danger. He, the new guy among men who'd already been here for close to a year, was not going to be the soldier to do that.

Even when it hurt so bad the only thing a man could focus on was stopping to rest, he knew there was still more inside, and he dug deeper to find it. There was always more. Mind over matter. Man versus mountain.

The echo of a single gunshot bounced between the peaks, and every man around him dropped into a crouch. Tuck dropped as well. He crab-walked to the edge of the path until his back was pressed flat against the rock, wondering if there was a sniper in the area, until the sound of machine-gun fire cut through the silence. Bullets began hitting all around them, pinging into the dirt and sending bits of loose shale into the air. Short bursts of rapid fire interspersed with the slow *pop, pop, pop* of slower rounds.

". . . we have TIC. I repeat, we have troops in contact. Request air support. Over." Between the louder bursts, Tuck heard one of the guys on the radio, calling back to base with their coordinates.

He glanced to his right, where Conseco, a soldier of Cuban descent from one of the tougher areas in Chicago, crouched calmly next to him. Beneath the dirt and sweat, his expression looked as calm as if they were waiting for a bus. The man glanced down at his boot as a puff of dirt was thrown into the air inches from his toes.

"That was a close one." Conseco made the statement

with a kind of detached excitement. Kind of like a fan watching his favorite baseball team on television when the runner had just made it safely to home plate. Like there wasn't anything he could do about it either way, but he was happy it had all worked out.

Incoming enemy fire from AK-47s, belt-fed machine guns, and RPGs all rained down hell upon them. It was apparent this wasn't a single sniper, but a full-out ambush.

"What do we do?" Tuck couldn't take his eyes off the enemy fire hitting the ground at their feet; he couldn't stop listening to the boom of the rocket-propelled grenades that had missed their mark. He felt more like the new guys everyone here called cherries than a man with nearly a decade in the service as well as combat experience behind him.

Conseco shrugged. "Wait 'em out. We're pinned down. We move, we die. They'll either run out of ammo or the Apaches will get them."

Tuck looked around him. Even the 240 gunner was pinned down, as helpless as the rest of them in spite of the thirty-pound machine gun he cradled against his chest as if it were his child.

"How long will that take? For the air support to arrive."

The Taliban fighters must have been on the next ridge, firing down at an angle. It was like shooting fish in a barrel. If Tuck and Conseco hadn't been able to get to the crevice barely as deep as their bodies . . . He didn't want to even think what would have happened. The rest of the squad had taken similar cover.

"An hour. Maybe less if we're lucky. Depends." Conseco shrugged.

At times the shots pummeling the area where the squad had taken cover were so close together it made one continuous din.

"What the hell? I thought with the drawdown there

wouldn't be much contact here anymore." Tuck shouted over the noise.

Conseco's response was a snort. "I guess the Taliban didn't get that memo." When Tuck frowned at him, he continued above the noise. "Don't get me wrong. The guys in the valley, before we pulled out of Korengal in two-thousand-ten, used to get hit like five, sometimes seven times a day."

"Seven times *a day*?"

"Oh, yeah. My buddy was there. They had a guy hit in the leg while taking a nap in his bunk. They'd get shot at while minding their own business trying to take a piss. We're usually only hit outside the wire. So yeah, I guess you can call that not much contact."

His back against the wall, Tuck was still trying to absorb that he supposedly had it good compared to some others when Conseco asked, "So, you got a girl at home, Jenkins?"

The rounds had slowed, but they sure as hell hadn't stopped. Maybe the enemy fighters were starting to run out of ammo and were forced to ration it. Good. Maybe they'd run out completely. That thought gave him a small amount of hope.

"You want to talk about home now?" Tuck still had to raise his voice to answer.

Conseco shrugged beneath his body armor. "Sure. Why not? You got something better to do?"

Tuck glanced at him. "I'd feel better if I were shooting back."

"We all would." Conseco blew out a sound of disgust. "If you'd like some ventilation holes in your helmet, go ahead. Stand up and try to take a shot. Otherwise, we're stuck here waiting."

They exchanged looks, and Tuck realized Conseco was

right. He gave in and answered. "No, I don't have a girl at home. Well, I kind of did. But not really. I don't know."

Tuck realized how pitiful that sounded. He laughed, but it was short, more like a wheeze as the bullets peppering the ground in front of him kicked up enough dust to make him choke.

"You don't know?" Conseco laughed.

"I'm not quite sure." Pressing back as close as he could against the wall—and safety—Tuck admitted the sorry truth. "I didn't mean to, but I think I might have totally ended any chance we had by leaving."

That he wasn't sure where he stood with Becca, where he wanted things to stand between them, was a pretty sad state of affairs. Especially since today could be his last.

"Sounds like there's a story there." Conseco angled just his head toward Tuck. "Tell me about her. What happened?"

"Seriously? You want to hear it all?" The incoming fire had slowed to sporadic bursts, making talking a little easier.

"Sure, I'm bored and we could be here a while. It'll help pass the time. I've heard all these other sorry bastards' stories a hundred times over the last nine months. It'll be refreshing to hear something new for a change."

Tuck had never felt so helpless, and Conseco was bored and wanted to chitchat. But in this situation the man next to him was the one with experience, and like it or not, Tuck was the cherry.

Since he hadn't been struck yet, he calmed himself enough to glance around them and reevaluate the hellish situation. Shooting back was out of the question. Even if his weapon was trained in on where the insurgents were hiding, which it wasn't, to get a clear shot he'd have to expose himself to their hail of bullets.

His teammate was right. The best thing to do was sit and wait for air support, or for the bad guys to run out of ammo. Either way, it was going to be a little while.

"All right." Tuck shrugged and was reminded of the weight of his pack braced against the rock wall.

Even though he'd never told the story in its entirety, not even to his best friends, he swallowed away the dry grit in his mouth and launched into the tale of two city girls who walked into a rodeo one July night in Oklahoma. He somehow felt he had to tell it, from start to finish. That another living person knowing it all would keep the memory alive because there was a very real chance he wouldn't leave this valley. At least not that way . . . alive.

He glossed over the very intimate bedroom details, but told Conseco everything else, right down to his deciding to leave when they got caught in the library on the security video and how he thought he had to, before they both got into trouble.

When he'd finished, Conseco shook his head. "That's a hell of a story. Sounds like true love to me. Like a damn fairy tale."

"Nah. We weren't that serious." The statement rang so false in his ears, he elaborated to make it sound more convincing. "Just having some fun together."

That didn't sound any more truthful.

Love. The other reason Tuck had left in such a hurry. Love was a word Tuck had deliberately avoided saying or even thinking, yet Conseco spat it out easily. Maybe daily near-death experiences did that to a man. The fear of love and getting hurt by it was starting to feel ridiculous as real pain, the kind inflicted by automatic weapons, loomed literally at their feet.

But as for the fairy tale? No. Tuck couldn't embrace that concept even a little bit, because being crouched against a rock face braced for the impact of the bullet that would

take his life while Becca was back in Oklahoma totally unaware of why he'd really left was certainly no fairy tale
ending.

"Here's my question." Conseco paused to spit a dribble
of tobacco-tinged saliva into the dirt. "If you were having
so much fun, then why the hell did you leave her and volunteer to come to this shit hole? I would have said fuck it
to the university and their fucking rules and kept seeing
her on the sly."

Another bullet hit close enough to Tuck he could hear
the whoosh of it passing his ear. To hell with it. If this
were the last thing he ever said, the last man he ever spoke
to, he intended on speaking the truth. That old saying was
true. There were no atheists in foxholes, and though he
would give a year's salary just to have a foxhole to hide in
right now, this shale crevice was close enough.

As if Conseco was a priest and Tuck at confession, he
finally spoke the truth. "I guess I left because I love her."

"Did you tell her you love her?" Conseco's dirt-
encrusted brows rose beneath the rim of his helmet.

"No." A round hit particularly close, sending shards of
rock into Tuck's face. He closed his eyes to protect them
and then blinked away the dust.

Conseco let out a snort. "You should have."

Didn't Tuck know it.

Chapter
Twenty-five

Through the haze of sleep, the ringing fit right into her dream. Becca crawled her way up out of the darkness and back to reality, or at least the fuzzy approximation of it.

She took a second to register it was her cell phone's ringer blaring away on the bedside table. She'd stayed up late looking at websites dedicated to troop support until she'd finally gotten so tired she'd given up and gone to bed.

It was crazy. She hadn't heard a word from Tucker since he'd left weeks ago—not a phone call or an e-mail or even a damn letter—but she was still obsessed enough to go searching for information about soldiers online just so she'd feel connected to him.

She'd been dreaming she was baking cookies to send to the troops, and the oven timer began to ring, over and over again. Consciousness now told her it hadn't been the timer.

There were no cookies. Only sleep deprivation and a really loud cell phone ringtone.

Becca flung one arm in the general direction of the annoying object and eventually connected with it. She juggled the phone, nearly dropping it as she somehow managed to answer. At least she assumed she'd answered it.

The ringing stopped, which was a relief, but there was no way she could focus her eyes on the glaringly bright display to see if she'd actually hit the right button or the caller had just given up.

Only one way to find out. She pressed the phone to her ear and said through what felt like a mouthful of cotton, "Hello?"

"Becca?" The static on the line cut away enough for her to hear a male voice, unclear and far away.

"Tuck?" Even in her semi-asleep state she knew it was he. She struggled to sit up against the pillows, more alert. Her heart began to pump blood faster through her veins just from hearing his voice. "Oh, my God. Are you okay?"

"Yeah. I'm fine. How are you?" he asked.

How was *she*? She wasn't living in a war zone like he was. Becca didn't need niceties from Tucker. She needed assurances. "I'm worried about you."

There was a pause. The amount of static on the line made her wonder if maybe he was speaking and she just couldn't hear him until he finally said, "Please, don't worry about me."

"How can I not considering where you are?" The pitch of her voice rose with the question.

"Because your worrying about me won't change anything, and while I'm here I'd rather picture you exactly how I remember you. Living your normal life. Pawing through dusty old volumes of Chaucer in the library. Eating take-out pizza and barbecue at your place. It helps, believe me. You don't know how much."

"All right." She was willing to give him anything he needed to ease this deployment. "Can I send you something? Do you need anything? Sunscreen, bug spray, baby wipes, beef jerky, flip-flops for the shower, disposable razors . . ."

What else had she read the troops needed in that area? She racked her brain for any other items he might need or want.

He laughed, a warm, genuine laugh. The laugh she'd first heard that night at the rodeo when he was still just a cowboy, amused by her city girl ways. It was a really good sound.

"That was some list, darlin'."

"I read online at one of those troop support websites that's what guys like to have over there in the warmer months of the year. But it's going to get cold soon so maybe you need socks? Or hand warmers?"

He chuckled again. "No, I'm good. Really."

"I want your address anyway. So I can at least send you letters."

There was another pause before his answer. "Letters would be real nice." When it came, his voice had softened, all amusement gone.

"I wasn't sure if I'd hear from you." Becca hated the doubt and insecurity she heard in her own voice. "You've been gone a while."

And wasn't that the understatement of the year.

"I know. I'm sorry. Communications are hard. There are a few shared computers with satellite Internet set up, but only here at the firebase. We take turns rotating back every couple of weeks from the outpost. There's only radio comm there."

Outposts. Firebases. Radio comm. These were all words—and a world—so foreign to Becca, Tuck might as well have been speaking another language. She vowed her next foray on to the Internet for research would be to learn some of the lingo.

"I can't stay on much longer." His voice broke into her relief over hearing from him, because now he'd have to go and she'd be left to wonder and worry. Even so, she couldn't seem to bring herself to ask him if and when he'd call again.

"Oh, okay." She wrestled herself all the way into a sitting position and pulled open the bedside table. "Do you know your address so I can mail you?"

"Yeah. Got a pen?"

Thank God for her obsessive organizational habits. That, coupled with her love of office supply stores, meant Becca had pads of paper and multiple pens in every room of the apartment, as well as in her office at work. "I do. Go ahead."

Tuck hung up the call with Becca, feeling both better and worse. Her voice had made him homesick in the worst way, but hearing she'd researched what he might need was a comfort. At least it meant she was thinking about him while he was gone. He'd wrestled with himself for weeks about whether or not to call her and what to say if he did.

Now he was glad he had.

Back at his bunk he pulled off his body armor, grateful to be free of it, as usual. While he was stripping, he pulled off his T-shirt and draped it on a nail sticking out of the wall so it would dry. It was soaked with sweat from the hike from the outpost. It would be stiff with salt, but at least it wouldn't be wet. It felt good to have air hit his damp skin, even if it was the stifling air of their living quarters.

Of all the many things they went without here—fresh meat, television, air-conditioning, flushable toilets—he thought he'd miss sex the most on this deployment. It turned out his nostalgia for daily showers was running a close second. On days such as today, the shower might even win out over sex. Even sex with Becca.

He glanced around at the raw conditions they lived in

and chuckled one more time at the list she'd spouted off of things she'd thought he'd want.

Conseco lowered a magazine Tuck hadn't seen him with before. They must have gotten mail with the last drop off of supplies. "What you laughing about over there? Tell me. I could use some entertainment."

"I just called my . . . uh, Becca." He still didn't dare call her his girlfriend, but after Tuck's foxhole confession a couple of weeks ago, Conseco knew her name.

"And?"

"And she offered to send me razors and shower shoes." Tuck scratched at the stubble on his chin. He hadn't gotten to shave yet today. Or yesterday. He thought he'd shaved the day before, but he couldn't be sure. Conseco's stubble was even thicker and darker than Tuck's.

The big brass back at home or in Italy, or hell, even in Kandahar, would be appalled. He'd have to toe the line when they got back to the real world, but here and now, during the height of the fighting season, anything that took time and energy away from keeping themselves and each other alive was a pretty low priority.

They were so far away from anything resembling a real base, little things like being clean shaven fell by the wayside pretty quickly. He'd seen soldiers here run for the guns in their underwear during a surprise firefight. Since a .50-cal could shoot through a wall, Tuck figured it really didn't matter if you were manning that bad ass of a weapon in boxer shorts.

Even though he could walk around shirtless and stubbly and not get into trouble, he wished the showers were a little more frequent. Rotating from a barebones outpost with no running water, back to a firebase with limited showers, meant they walked around dirty. Basically they all looked like Pigpen from the Charlie Brown comics.

Conseco let out a snort at the offer of razors and shower

shoes. "Tell her if she wants to mail you something, she should send some nice pictures of herself. The less clothing the better. Those kinds of care packages are always appreciated."

Tuck laughed. "I don't think we're at that stage in our relationship."

"You two were doing the deed before you left, right?" One dark eyebrow rose in question.

"Yes." Tuck inwardly cringed, feeling a little guilty now he wasn't in the heat of battle that he'd spilled so many of the details of his time with Becca.

"Then you're at that stage. Trust me." Conseco raised the magazine resting on his chest, but it didn't stay there. He lowered it again. "And speaking of relationship—you tell her you love her on that phone call?"

"No . . . It didn't seem like the right time." Tuck rushed to explain when he saw the judgmental look Conseco sent him.

There wasn't even a lecture. Conseco simply pressed his lips together, shook his head, and went back to his reading.

Tuck didn't need him to say anything. He knew exactly what Conseco was thinking. Time was the one thing none of them could be sure of.

"By the way, you got a package. Jinx dropped it off. I told him to put it on your rack." Conseco delivered that news from behind the pages of his magazine.

There was a big brown envelope on top of his blanket. Not sure who would be sending him anything, Tuck frowned. Not that he was unhappy to see it. In a place where the only entertainment was a good firefight, a package was a welcome sight. He sat and picked it up to see who it could be from.

Tuck grinned when he recognized the return address. Good old Jace had sent him a package, though God only knew what he'd put inside. Probably something against the rules, like porn. Of course, way out here, who the hell was going to catch him or care if he had a girly mag under the mattress? He'd rather have a picture of Becca, though.

He tore the flap open and slid his hand inside to find a slick, colored poster the exact size of the eleven-by-seventeen-inch envelope. It took a bit of doing to slide it out without wrinkling it more than transit already had or getting it dirty because his hands weren't all that clean right now. In this place, everything eventually turned the color of dirt.

Finally he coaxed the poster out, and in front of him were the smiling faces of his rodeo team. He laughed when he saw Jace had somehow wiggled his way into the team photo. That was fine. Jace looked good there, grinning ear-to-ear at the end of one row of students. It was an advertisement for an upcoming charity rodeo the team would be competing in. Every member had signed it.

For a guy who was generally a joker and a dumbass, Jace could be really thoughtful sometimes. Just looking at the poster made Tuck smile, but it upped his homesickness another notch. He sized up an empty section of plywood sheathing and then glanced across the room at the other bunk. "Is it okay if I hang something on the wall?"

Conseco lowered his sports magazine and cocked a brow, pointedly glancing at the wall to the right of his bunk where there were numerous advertisements featuring scantily clad females. "I think that might be all right. I wouldn't hang a picture of your girl up there, though. That's just asking for trouble. The other guys are going to comment until you're good and pissed off. I can promise you that. I stick with the pros myself."

Tuck glanced at the Hooters calendar next to Conseco's head. "So I see."

"Here. You can have this."

A tack came flying across the room. Tuck caught it in mid-air. If nothing else, combat was good for your reflexes. "Thanks."

With his thumb, he pushed the point through the poster and sank it into the wood. "Home, sweet home." Tuck stood back and admired his work.

"What the hell is that?" Conseco frowned at the poster and swung his feet to the ground.

Apparently even though he didn't know what it was, it was interesting enough to get him up off his mattress to come over and take a closer look.

"That is the Oklahoma State University rodeo team," Tuck said with pride.

"I see." Conseco nodded. "And might I ask what the hell you're doing with it?"

He laughed. "I used to be their coach. Guess I still will be when I get back." Unless Jace refused to give up the position, in which case he supposed they could share it.

"Rodeo coach. What the fuck do you know about rodeo?"

"I took the state championship in bull riding and came in second in roping." When Conseco stared at Tuck as if he'd grown dick antlers, he elaborated. "I won the state buckle years ago. Back when I was on the circuit full-time, before I enlisted. Nowadays I only ride bulls. I haven't roped competitively in years. With work and workouts, I just don't have the time it would take to get a good cutting horse up to competition level . . . What?"

He stopped when he noticed Conseco's mouth had dropped open.

Tuck laughed. "Close your mouth before something flies in it."

He did, but it was only to open it again. "You're kidding me, right?"

"Um, no. Why?"

"You've been here for what? A month? And you never told me you're a fucking cowboy?"

"It didn't come up. I guess I never thought it was important." Tucker shrugged.

"That you willingly get on the back of a freaking bull and ride on a regular basis isn't important?"

"No. Not really." They were in a province where there was a very real chance some of them wouldn't make it out. And if they did, it could be with a good amount of shrapnel inside them. The fact he hopped on a bull a few weekends a month didn't seem all that important in comparison. "Sorry. I didn't think you'd care. I did tell you I met Becca at a rodeo."

"Yeah. I thought you were there to watch. Not, you know, do. A bull rider? Jesus!"

Tuck had played football in school. He wondered if he'd get shit for not telling Conseco about that as well. "Anyway, now you know."

"Yes, I do. And from now on, your name is Cowboy."

"Oh, no." Tuck shook his head. "You've been calling me Jenkins since I got here. No need to change now."

"Only because I was waiting for the proper nickname to present itself. Now it has, don't think I'm not taking full advantage of it."

"Come on. Everyone is not going to start calling me something different a month into my being here."

"Yes, they will. Do you know Jinx's real first name?" Conseco looked a little too smug for Tuck's liking.

"No." He had a bad feeling his answer was going to work against him.

"Exactly." Conseco gave him a single nod of victory. "And I didn't give him that name until we were a good month into the deployment."

"And how exactly did he earn his handle?" He was almost afraid to ask.

ONE NIGHT WITH A COWBOY   243

"Every damn patrol the kid went on got hit. Meanwhile, there were other patrols going out without him
who never saw any action at all. After about the third
time, I finally said, 'You know what, kid? You're a jinx.
That's going to be your name from now on.' And that
solved the problem. After I gave him that name and we all
started calling him Jinx, he went out on another patrol and
not a shot was fired." Another nod from Conseco told him
the story was over and he had no hope of getting rid of his
new name.

Conseco pulled a marker from a pocket, making Tuck
wonder what else he had in there, but only until he was
distracted by what the man was doing. He grabbed a
grenade and wrote in big bold letters COWBOY. He
handed it to Tuck. "There. Now the bastards will know
who's shooting at them."

Tuck accepted both the grenade and the nickname with
a sigh. "Thanks."

"Not a problem." With a grin, Conseco flung himself
back onto the mattress, his torture obviously done for now.

Thompson came through the door with a bang and a
curse, stripping out of his gear and shirt as he walked.
"Why is it still so fucking hot out there? Isn't it like Sep-
tember or October? Shouldn't it be cooling off?" He
glanced up and nodded to the two of them already inside.
"Conseco. Jenkins."

"It's Afghanistan. Nothing happens like it's supposed to.
And we call Jenkins Cowboy now," Conseco informed
him.

"Okay." Thompson barely spared a look for Tuck and
then flopped backward onto his bunk. He closed his eyes,
apparently accepting the name without question so he
could take a nap.

With Thompson napping and Conseco back perusing
his magazine, Tuck was left to read the letter that had

come in the envelope with the poster. Jace wasn't exactly a wordsmith, but he got his point across. Tuck was laughing out loud reading Jace's description of how he'd gotten on a practice bull to show the kids how it was done, only to end up hanging from the rails as the bull came after him. He had just opened his mouth to relay the story to Conseco when an explosion in the distance had all three of them on their feet.

There wasn't time to wrestle into his wet T-shirt. Tuck pulled his body armor on over his bare torso and reached for his weapons.

As the three ran out the door, there was the sound of answering fire.

Conseco was right. Tuck should have told Becca how he felt, but there was no more time for regrets as they ran for the Hescos and dove for cover behind them.

Chapter
Twenty-six

Becca barely cleared the doorway and had just dropped the handle to her suitcase when Emma enveloped her in a huge, sisterly hug. "I'm so happy to have you home."

"Thanks, Em. Me, too." It felt good to be back in New York, where everything seemed as familiar and comfortable as an old pair of shoes. And where she didn't imagine she saw Tuck's truck driving down the road, and she didn't get sad while trying to eat her take-out dinner because it reminded her of him.

"I'm still mad at you for not letting me pick you up at the airport, though." Emma finally released her so she could take off her coat and scarf.

"I told you, there was a special deal on rental cars for the holiday weekend. It made sense for me to get one so I can run errands while I'm here."

"I guess, but you know I would have driven you anywhere you wanted to go."

"I know." But she probably also would have had comments to make about Becca driving over to Vassar on the way from the airport to say hello to her former co-workers—and see who'd replaced her.

It was well worth the eighteen dollars a day plus tax for the rental just to have the freedom from Emma's lectures.

Now all Becca had to do was free herself from the demons of her recent past. It seemed she was more obsessed with them than ever. Especially one in particular. Tucker.

She hadn't heard from him in what felt like months. Not since that one and only call. Though it was probably closer to just a month since he'd called, it was still too long. All that time left her wide open to obsessively worry about him. About whether he was all right.

That worry had soon turned into anger. Why hadn't he called? Surely he could get one little communication out. He had before.

While she was angry with him, she remembered how mad she'd been about being let go from Vassar. And since she was back in New York, why not obsess about her old job? It was all a vicious cycle.

But as she stood inside the warmth of Emma's home, the anger faded. Acceptance had begun to set in. Her job was gone. Tucker was gone. Holding on to anger wouldn't change any of that. Seeing how the rest of the professors had all taken on extra classes in addition to their usual workload because of the budget cuts and her dismissal, she really couldn't be angry about that anymore.

It was as if she'd gone through the stages of grief. What were they again? Denial. Anger. Acceptance. There were a bunch more she couldn't remember right now, but she was fairly certain she'd run through them all since Tucker had told her he was leaving for Afghanistan.

Now she simply felt tired. Exhausted really. It came on suddenly. As if she'd walked into Emma's house and all the hot air keeping her balloon afloat whooshed away, leaving her deflated. Her energy and her spirits sinking after she'd worked so hard to keep both up for her students and for Tucker's sake.

Maybe being back in a familiar place amid people who

loved her had done it, allowed her to let go. She felt too tired to even remain upright any longer. "Can we sit?"

"Of course. Sit. I'll open wine and then we can catch up." Her sister headed toward the kitchen.

Becca accepted Emma's offer of a seat, but catching up with her sister might be beyond her at the moment in her current state. "We talk at least once a day on the phone. What do we have to catch up about?"

"I don't know. We'll find something." Emma returned with a corkscrew in one hand and a bottle of red wine in the other, and Becca had no doubt her sister was right.

"Oh, my God. I knew I had something I had to tell you." Emma planted the bottle on the table so hard, Becca feared it would break. She spun toward Becca on the couch, hand on her hip. "You won't believe who I saw this morning while I was out running errands."

"I don't know. Who?" The sofa back cushioned Becca's head nicely. It was so comfortable, she could probably fall asleep right here. If Emma wasn't still talking . . .

"Jerry." Emma announced it with a scowl.

That name got Becca's attention. Tired or not, she sat bolt upright.

Jerry—the one loss of her past she had managed to not obsess over. Unlike her former job and her former . . . whatever Tucker had been or currently was, she had no regret that Jerry was gone from her world. She didn't even like the intrusion of his name being mentioned now, keeping her from the wine her sister had yet to open.

"And?" Becca cocked a brow.

"And he was feeling me out for information."

"About what?"

"About you."

Oh, this was not good. "Emma. I seriously hope you didn't give him any."

The rotten bastard didn't deserve any information about her.

"Becs, I had to tell him something. He was being such a cocky ass."

What else was new? Becca groaned. "Oh, God. What did you tell him?"

"Just that you'd gotten a great new job at OSU with an advancement to associate professor."

All right. That wasn't so bad, but knowing Emma, that wasn't all. "What else?"

"Well, after he started saying how he was sure you'd taken a huge loss selling your condo in this market, I had to tell him you didn't sell. That you rented it fully furnished to a wonderful tenant and were making a nice monthly income from it."

Not exactly true, but the rental income covered the monthly mortgage and that was really all she wanted.

"All right. That's fine. You didn't say anything else about . . . anything, did you?"

"Like what?"

"Like Tuck," Becca accused. She held her breath, hoping the subject hadn't come up. That sneak Jerry shouldn't have the privilege of knowing anything about her personal life . . . such as it was.

Emma looked insulted. "No. Of course not. What do you think I am?"

She thought it best not to answer that question. Instead she eyed the still corked bottle Emma had abandoned on the table. "That wine coming anytime soon?"

"Oh. Yeah. Sorry." Emma cringed and reached for it. "But I think it's good Jerry knows you've not only moved on with your life, but you're also doing really well."

"I guess." Still, even if it was only about her job and apartment, Becca hated the idea of his knowing anything

at all about her after the cowardly way he'd ended their relationship.

The blessed wine was winging its way toward the sofa,
transported by the hands of Emma, when Becca's cell
phone rang.

"What now?" She'd been so close to finally relaxing.
Becca let out a sigh filled with all of her frustration and
glanced at her phone. The number was a local area code,
but unfamiliar. Wondering who it could be wouldn't get
her the answer, so she hit the button and said, "Hello?"

"Miss Hart? It's Jim Mooney."

"Uh, hi." Who the hell was Jim Mooney?

With one wineglass in each hand, Emma perched on
the sofa and whispered, "Who is that?"

Becca shrugged and silently mouthed, "No idea."

"Um, I'm at the condo and there's a man here who says
he used to live in this apartment with you, and the wall
unit belongs to him. He wanted to take it today."

Jim. The condo. The pieces began to fall into place. Jim
was her tenant, though his checks were imprinted with
James R. Mooney III so it was no wonder it had taken her
a few seconds to put it all together. But it was the other
piece of the puzzle that had her blood pressure rising until she could hear the pulse pounding in her ears. "Jerry is
there?"

"Yes, that's the name he gave me."

"There right now. Inside the condo?" She was having
trouble wrapping her head around that concept. How dare
Jerry think he could go to her condo and try to take the
furniture.

"Yes. I didn't want to turn it over to him without
checking with you. And I kind of was counting on the
shelves staying here. I've got my TV and my stereo—"

"Oh, no, Jim. That wall unit comes with the apartment,

and if he tries to take it, call the police. I'm on my way over now."

"But I thought . . . Aren't you in Oklahoma?"

"No, actually. I'm home visiting family. I can be there in five minutes. If you could ask Jerry to wait outside for me, I'd appreciate it. And if he doesn't want to go, tell him not only will I call the police, I'll also be calling my father, the retired cop who still has a sidearm."

"Oh." There was a pause, and then Jim said, "All right, then. I guess I'll see you in a few minutes."

She might have scared her tenant off for good, but it would be worth it. Becca disconnected the call and stood. "Son of a bitch! You won't believe this. Jerry is at the condo trying to steal the wall unit."

"What?"

"I'm sure he got the bright idea from talking to you this morning. When he heard the furniture was here but I was in Oklahoma, he probably figured he could get away with telling the renter it was his and it would be too late for me to do anything about it by the time I found out." Becca's blood pressure rose so high she felt light-headed.

"Why would he do that? Does he have any claim to it?" Emma stood, glass in each hand, looking like she didn't know what to do.

"No. I mean he paid for half of it when he moved in, but that's because he needed it for all his damn video game equipment."

Emma waffled her head side to side. "Well . . ."

"Don't you defend him." Becca gave her sister a scathing glare. "If he wanted it, he should have taken it when he moved out. And he should have given me my half of the money back. He didn't. He left it and he can't come get it months later."

"Then by the same token, if you're going to keep it, you owe him half the cost—" Emma took one look at

Becca and clammed up. "Never mind. Um, do you want me to come with you?"

"If you want to." Becca had her coat on and her purse in her hand when Emma trotted after her. She eyed the wineglasses still in her sister's hands. "You can't bring that in the car."

"What if I get a to-go cup?"

She frowned deeper. "No."

"Oh, you're no fun." Emma put the glasses down on the table in the entry hall and grabbed her coat. "I hope this doesn't take too long."

"You and me both." Becca opened the door and got hit with a brisk November wind.

"Is your tenant cute?" Emma followed her out and pulled the door closed behind them.

Becca frowned at her sister. "You need to get yourself a boyfriend."

"I'm trying. Why do you think I asked about your renter?" She pulled the two sides of her coat tighter together. "Come on. Let's go so we can get back. I have a lasagna in the oven."

That news gave Becca one more reason to dispense with Jerry quickly, before he ruined her appetite for Emma's homemade, extra cheesy and oh-so-tasty lasagna.

The drive to the condo wasn't a long one, but by the time they arrived, Jerry had already left. Perhaps the threat of the police, or their father, had been too much for him.

She'd always known he was a coward, so it was no surprise really, but it did make Becca extra glad she'd changed the locks right before her tenant moved in. She wouldn't put it past Jerry to try to use his key to sneak in when no one was home and help himself to what he felt he was entitled to.

After Emma had determined that Becca's tenant, though a handsome man for his age, was too old for her, they left again and headed home. She pushed through Emma's door more exhausted than before, but the smell of the lasagna and the sight of the wine greeted them, and that was enough to revive her spirits.

Becca gulped a swallow of wine, still so angry with Jerry she had no hope of even tasting it, forget about appreciating the flavor. "You know what really pisses me off?"

"Do tell." Emma grabbed her glass and headed for the kitchen, leaving Becca to follow.

"That I dated him at all. I wasted two years of my life on that man." Two years of her life were gone, and she wasn't getting any younger.

"So what are you going to do about it?" The sound of the oven door squeaking open accompanied Emma's question.

"What can I do? I mean I'd love to get revenge but . . ." Becca considered that idea.

Maybe she could somehow put bedbugs in his mattress. How would one go about obtaining and transporting those nasty things? Too risky. She'd probably end up becoming infested herself.

"I'm talking about Tucker. You've got a great guy who is obviously into you and all you keep telling me is how you don't want a relationship with him."

Becca had already made the comparison between the two men herself. Where Jerry seemed to run from any sort of confrontation as if his life depended on it, Tucker ran toward it. Literally, and his life did depend upon it. "I was trying to not rush into something. After the disaster with Jerry, I thought that was the smart thing to do."

"Mmm, hmm." Emma had a knack for agreeing in the most judgmental way.

"What am I supposed to do? He doesn't call. He doesn't write, even though I've written him." She was getting pretty tired of this total lack of communication. Of course he was at war, but still. He'd managed to call her once. Surely he could do it again. Becca realized she'd somehow gotten back to the anger stage again, and took another sip of wine.

"Becca, come on. It's not as if he's ignoring you to go hang out with the guys to drink and play pool or pick up women. He's at war, for God's sake." Emma cocked a brow. "So let's move forward, past right now while he's somewhere in Afghanistan serving our country, and think about the future. What are you going to do once he's home?"

She hated to admit it, because her sister would just gloat, but Becca had no choice. "*If* he wants a relationship, and that's a big if considering he hasn't been in touch"—she watched Emma make a face that told her to move past that issue and continued—"then I'd be willing to explore getting serious with him."

Emma let out a huff. "You are unbelievable."

"What's the matter now?"

"You'll *explore* getting serious? You can't give in just one tiny bit." Emma shook her head.

"I did give in. I said I'd be willing. And you know what, I'll go one step further. When I get back I'll talk to his military friend Logan. He might be able to tell me more about where Tucker is and why he isn't calling." Because in spite of waffling between hope for a future together, and anger over the present, there was a steady undercurrent of concern for Tucker's well-being that Becca couldn't shake.

"That's a very good idea. I approve. Now, until then, can you please try to enjoy your visit?"

Becca was goal oriented, but there was nothing she could do about Tucker, short of looking up Logan's number and calling him during their Thanksgiving break.

She'd just have to wait and do as Emma suggested, enjoy her visit home. "Okay, I'll try."

After the hike from the outpost, Tuck and the squad finally arrived at the base, sweaty, dirty, and happy to be there. He dumped his pack next to the rack he used when he rotated back.

He let out a long breath. It was cooler now than when he'd first arrived, but hiking in full gear still worked up a sweat. "It's good to be back. I need a shower."

"I'm more looking forward to decent chow." Conseco dumped his own pack on the floor. The body armor and helmet he hung on a nail.

Thanksgiving had already come and gone without a whole lot of hoopla or any turkey, but real food cooked at the base rather than meals eaten out of foil packs at the outpost was something to be excited about. That, and the phones. Tuck needed to call home, and to call Becca.

Speaking of Becca . . . there was a stack of white, or what had once been white, envelopes on the one and only table in the room. One look at the 'to' and 'from' addresses penned in neatly looping feminine script told him they were all from her.

Letters. For him. His pulse quickened. That happened pretty often nowadays, but it was usually because someone was shooting at him. It was nice to feel excited about something other than combat for a change.

"I'm guessing that goofy-ass grin on your face means those are from your girl." Conseco dropped onto the cot.

"Yup." Tuck checked and he was grinning from ear to ear. He couldn't have controlled it if he'd wanted to.

"You tell her you love her yet?"

This had become a regular thing between the two of them. Every time they rotated back to the base, Conseco would ask the same question and Tuck had to deliver the same answer. No.

At least this time he had a good excuse to go along with the no. "I haven't called her because the last few times we were back here, the satellite was down."

"Don't need a satellite to mail a damn letter. And besides, I'm betting it's not still down now."

"We just got back . . ." Tuck noted Conseco's disapproving expression and gave in. "Fine. I'll go over now."

"Wait. Aren't you going to open those first? There could be some nice pictures in there." Conseco waggled his eyebrows.

"No, I'm not going to open them first." He would have liked to read her letters now, but talking to Becca would be far better. Then he could save the letters for later. Open them in private when Conseco wasn't watching him so he could savor the time with each one. He grabbed his body armor and pulled it on. "Be back in a bit."

"Fine. I'm taking a nap." Conseco waved a hand in Tuck's direction and closed his eyes.

After planting his helmet on his head and grabbing his rifle, Tuck headed out and across the base. He was just pulling open the door of the communications center—if you could call the tiny brick and mortar building with a few shared computers and phones inside that—when he heard the explosion.

Tuck ducked low and ran to take cover behind the ammo hooch. He tried to hear where the sounds of the attack were coming from. The base became a whirlwind of action around him with men running for their gear or their post.

Thompson sprinted the distance across the open area and dove, hitting the ground next to Tuck. He was breathless as he said, "The outpost is under attack."

The same outpost where Tuck had been an hour ago. He should have been there to help defend it. Instead he was here.

From his position behind the makeshift walls, he could look across the base and see Smith in the guard position manning the Squad Automatic Weapon. He opened it up, raining fire upon the hill where the insurgents were taking cover while they targeted the outpost. The nearly deafening noise drowned out the more distant sound of the squad at the outpost defending themselves against the attack. The SAW jammed from the heat created by the sheer number of rounds Smith fired. While he cursed loud enough for them all to hear it over the ringing in their ears, a radio nearby squawked.

Seconds later, Conseco joined them. "The forward observer radioed in. The fucking Taliban bastards are trying for the wire."

Tuck gripped his M4 tighter. "If they get inside the wire . . ."

"Yeah, I know." The expression on Conseco's face clearly showed what he was thinking. It was the same thing as Tuck and Thompson and every man there.

Every one of them knew if the insurgents made it inside the boundaries of the outpost, the men inside were on their own. The base's mortars were ranged in but how could they fire when the enemy was inside the American outpost? The .50-cal wouldn't be able to protect the soldiers on the inside any better. The base couldn't fire at the bad guys nor could air support when they finally arrived in an hour, for fear of hitting their own men.

The outpost would be overrun. For the occupants it would be a close-range battle to the death. Or worse— every American soldier's worst fear—they'd be captured. Dragged away to be used for propaganda. Put on television for their families, their country, and the world to see before the Taliban finally decided to finish them off on video.

In a choice between taking his own life and being taken alive by the enemy, there was no choice. Tuck touched the grenade in his pocket. They each carried one, just in case.

"Conseco, Thompson, Jenkins." With a radio to his ear, the captain shouted in their direction. "You three, get over there!" He issued the order and then spun to yell to Smith on the gun.

Without even remembering how he came to be there, Tuck found himself as part of the three-man relief team, sprinting full out across open terrain as Conseco and Thompson covered him. His pack was loaded with as much weapons, ammunition, and medical supplies as he could carry.

He hit the ground behind a shale outcropping, took a knee, and provided covering fire for Conseco and Thompson as they sprinted past his location. Then it would be his turn again. They'd move this way, bounding, until they covered the distance between the base and the outpost. It was like a deadly version of a child's game of leapfrog.

They were taking too long. The only thought in Tuck's mind was that he hoped there would be someone left alive to help by the time they got there. Actually, one other thing crept into his mind on the side of that mountain amid the gunfire and gnarly spiked-leaved holly trees. It hit him unbidden and was enough to have him setting his jaw and running faster than he thought he could, determined to save both his squad and himself.

Becca.

The sound of the enemy fire was overwhelming, while outgoing fire had dropped to almost nothing. Tuck guessed they were getting hit so hard and so steadily, the men inside couldn't even get to the mortars to fire back. And by now, the outpost's machine guns had probably overheated and jammed just as Smith's had.

If they took much longer to get there, it might be too late.

"Fuck the bounding. I'm sprinting the rest," he shouted to Conseco and Thompson, who'd just passed him and ducked behind cover.

"All right. We'll cover you," Conseco yelled back.

Tuck ran full out in a straight line toward his destination, covering as much distance in as little time as he could. He somehow made it to a spot right outside the wire without getting hit. The enemy was too damn focused on firing inside the outpost. He turned to cover his teammates and they matched his sprint, hitting the ground next to him, panting for breath.

Conseco picked up his radio and was mid-sentence with the captain, telling him they were at the gate and about to enter, when a heavy barrage of grenade blasts hit inside the wire. That was followed by a deafening sound from the radio. Conseco stared down at the device in his hand and then looked up and shook his head. "The frequency's jammed."

Which meant none of them had radio contact with each other, the outpost, or their backup at the base.

"We've got to get in there." Tuck sized up the distance to the gate, so close. Mere yards now.

Conseco glanced at them both. "One at a time will give them time to pick us off."

"Then we all go together. On three?" Thompson suggested.

"On three," Conseco agreed.

Tuck nodded and shifted his weight, ready to move. On Thompson's count of three, he bolted through the gate and into the middle of hell.

Inside it was a tough decision where to go first. They had to both defend the position and help the wounded. That raised the question of where the wounded were and whether any of them were still alive to be helped.

Ducking behind a Hesco, Tuck shouted, "Any suggestions?"

"They're targeting that bunker hard. There must be friendlies alive inside," Conseco shouted back.

But the incoming fire seemed to originate from everywhere. They were completely surrounded. How could three men defend an outpost against that? Frustrated, Tucker glanced at the sky. "We need those Apaches here now."

Tompkins shook his head. "Not gonna happen. We're on our own for a good thirty minutes more."

Tuck drew in a bracing breath and made a decision. "I'm going for the gun at the guard position." Maybe it wasn't jammed or out of ammo. Maybe there was just no one left to man it, as sickening a thought as that was.

Conseco nodded. "Thompson and I will get closer to that bunker. If there's anyone in there, they may need weapons or first aid."

"Okay." With one final glance at his teammates, Tucker turned toward the guard position, determined this would not be the last time they all saw each other alive.

Ducking behind cover when he could, and sprinting when he couldn't, he made it to the guard position. Not a surprise, he found the machine gun jammed. The men had obviously fired at the attackers until the barrel melted.

Tuck still had the weapons he'd carried in with him, and a good spot to shoot from. He scanned the area, trying to determine the locations of the incoming. That's when he saw it—a sight that made his blood run cold. An enemy fighter was dragging a heavily loaded tarp away from the outpost. The barrel of an automatic weapon stuck out from one of the folds. Tuck swung the sights of his 240 and fired, just as the enemy ducked behind an out-cropping.

"Fuck!" He shouted to nobody, because that was exactly who was near enough to hear him—no one.

He couldn't let those weapons remain in enemy hands. Not so they could be used to kill American troops in the foreseeable future.

Conseco and Thompson must have made it to the bunker. Tuck heard fire coming from the other side of the outpost now. His teammates would help the survivors while he went after those weapons. Getting hit by friendly fire was a real danger, but he couldn't radio anyone to tell them where he was with the platoon's radio frequency jammed. He'd have to risk it. The Apaches wouldn't be here for another half hour, and with any luck, he'd have gotten the bastard and those weapons back by then . . . or have died trying.

With adrenaline pumping, he left the relative safety of the outpost and set out in pursuit of the fighter and those weapons.

Chapter
Twenty-seven

The door to Logan's office was open, but Becca couldn't bring herself to walk through it. Instead she stood in the hallway of the military science building trying to gather the nerve to approach him.

Back in New York, with a glass of Emma's wine in her belly fueling her emotions, she'd been ready to fly to Oklahoma, barge right in on Logan, and demand he find out for her what was happening with Tucker half a world away. Now, it seemed her nerve had abandoned her along with her wine buzz.

What right did she have to question Logan or anyone else about Tucker? She had no claim on him. Nothing more than the fact they'd had sex.

But he had promised he'd call her again and hadn't.

"Miss Hart?"

Uh-oh. Now it was too late to change her mind and sneak away. Logan, being a soldier, must have sensed her standing there. Or maybe he'd heard her. That wouldn't have been too hard, the way she was having trouble breathing from her nerves.

Time to throw on a brave façade. Becca tried to ignore how her heart pounded with fear that she might not like Logan's answer to her question and pasted on a smile. "I thought we'd agreed on first names."

Logan donned a smile to match hers. "I do believe we did. My apologies, Becca. Please, come in."

"Thank you, Logan." A little flirting could go a long way. She was determined to see exactly how much information it could get her without having to disclose the extent of her relationship with Tucker to Logan since she didn't know how much he did or didn't already know.

"It's a pleasant surprise to see you again." The subtext of Logan's comment was clear to her—*what the hell are you doing here?*

How to play this? Lying was an option. More like stretching the truth actually. Really, really stretching it. "I've been meaning to stop by, and since I was nearby, I thought I'd pop in and say hi."

"Oh, really?" One dark brow rose.

"Mmm, hmm. So how have you been?"

"Good. Very good." His eyes were a little too intensely focused on her for her taste.

"The semester going well? The ROTC . . . stuff and all." Becca realized she didn't know enough about what Tucker taught to even fake asking Logan about it. That would change when he got back. She'd make sure to take an interest in his job . . . If he was interested in a relationship, that was.

"Yes, all of our *stuff* is coming along very nicely. Thank you." A smile tugged at the corners of his mouth. "And you? The English department treating you well?"

"Oh, it's great. Everyone's been so nice." She ran a hand along the back of the chair she was still standing near rather than sitting in.

"Good to hear." Logan nodded and then sat silently, hands folded.

Time to get this recon mission moving forward or he'd think she was a nutcase. "So, I . . . uh . . . haven't heard from Tucker in a while."

"That's not too surprising, given he's in Afghanistan."

"Oh, I know. He told me he was going there."

Logan wasn't giving an inch or making this any easier for her. He just stared, unblinking, waiting. Dammit. She was going to have to tell the truth.

She sat in the chair and leaned forward. "Look, Logan, I'm not sure what you know about my relationship with Tuck—"

He held up one hand. "I know enough."

Logan was obviously not a man who wanted details, so she decided not to go into that portion of the truth and skip right to the point of her visit. "Okay, well I'm worried. He called over a month ago from Afghanistan. He told me they had phones at the . . . I can't remember exactly, but there was a base and an outpost and he could call from one and not from the other. But the point is, he promised he'd call and he hasn't. He hasn't written, either, even though I wrote him a few times and now I'm worried something's happened."

Logan drew in a deep breath, then rose. He walked around Becca, closed the office door, and then went back to his seat. She wasn't sure why he thought they needed privacy. All she had done was ask whether he knew if Tucker was all right.

He folded his hands on the desk in front of him again. "I haven't heard from him, if that's what you're asking."

"You haven't?" Becca didn't know what to think of that. Maybe Tucker and Logan weren't as close as she'd assumed. They could be just coworkers and not good friends as she'd thought.

"No. But knowing the kind of . . . conditions at the firebase where he is, I'm honestly not at all surprised I haven't gotten a call."

Huh. She hadn't realized things were that primitive there. She figured today's modern army would have state-of-the-art communications and technology at their bases, but Logan was telling her otherwise, and she supposed he should know. "Hmm, then I guess I should be the one surprised he called me at all."

Logan's burst of a laugh had her looking up. "I'm not."

"You're not?" Becca frowned. "But you just said—"

"Becca, the man volunteered to go to the Kunar Province because of you. So no, the fact he called you from there is not a surprise to me. Not at all."

This visit was creating more questions than it was answers. "Okay, so then you're saying I *should* be worried he hasn't called again or I *shouldn't* be?"

"I'm saying I don't know. In that region anything is possible." Logan spread his hands.

This was not the reassurance she'd hoped for. "Can you find out if he's all right? I mean is there someone you can call and check? If he's busy and can't call, or the phones are down or whatever, that's fine. I'd just like to know he's okay."

Logan took his time answering again. This man should be in charge of military interrogations or something. It was really unnerving the way he kept pausing before he answered, all while staring at her. Finally, he nodded. "All right. I'll call his parents. If anything has happened, they'd be the first ones notified."

If anything has happened. Becca's stomach fell as she pictured the men in uniform knocking on the door of Tucker's parents' house to deliver the news that would change their lives forever. She'd seen it happen in movies and on television shows, but this was real life. Horrifying, sickening reality. She swallowed away the nausea. "Okay. But don't scare them when you ask, just in case nothing's wrong."

"Don't worry. I'm an old friend of the family. My parents still live next door to them. I spent half of my youth in the Jenkins kitchen eating cookies, so it's long overdue I call and check in with them anyway. They won't think it's out of the ordinary." Logan glanced at the watch on his wrist. "They'll both be at work now, but I can call later tonight."

"Good. That's good. And then you'll call me?" Knowing her worrying would soon be over once the Jenkinses told Logan everything was fine made Becca feel enormously relieved.

"Right after I talk to them. I promise."

"My number's in the faculty directory."

"Yes, ma'am." He nodded.

Everything would be fine. Logan would confirm with Tucker's parents that he was okay, he'd call her, and then she could rest easy knowing he was very busy there and probably couldn't call even though he wanted to.

"All right. I feel better now. Thank you."

"My pleasure."

"I'll let you get back to work." Becca stood and turned toward the door, about to take her leave when something he'd said hit her. "Um, you said something before. That Tucker went because of me. What did you mean by that?"

For the first time since she'd entered the office, Logan looked uncomfortable. "Nothing. I'm sorry; I misspoke."

Becca was a terrible liar, but that meant she was good at identifying other people with the same affliction. She zeroed in on Logan's face and decided his comment had definitely not been nothing. "Logan, what did you mean? Why in the world would Tucker go to this Kunar place because of me?"

"Becca, it's not for me to say. You'll have to discuss this with Tuck."

"That's exactly why I'm here. I can't get in touch with

him." Her voice rose higher along with her rising panic. She leaned both palms on the edge of the desk. "And if he doesn't ever come home and it's because of me . . ."

"I'm sure he's fine." The expression on Logan's face told her he wasn't sure at all.

"Logan, I swear to God, if you don't want a very loud and hysterical woman in your office, you had better tell me everything."

That seemed to scare him. Good. Becca took great satisfaction in that since he'd sure done a good job of scaring her.

She tried desperately to remember Tucker's exact words the last time she'd seen him, the day he'd told her he was leaving. She didn't remember anything about his going involving her. In fact, he'd acted as if he'd had no choice in the matter. That the army was sending him, or was that just what she'd assumed?

"Logan. Please."

He leveled his gaze and finally said, "He volunteered to go."

"Why?" She couldn't even begin to think of a reason.

"He left to save your job."

Chapter
Twenty-eight

The image filled Becca's laptop screen, frozen in the spot where she'd pressed pause. The shot of a combat boot sticking out from beneath a tarp.

That scene had been what finally got to her. Though since the whole documentary had her in cold sweats and feeling ill, perhaps it was more accurate to say that shot had been what finally knocked her into motion. Pushed her out of her frozen state. Her eyes riveted to the screen as she watched the physical and emotional breakdown of a soldier in the middle of a firefight when he's told his teammate is dead.

All of the horrifying sights and sounds of the ambush had been caught on video in the midst of the action, recorded in the same region where Tucker was right now.

Immediately after Logan had told her how Tucker had left OSU and gone to Afghanistan to save her career, she'd driven home in a shocked daze. The moment she walked in the door, she headed directly for her laptop and started to research the war in Afghanistan in earnest. Not like the other times when she'd cruised the troop support pages that focused on trivial things, like informing supporters not to mail chocolate to troops during the heat of the summer.

She didn't go to the feel-good sites where they posted

pictures of smiling men in uniform and upbeat thank-you notes from soldiers who'd received the care packages. Instead, Becca set out to do some real research about the region where Tucker had been sent . . . Actually, where he'd volunteered to go. Because of her. The knot in her stomach tightened.

Before today, she hadn't been able to tell where exactly he'd been sent. The address he'd given her for mail didn't say. She assumed a military APO address was kind of like a post office box. The mail got there, but the sender never knew specifically where the receiver was located.

But Logan had mentioned the name Kunar, and if nothing else Becca had absorbed some of Emma's search engine savvy. She searched and there was plenty to find on the happenings in the Kunar Province in Eastern Afghanistan, but what she discovered did nothing to relieve her worry. It only made things seem a hundred times worse.

Where was her phone? She needed her cell phone now. Her panic about Tucker overshadowed every other part of Becca's world. Small, everyday tasks seemed impossible. She was shaking so hard, she could barely hold the phone, forget about dial. Somehow she eventually managed to hit the right buttons and make the call.

When her sister answered, Becca's fears came tumbling out in a cascade. "Emma, I'm watching this war documentary and so many of them get killed. I still haven't heard from Tucker, and Logan hasn't called me back yet. What if he's dead?"

"Wait, Becca, slow down. I can barely understand you. What happened? Why are you crying?" Emma sounded wide awake even though Becca had called her when she knew her sister was usually sleeping. Even fully awake, Emma's voice coming through the phone did nothing to calm Becca's sobs. "Calm down and tell me exactly what happened."

She wheezed in a shaky breath and began, "I went to see Tucker's army friend before I left work. He told me Tucker didn't get assigned to go to Afghanistan. He volunteered to go."

"Why would he do that?"

"Because the university has a non-fraternization rule I didn't know about and he was afraid if he stayed, I'd get fired."

"How would anyone know if you were *fraternizing*?" Emma's emphasis of the word made it all sound as ridiculous now as it had to Becca in Logan's office.

"Apparently we got caught on the security video in the library." Thinking back, was that the last time she'd felt truly happy? Tucker, wanting her so badly they were like two teenagers making out against the stacks.

"Rebecca! You and Tucker had sex in the library?"

"No. We just kissed a little." Or a lot. She glanced back at the picture on her computer and got a cold hard reminder of exactly where Tucker was because of his attempt to do the right thing. "None of that is important now. What is, is that I spent all of tonight researching where he is. And . . . Emma, it's horrible."

"War is horrible, Becca. But remember, for centuries men have been going and coming back again. I'm sure he's fine. He'll call again when he can."

Becca glanced at the screen on her computer, and the tears began anew. She couldn't shake the images running through her head. What she'd read. The hatred the insurgents had toward Americans. The jihads against coalition soldiers. That one combat boot . . .

Emma's usual solution to everything—to look it up online—had backfired this time. Every piece of information Becca unearthed was worse than the last.

"No, Emma. Something's wrong. I know it."

"No, you don't."

"I do. I can feel it. I dozed off on the couch tonight and I had a nightmare. Tucker was lying there in the dark, all alone." Becca hadn't wanted to speak it aloud, as if that would make it true. "It's freaking me out. I know it sounds crazy and I don't even believe in stuff like that—premonitions or whatever, but—"

"Becca, stop. It was just a bad dream."

"But the number of casualties—"

"You can't think like that. It's war. Of course there are casualties. But there is always going to be a risk. When isn't there? I could get killed crossing the street."

"You don't understand. He's not just at war. He's in the worst place there is in the war. The place where like eighty percent of all the casualties of all the forces occur."

"Where are you getting these statistics?" The doubt was clear in Emma's tone.

"Online, the same place where you get your facts and statistics." She threw that indisputable detail at Emma as a defense against her doubt. "Look it up yourself and see. Search for U.S. military forces in the Kunar Province in Afghanistan. It's absolutely horrifying. Worse than I ever imagined. There was a reporter embedded there, and he wrote a book and took video and made a documentary."

"Tell me you didn't watch that documentary." Emma had used her mommy voice. Becca ignored that.

"I had to, Emma." And after watching it, she might never sleep again without nightmares. "The camera was there filming live during an actual ambush. Men were shooting and shouting and bleeding . . . Em, they showed . . ." She couldn't even finish the sentence.

"Okay. Rebecca Hart, you listen to me. You turn off your computer right now. You stop reading and watching anything about Afghanistan."

"But—"

"Don't you *but* me. Just do as I say. What you found

isn't up to date. Books and movies take time to produce and release. I'm sure things change month by month over there, so the situation could be totally different now. Remember the troop reductions we talked about when you first told me he was going?" Emma didn't wait for Becca to respond but instead surged on. "I searched it after you told me, and it's definitely happening. We're pulling troops out and turning things over to the Afghan government and their army."

"Really?" Becca drew in a shaky breath.

"Yes. And that wouldn't be happening if things were still as bad as you say they were when that reporter was there and the video was being filmed."

She hated to admit it, but what Emma was saying made some sense. The moment she hung up, she'd go back and check the date on the documentary again. Wouldn't it be wonderful if everything was settled down over there by now and she'd worried for nothing? "You really think so?"

"Yes, I do."

Becca would give anything to believe that. "Okay. I guess you're right." She wiped her eyes with her last remaining tissue. She'd have to buy more. She had a feeling she'd need them if Tucker didn't call her very soon.

"You have to try and get some rest, Becca. Staying up all night watching nightmarish videos and reading about troop casualties isn't going to help your state of mind any."

"I know, but I don't think I'll be able to fall asleep." She hadn't even been able to eat anything for dinner, which might be contributing to the sick feeling in her stomach as much as the fear.

"Just try to rest, and tomorrow go and get some of those over-the-counter sleeping pills."

Becca generally wasn't the sleeping pill type. Herbal tea and maybe an old movie on television before bed had always been enough to lull her into oblivion, but there was no way she'd be able to sleep with the sounds and images from that documentary's battle replaying in her mind. "All right, I will."

"Promise?"

"Yes. I'll go to the pharmacy and buy some, I swear." She needed to be well rested if only to keep herself on an even keel mentally.

If Tucker was able to get in touch with her, she didn't want him to hear how worried she'd been. She needed to be able to respond to his e-mail or phone call like everything was fine, so he could concentrate on keeping himself safe without her being a distraction. That was *if* he called or e-mailed. If he wasn't . . . the word *dead* echoed in her head and increased the nausea.

As that thought resurfaced once more, she pressed her hand to her mouth to stifle a fresh sob. She was a wreck. Emma was right. She needed to sleep, and to eat, and to calm down.

"I think I have some of those nighttime pain relievers here. They always put me to sleep." She'd cried herself into a headache anyway.

"Good. Go take those. It's the weekend. You don't have classes. Do you have anything else you absolutely have to do tomorrow?"

"No."

"Then you go and take two. Close the blinds and curtains tight, go to bed, and sleep late. And if you can't fall asleep in like half an hour, you get up and take another pill."

"But the label says the dosage is one to two tablets."

"You'll be fine taking three. Trust me. I've gone up to four."

Emma was usually a champion sleeper. Becca frowned. "When did you ever need to—"

"Never mind. This isn't about me. It's about you, and

you need to rest. You'll feel so much better after some sleep. Everything will look different in the morning when you're well rested."

Good, because even breathing seemed harder than it should right now. "Okay. I'll give it a try. I'll call you to-morrow."

"You better."

Becca hung up with Emma and had just pushed herself off the couch, when there was a knock on the door. The sound made all the calm Emma had instilled in her disappear.

She hadn't ordered delivery. Who could be here this late on a Friday night? Not for the first time, Becca considered how she should have pepper spray or something for times like this, but one look through the peephole allayed the fear she was about to be attacked.

It was Logan. She couldn't get the door open fast enough to let him inside. "Did you hear from his parents?"

"Becca." The expression on his face told her the answer. He knew something, and whatever it was, it wasn't good. If everything was fine, he would have called. He wouldn't have shown up here looking like this.

"No. Logan. No." She shook her head. It couldn't be true. "Do not tell me they told you he's dead."

When the room began to sway, Logan reached out and grabbed her by both arms. As she concentrated on the black letters spelling ARMY on the front of his gray sweatshirt, Logan held her steady and said, "We don't know he's dead. But he's missing."

Chapter
Twenty-nine

It was a hellish night followed by a pretty horrendous day. Hour after hour of waiting and uncertainty. Becca definitely was not going to fall to sleep and she didn't take anything to help. How could she when she was waiting for word about Tucker?

She'd never felt so alone. Tucker's mother was not handling the news well, and Logan had driven to be with her. But he promised if Tuck's family was notified with any updates at all, he would call. Day or night. Good or bad.

The phone rang more than ever, sending her into a near heart attack each time. Ninety-nine percent of the calls were from Emma, checking on her, asking if she'd heard anything new. A few times it had been Logan checking up on how she was doing. Asking one more time if she wanted to drive to Tucker's parents' house to wait with them.

That would have been interesting. How the hell would she have explained her position in his life? *I used to have sex with your son, before he volunteered to put his life in danger because of me.*

No, she was better off in her apartment where she could cry and look like a mess in private without adding to his parents' already overwhelming stress.

She'd grown so accustomed to jumping for the phone

each time it rang and seeing Emma's number come up, it was a shock to see an unknown number on the display.

"Hello?" Shaking, she answered and held her breath, waiting for what she hoped would be good news.

"Becca."

"Oh, my God. Tucker." Air whooshed out of her as she grasped for the arm of the couch and lowered herself onto the cushion. The sound of his voice and her relief at hearing it took Becca off her feet. "They told me you were missing."

"Yeah, I know. That wasn't quite the truth. I mean I knew where I was, but the radios were down so no one else did, but I'm fine."

"I was so worried." She bit back anything else, about exactly how panicked she'd been. About how she'd practically paced a hole in the floor of her apartment over the last day. Now was not the time to complain about how bad things had been for her, because they had to have been infinitely worse for him.

"I know. I'm sorry to worry you. I called as soon as I could. The minute I got off the bird here at base, the captain told me they'd informed my parents I was missing. I hung up with them and dialed your number. I figured I'd better call my mom first—"

"No, no. Of course. I'm glad you called her. She was really worried. Logan is there with them."

"Yeah. He was on one of the extensions on the house phone. He told me to make sure I called you."

"He told you to call me in front of your family? Didn't they wonder why? Or who I was?"

"Nah. I doubt it. No one said anything to me about it anyway. It was a little chaotic there with both my parents, and my brother and sister and Logan all in the house trying to be on the line at once." He paused. "It's really nice to hear your voice."

She let out a laugh that sounded too much like a sob about to break through. "It's good to hear yours, too."

That was an understatement.

She needed to tell him how she felt before it was too late and he hung up and something bad happened.

"Becca—"

"Tucker, I—" Her words tumbled out on top of his.

When they both stopped talking at once, Tucker said, "Sorry. You go first."

"No. It's fine. You first." She was having enough trouble breathing. She could use the delay.

"Okay. I wanted to . . . to tell you I love you." He paused for a second as her pulse thundered at his words. "You don't have to say anything, but I wanted you to know."

"I know I don't have to say anything, but I really want to. I love you, too." Relief flooded Becca. Now he'd said it, and she'd said it back, it seemed as if she'd opened the floodgates and she couldn't close them again. She began to babble. "When you get back I don't want to be only friends, or even friends who have sex. I want us to be together for real. And eat fried bologna sandwiches and go to the rodeo and . . . I don't know. Do everything and anything together."

"That's really good to hear. I'd like that." There was a smile in his voice.

Becca was smiling, too, until she remembered the damn university rule, which had caused this mess to begin with. Now was not the time to get into that with him. Not with him still a world away and in danger.

"And I don't care what I have to do to be with you. We'll work it out somehow. Okay?" She'd start looking for a new teaching position tomorrow if that's what it took to be with Tucker.

"Okay." He let out a huff of air. "God, I wish I could hold you right now."

"Me, too."

"No, really. You have no idea how much I've wanted to tell you how I feel, and to see you . . . and to touch you." His voice dipped low and sexy. It caused a craving deep down inside her.

"I know what you mean. Me, too." But as much as she'd love to fall into bed with Tucker and show him exactly how much she loved him, the relief of knowing he was fine now couldn't dispel the fear she could lose him again. "How much longer until you come home?"

"Things change a lot around these parts, but the platoon is scheduled to be here until spring." Tucker laughed. "Sorry about the shitty timing. I tell you I love you and then follow it up with how I won't be able to see you for months."

"It's okay. I'll wait as long as I have to."

"I'm sorry I didn't tell you how I felt before I left. I should have. I guess I was too chicken."

Becca wasn't certain she could have handled hearing it before he'd left anyway. Not when she'd been so confused about his leaving to begin with. Before she'd known the true reason why he'd left. Before she'd realized the depth of her own feelings for him.

"Tucker Jenkins, you are anything but chicken. You're a hero, just for being there where you are and doing what you do."

"No, not really. Any one of the men in my squad has done the same and more every day, but thanks for saying so. Look, I can't tell you how much I hate to say this, but I've used up more than my share of phone time."

"Of course. Go. It's fine."

"I don't know what's going to happen around here over

the next few days. The rotation schedule's . . . It's a little messed up right now, but I'll try my best to call you back soon. Okay? Keep your phone nearby."

"I will." It had been practically glued to her body since yesterday anyway while she had been waiting for word. After he said that, she wouldn't let it out of her sight.

"I love you, Becca."

She smiled as the tears escaped and spilled down her face. "I love you, too."

"Jinxy. Get the hell up and make room for the return-ing hero."

"Shut up, Conseco." Tucker rolled his eyes. If he hadn't been starving, he would have bypassed the base's building where the cook served a hot meal once a day, and headed directly for a shower and then bed.

"Sure, sure. No problem. Hero gotta sit, don't he?" Jinx shoved to the side and made room on the bench next to him. Not that Tucker wanted to sit with them given the mood these guys were in. Now that they knew he wasn't actually dead, it seemed they were determined to taunt him until he wished he were.

"Hey, Cowboy, tell us what happened. Did you really fend off a camp of enemy fighters with your bare hands?" Tompkins grinned.

"No, not bare-handed. I heard he used his cowboy bull-whip. You know, like Indiana Jones." Conseco made a whipping motion and sound.

Tuck shook his head and tried not to laugh. ·

Post-battle adrenaline, he guessed. They were still all riding a high from the attack, as well as trying to deal with the losses, each in his own way. With no more fighting as the enemy hid and licked their wounds, the squad needed an outlet. It seemed for some of them, teasing Tuck was it. Lucky him.

"Oh, is that how he did it?" Jinx nodded knowingly.

"Here ya' go, Cowboy." The cook planted a hot sandwich right off the grill in front of Tuck. "And bull riders don't use whips, you idiots."

"Thanks, Jonesy. And you're right. They don't." Maybe he had one ally here, after all.

"You see in bull riding, it's all in the hips. Like this." Jonesy made some pretty obscene hip thrusts with accompanying sexual noises, and Tuck sighed.

"Ah. Gotcha." Conseco laughed along with the rest of the guys in the room.

"Yeah, yeah. Real funny." Tuck scowled and took a bite of the sandwich. Since he was there and enduring this torture, he might as well eat. At least the food was good, even if the company wasn't.

"Cowboy. How many bastards were there at the weapons cache? I heard a dozen." Smith leaned across the table and spoke low.

Somehow the story had grown to epic proportions in the past few hours. After he'd tracked the fighter he'd seen dragging the weapons away from the outpost, Tuck figured out two things. One, he was far from help and outmanned, judging by the number of insurgents who'd been bombarding the outpost. A single shot would take out the fighter with the weapons, but it would also reveal his presence and location. He'd be hard pressed to retrieve those weapons and get back to the outpost before the enemy knew he was there and alone. And two, if this guy was bringing the stolen weapons to the place the coalition forces had yet to find, the spot where the bastards hid their stash, it would be more valuable for Tuck to follow him than to kill him.

The plan worked. The fighter brought the guns to a group of men, where there was much inspection of the booty and rejoicing before they hid it. All while Tuck hid

and watched. It had taken all night to wait out the fighters, who eventually left once the Apaches had stopped
sweeping the area and chewing up the hills with their fire.

It had taken Tuck another hour to convince himself
they were really gone before he dared try the radio. Thank
God it had worked. He called in his location in a whisper,
and more important, he told the captain the location of
the cache. He didn't dare go in to recover the weapons
since more than likely the cache was wired with explo-
sives. Instead, he moved as slowly and silently as he could
to the designated landing zone and waited to be extracted.

"No, man. Not twelve. There were only four," Tuck
told him.

"Four." Smith shook his head, slow and steady.

Smith and the forward observer at the outpost had been
friends. Tuck had learned the FO took a direct hit with a
grenade while on the radio calling in an update to the
base. That's what jammed the platoon's frequency.

Tuck knew what Smith was thinking. How could so few
do so much damage? "There were way more at the outpost, Smith. They just didn't make it back to the weapons
cache because we got 'em."

"Yeah, we got 'em." Smith nodded. He stared at his
plate for a bit. Not eating. Just staring. "And after the bird
picked you up? What happened?"

"We blew the shit out of their hidey hole."

Smith's head bobbed in another nod, and then he went
silently back to his meal.

Tuck finished his sandwich in two more big bites and
then stood. "Well, it's been fun, boys, but there's a shower
in my future."

He was filthy. Though what else was new? He dumped
his trash in the bin and headed for the door.

"Hey, Cowboy."

Resigned to getting more crap from his teammates,

Tuck stopped in the doorway and turned back toward Conseco. "Yeah?"

"You tell her yet?"

Tuck grinned. "Yeah. I did."

Conseco nodded once, then turned toward the grill. "Jonesy. Got another one grilled up for me?"

Tuck didn't miss the satisfied smile tugging at the corners of his teammate's mouth.

Chapter
Thirty

Becca held the cell phone in one hand and struggled to hit the button on her key to unlock her car with the other. Both tasks were harder than they should have been with her fingers chilled to the bone as they were.

"So what are you doing for Valentine's Day tomorrow?"

The better question was why did Emma sound so enthusiastic about this dumb holiday they'd both be spending alone?

She groaned and slid behind the wheel. "I'll be doing nothing, thank you. And thanks so much for reminding me of that depressing fact." She slammed the door and started the engine, willing the heat to kick in soon.

"Hey, at least you have a boyfriend."

"Yes, a boyfriend thousands of miles away in a war zone." She rolled her eyes.

Having a boyfriend didn't do her much good on a cold gray day like this when she would really love having Tucker and his big, warm body here to snuggle up against. He couldn't even give her an exact date he'd be coming home so she could anticipate when she'd have him back with her again.

"I don't care. It doesn't matter where he is. It still counts."

Emma was right. Becca's heart warmed just thinking about him. Tucker loved her, and she loved him, and whenever the stupid army let him come home, they'd be together. "You're right. It does count. At least I'm not totally without a boyfriend on Valentine's Day."

"Like me, you mean? Yeah. Thanks."

"Just teasing you, Em." She smiled.

"Mmm, hmm." Emma didn't sound convinced.

Becca didn't worry her sister would stay mad for long. She'd sent flowers and chocolates to be delivered to Emma's house tomorrow to make up for the fact she wasn't in New York. If she had been, they could have drowned the sorrow of their Valentine's Day lonesomeness together.

She gripped the ice-cold steering wheel, knowing full well she'd be home just about the time the car started to warm up. Next teaching position she applied for was going to be in Florida. Or maybe Hawaii. That idea was sounding better by the day. Especially today when she'd forgotten her gloves.

Funny how she'd remembered to order flowers for Emma, yet she couldn't remember to wear her damn gloves when she left the house. She'd been forgetting things a lot lately. This sit-around-and-wait game, wondering when Tucker would finally be coming home, was enough to make anyone a little scatterbrained.

"So what are you—" She'd been about to ask Emma what she had planned for tomorrow when her driveway came into view. The sight of Tucker's truck parked there had her stopping mid-sentence and slamming on the brake. "Em, I gotta go."

She hit the button to disconnect the call before she shoved the phone into her pocket. Swinging in behind his truck, Becca parked so crooked the car was nearly sideways. She didn't care as she flung the transmission into park, turned the key to off, and nearly choked herself trying to get out with her seat belt still latched.

She finally freed herself and opened the door.

Where was he? She'd expected him to be waiting in the truck, but it was empty. Becca sprinted for her door. It opened just as she approached, and there stood Tucker, inside her apartment and dangling her spare key between two fingers.

"I see you're still hiding this under the plant. I can tell you one thing, *that's* gonna change now I'm back." He looked so good in his jeans and a long-sleeve shirt with not even an inch of camouflage anywhere, it was enough to bring tears to her eyes. It was really over. He was back.

"Oh, my God, you're home." She flung herself at him so hard, she probably would have knocked over a smaller man.

He caught her easily, lifting her in his arms as he crashed his mouth against hers. The apartment door was still open, and her coat was still on, but she didn't care. All she cared about was that he was back, safe and sound and kissing her again.

With her arms and legs both wrapped around him, she pulled away from the pleasure of his lips to say, "God, I missed you."

"I can pretty much guarantee I missed you more." He kicked the door shut and carried her toward the bedroom. "I gotta warn you, it's been six months. First time's gonna be insanely fast and probably not very good."

And she could pretty much guarantee the second time would be very slow and incredibly good.

"That's fine with me." As if she could possibly care about that anyway, when he was home safe and about to make love to her.

"Do you know how much I love you?" He dropped her onto the mattress.

"Nope. I think you have to show me." Pulling off her coat, she tossed it to the side and watched as he toed off his boots—cowboy boots, *not* combat boots.

The significance of that seemed enormous as she struggled to keep the tears at bay. She didn't do a very good job.

Tucker kneeled on the edge of the bed, still dressed. "What's the matter, darlin'?"

"It's okay. Happy tears." She forced a smile as proof.

"Hmm. I suppose there are going to be more of those coming. At least I hope there are." Tucker grabbed her hand and pulled her upright until she was sitting on the edge of the bed with her feet on the floor. He reached into his pocket and dropped to one knee.

Realization dawned when he held the diamond ring in front of him. Her eyes widened. "What are you doing?"

She had a feeling she knew the answer, but she was too shocked to be sure.

"Rebecca Hart, will you be my wife?" He took her left hand and slid the ring onto her fourth finger. It was a tad big, but it would do for now.

Becca's throat felt too tight for her to even try to speak, not that she would have been able to through the tears that flowed freely now. She managed a nod and what sounded more like a squeak than any actual word in the English language, before she grabbed and kissed him.

He sank his hand beneath her hair and cradled the back of her head as he angled his. His tongue plunged into her mouth. His weight pressed her to the mattress. She could feel the outline of his erection crushed between them.

Tucker pulled back just enough to ask, "So that's a yes?"

"Yes." She laughed through the tears.

"Good."

Somehow, reality crept in through her joy. "But what about the university's non-fraternization rules?"

He smiled. "They don't count for married couples. I already asked."

"You asked?"

"Mmm, hmm." Tucker's attention seemed to be wavering as he stared at her lips and pressed his pelvis harder against her. "Well actually, Logan asked your boss for me."

She braced one hand against Tucker's chest and held him back as he leaned toward her lips. "Is that why you're marrying me? So we both won't lose our jobs?"

He pulled back and frowned. "You are a crazy woman, do you know that? I don't want to marry you because of a job. I want to marry you because I don't want to spend another minute of my life without you. Afghanistan proved that to me. I was going to give up my billet at OSU and hope to get recruiting duty locally so we could be together—together *and* married. But then I thought, hell, maybe being married changed the rules. Turns out, it does."

"Wow." It was a lot to absorb in a short amount of time.

He brushed one finger down her cheek. "You okay now?"

She flicked the remainder of a tear away, and the sparkle of the diamond caught her eye. "Yes, very okay."

"Good." He ran both palms down her sides and groaned. His eyes narrowed. "Can we get naked now?"

"Yes." She couldn't think of anything she wanted more.

Her cell phone rang in her pocket, where it had lived steadily since November when Tucker had told her to keep her phone nearby in case he could call.

"Give me." He held out his hand and raised a brow.

She wiggled the phone out of her pants and handed it to him.

Tucker glanced at it and then hit the button. "Hello, Emma . . . Yes, I'm back and I'm about to ravish your sister. It's probably gonna take all night, so don't call her. She'll call you. Oh, one more thing. We're getting married. Talk to you soon. Bye."

She heard Emma's squeals as Tucker disconnected the call and then went another step and pushed the power button, shutting the phone completely off. He glanced back at her as he tossed it onto the nightstand. "Thought I'd throw her a bone and give her the good news."

Becca laughed. "You're probably going to drive her completely insane, telling her that and then shutting off the phone."

"She'll get over it." He shrugged and crawled back over her body until he hovered above her. "Now where were we?"

At the start of a brand-new, wonderful life together. "About to get naked, I think."

Tucker leaned lower. "Oh, right."

Don't miss the next book in Cat Johnson's Oklahoma Nights series, *Two Times as Hot,* coming in October. Read on for an excerpt from chapter one, as plans for Becca and Tuck's wedding get under way . . .

"This'll be your first time meeting Bec's sister, won't it?"
Logan dipped his head in a nod. "Yes, sir. It sure will be."

"I'm not worried about Emma fitting in. Everyone loves her. It's the rest of the relatives I'm concerned about." Becca screwed up her face into a scowl. "My father, Mr. Punctuality, is beside himself they're not here an hour early and it sounded like my mother was already well into her sherry. She bought a bottle at the duty-free shop at the airport."

"Sounds like a hell of a start to a party." Jace walked through the door and scooped Becca into a hug that lifted her feet right off the ground. "Hey there, darlin'. You look great, as usual."

Speak of the devil . . . Jace gave Becca a kiss and set her on the ground.

Becca laughed. "Save some of those compliments for later when my relatives from New York are here and I'm tearing my hair out. I may need to hear them."

"You got it. And just send me the signal and I'll sneak you some booze too, if you want it." Jace winked at her and slid a flask out of his pocket.

"I'll keep that in mind. A visit with my parents might

require some alcohol." Becca glanced at Tuck. "I'm going to go see if your mom needs any help in the kitchen."

"Sounds good, baby." Tuck nodded.

Jace watched Becca leave as he walked over to Tuck. He stuck out one arm to shake the groom's hand. "Hey, man. How you holding up? I got the truck filled up with Diesel and coolers full of ice-cold beer. It's parked right outside, just in case. You ready to bolt yet?"

Logan shook his head. Typical Jace. As changeable as the wind. Sucking up to the bride with one breath, and offering to help the groom escape with the other.

Tuck's gaze cut to the doorway Becca had left through before he answered, "Not at all. I'm loving every minute of it. Nothing more fun than planning a big ol' wedding. You want a beer? I'm getting myself another one."

Logan glanced at his own bottle. He wasn't even half way done with his own beer yet but Tuck's was empty. Tuck might pretend he was calm, cool and collected about the wedding and all it entailed, but the empty bottle told another story.

Out of town relatives. Nervous brides. Rentals. Last minute errands. Saying *I do* for the rest of your life . . . Yup, Logan sure was happy he'd be on the ushers' side of the altar rather than directly in the line of fire like the groom.

"Definite yes on the beer." Jace answered Tuck and turned to extend a hand toward Logan. "Lieutenant Colonel Hunt, sir. What's the status of the Oklahoma State ROTC program?"

Logan laughed as Jace lowered his tone of voice and spoke more like a battalion commander than a bull rider. "A little slow right now since we're between semesters for the summer, but thanks for asking. How you been, Jace?"

"Good. Rodeoing quite a bit now that it's summer. Dragging Tuck with me when I can convince him to ride."

"Just don't break him, please. Tuck may be a bull rider part time, but full time he's one of my soldiers, and one of my department's best military science instructors. I need him with two good working legs for when we go back to working out with the cadets. Got it?"

"Sure thing. Let's just hope Becca doesn't break him during the honeymoon." Jace waggled his eyebrows. "As for rodeo, he usually ends up getting his ribs broken when he wrecks, not his legs, so we're good. Broke ribs hurt like a son of a bitch, but he can still run with 'em."

Jace grinned and accepted the beer Tuck handed him. "Thanks for the vote of confidence, Jace. And I only broke my ribs once or twice, thank you very much."

"Once or twice, my sweet ass. You can't seem to keep yourself out from under hoof. You're too tall for a bull rider, if you ask me. You need to be small and quick like me. You should have stuck with team roping."

Watching the two men bicker, Logan sipped his beer and stayed out of the fray. He wasn't about to enter that debate. Bull riders were crazy.

Sure, Logan had joined the Army knowing there'd be times during his career he was going to be up against an enemy who wanted him dead, but to get on the back of a bucking bull knowing you were going to be thrown in the dirt every damn time? Nope. Not for him.

While Jace and Tuck continued to banter—something about which bull Jace drew last time he rode—motion out in the driveway caught Logan's eye. He turned to watch through the window as a hot as hell woman in a short, black dress reached one long, bare leg out of the car. She stepped out of the open passenger door and even doing nothing but standing in the driveway, she was sexy enough to make a man take notice. Her blond hair and resemblance to Becca told him this must be her sister Emma.

Logan glanced at Tuck and wondered how bad of a

friend he was that Tuck's soon to be sister-in-law was giving him a hard-on. Just from his thinking about what the curves that dress accentuated so nicely would feel like beneath his touch.

Imagine if he ever actually got his hands on her?

An older woman and man got out of the front doors of the sedan and joined the blonde. They had to be Tuck's new in-laws. Their presence should have diminished Logan's amorous fantasies about Emma. It didn't. It seemed Emma had captured his attention and she wasn't letting go. He managed to block her parents right out as he wondered what her hair would feel like against his cheek while he ran his tongue down her throat.

"Hey, Tuck. It looks like Emma's here." Jace came to stand next to Logan at the window. He let out a slow whistle. "Boy oh boy, is she looking good."

The tone of Jace's voice made Logan turn to get a good look at him. The man had a knowing expression on his face that didn't sit well at all. "You know her?"

"Ohhh, yeah." Jace dragged the two short words out to be obscenely long. What the hell was that about? Logan's brows rose. He turned to glance at Tuck.

"Emma was here with Becca the first time she came to Oklahoma for the job interview at OSU. You know, the night she and I met at the rodeo," Tuck had answered without Logan having to ask, but that sure as hell didn't explain the rest. Such as why Jace was acting as if he and Emma had done more than just meet that night?

Those were details Logan was more than interested in having. "Yeah, I remember you telling me about the rodeo."

But not that Jace and Becca's hot sister from New York had had a little one night rodeo of their own.

Of course, Jace liked to exaggerate. It didn't matter if it was about conquering a bull or a woman. Logan had known the man for years through Tuck. Since the two had ridden on the rodeo circuit together before Tuck had enlisted in the Army. If nothing else, he knew Jace could throw the shit with the best of them. It was very possible nothing at all had happened between Jace and Emma, except in Jace's own overactive imagination.

He decided to run with that theory and see how things progressed. It was far better than the alternative—assuming Jace had a prior claim and having to back off. A lot could happen over a short period of time. Look at how one night between Tuck and Becca had changed both of their lives. Logan had an entire weekend and a wedding reception to work with. There'd be sentimental speeches and tears, music and a fully stocked bar. Everything to put the partygoers—and Emma—in the mood for romance.

Not to mention Logan had Tuck on his side, pulling for him, putting in a good word. At least Tuck had better be on his side. Jace was Tuck's friend, yes, but Logan was like a brother. Not to mention his boss and a superior officer. If it came right down to it, Logan would pull rank. Hell, he could order Tuck to put in a good word for him with Emma or else.

When it involved leggy blondes with curves like Emma's, a man had to bend the rules a little sometimes.

Red.